**R. T. RAICHEV** is a researcher and writer who grew up in Bulgaria and wrote a university dissertation on English crime fiction. He has lived in London since 1989. His previous book, *The Hunt for Sonya Dufrette*, was published by Carroll & Graf last year and has received much praise for its ingenious plotting.

### Praise for *The Hunt for Sonya Dufrette*

'This will be pleasing to more than traditionalists, because it adds a P. D. Jamesian subtlety to the comfortable Christie formula.'
*Booklist*

'Do you believe librarians lead dull, quiet lives? If so, you are about to change your mind as you open this well-told tale by talented author R. T. Raichev. Recommended for any mystery fan who likes surprises. Enjoy.'
*New Mystery Reader Magazine*

'Fans of cosies will love the light touch of Raichev's debut, right down to the charmingly titled chapters.'
*Kirkus Reviews*

Also by R. T. Raichev

*The Hunt for Sonya Dufrette*

# THE DEATH
# OF CORINNE

R. T. Raichev

Carroll & Graf Publishers
New York

Carroll & Graf Publishers
An imprint of Avalon Publishing Group, Inc.
245 W. 17th Street, 11th Floor
New York, NY 10011-5300
www.carrollandgraf.com

AVALON
publishing group incorporated

First published in the UK by Constable,
an imprint of Constable & Robinson Ltd 2007

First Carroll & Graf edition 2007

ISBN-13: 978-0-78671-991-4
ISBN-10: 0-7867-1991-5

Printed and bound in the EU

For Francis Wyndham

## *Author's Note*

This is a work of fiction. All the characters are imaginary and bear no relation to any living person.

R. T. R.

# Contents

# Prologue

*She lay sprawled on her back, the black beret still incongruously on her head. The ugly lopsided face was the colour of tallow, which is also the colour of tripe. I remembered that in France tripe soup was a favoured dish, and for a moment I feared I might be sick. I breathed in and out deeply, but my eyes remained fixed on her face. It was frozen in a ferocious grimace: eyes bulging, mouth open, teeth bared. One received the impression she had been snarling when death found her. Her tongue protruded between her teeth and it looked completely black, but that was probably due to the poor light in the greenhouse.*

*She had been shot. A lot of blood had oozed from the round hole in the side of her neck – it looked as though some monstrous wasp had stung her there. The bullet seemed to have hit the jugular. Her jacket and the scarf round her neck were stiff with blood and there was more, a congealed pool, surrounding her. The blood too looked black. It was obvious that she had been dead for several hours. Her mobile phone stuck out of a pocket in her breeches. The electric torch and the niblick we had seen her brandish the night before lay beside her, respectively on her left and her right sides. I found myself staring at her hands. On her right she wore a glove, but her left hand was bare. Her nails were long and scarlet and she wore two large-stoned rings.*

*It was then that I noticed the freakish detail. The little finger of her left hand was as long as her index finger. In some way I knew that to be important, extremely important, only I couldn't think how.*

*I started feeling nauseous again and looked away from the corpse. That was the first time I had been inside the greenhouse. I saw shrubs and plants, some as tall as trees, whose names I did not know. Some of the plants were in a state of decay. I remembered Lady Grylls saying she couldn't afford gardeners. Empty pots – blue-and-white Chinese containers – censers – garden tools. A garden bench. A rickety-looking bamboo table with a matching bamboo chair. A mobile phone lay on the floor beside the chair. I blinked. A second mobile phone? Whose phone was that?*

*I felt a violent tug at my arm. Nicholas. I had completely forgotten about him. 'Miss, look! Over there –'*

Antonia stopped writing and looked up with a frown.

I am making it sound like a *story*, she thought. She was writing in her diary, but it didn't read like a diary entry at all. It read like a detective story . . . *Death at Chalfont* . . . Some such title.

She knew the significance of the long little finger. The reason for the death had been fully explained. She knew how the killer had got hold of the gun. (All right, not for certain, but they had a viable theory.) Most importantly – the identity of the killer was no longer a mystery. The whole enigmatic affair had been elucidated, yet, when she wrote in her diary about it, she indulged in deliberate obfuscation and set out to create suspense . . . *Miss, look! Over there* – Why, she had even broken off on a cliff-hanger! It was almost as though she were writing for an *audience*.

Antonia bit her lip, at once amused and annoyed with herself. She couldn't help it, she supposed. Well, once a detective story writer, always a detective story writer, but then how many detective story writers got involved in real life murder mysteries? Not many, to her knowledge. In fact she couldn't think of a single one outside fiction.

Her thoughts turned back to the fatal night . . . Dinner over, they had sat in the drawing room, sipping coffee. *Rich and dark as the Aga Khan*, Lady Grylls said. Hugh started describing some money-spinning *son et lumière* venture with Chalfont at its centre – an ingenious installation involving wires and cables and hundreds of lights, all controlled from one point – wouldn't his aunt consider it? Then the phone call had come.

What would have happened if they had called the police immediately after? That would have been the logical thing to do, wouldn't it? Corinne had said they would do it the following day – but what if they had done it that same night? (Antonia couldn't resist what-if questions.) Well, the police would have searched the grounds and they'd have managed to catch Eleanor Merchant without much difficulty. What then? Well, then there'd have been no murders.

No murders . . . Was it really as simple as that? What would have happened next? Antonia tapped her teeth with her pen. That poor girl's misery would have continued and intensified and, sooner or later, she would have run away with the man she loved. Or would another murder attempt have been made *before* that?

It was the afternoon of 5th April and they were still at Chalfont. Antonia was sitting at the oak desk in what had once been Lord Grylls's study. Her eyes passed absently over the ancient tobacco jar with a picture of a grouse in languid flight, the fleur-de-lis paperweight, the several outdated copies of *Punch*, the stamp albums bound in red vellum, *The History of Quadrupeds* and a book with the tantalizing title, *Making Friends With a Badger*. She glanced out of the window at the magnolia tree covered in unfurled buds, at the iron-grey sky above, then across at the yew-hedged garden, misty and dreamlike in the drizzle . . .

Looking down at her diary, Antonia started turning over the pages, going back. The funny thing was that she hadn't *read* what she had written – not from start to finish. She was curious about the manner in which she had recorded the sequence of events leading up to the murders. She went back four days, to the first day of the month.

April Fool's Day.

That was when it had all started . . . They had had no idea at the time how appropriate the date would turn out to be.

# 1

# A Murder is Announced

'Somebody wants to kill her?' said Antonia with a frown, her eyes on the photographs on the mantelpiece.

'Well, she's been receiving death threats through the post. She sounded absolutely terrified. I knew you would be interested, my dear. This is up your street, isn't it?' Lady Grylls wheezed and she adjusted herself in the large chintz chair to hand Major Payne his cup. '*Quite* up your street. Do have some cake. You investigated that extraordinary business of the lost child together, didn't you? That's how you met. Talk about whirlwind romances!'

'I wouldn't call it investigating. We just went nosing around, asking questions. We were curious,' Antonia said lightly. It had been more than mere curiosity on her part, at least at the start. She had been racked with guilt. A totally irrational reaction, she had realized soon enough.

'Do you think you might use all that as "copy"? Not necessarily for your next novel but one day?'

'I don't think so.'

'Really? Not even if you changed all the names and the setting? Poor taste, I suppose. Pity. It'd make a marvellous book. One of those that keep you up all night. Why do extraordinary things happen to some people while others lead such perfectly dull lives? I know I may live to regret my fatal craving for the picturesque and yet I can't help myself. The tea's not too weak, is it, Hughie?'

'It's just right, Aunt Nellie,' Major Payne reassured her.

Lady Grylls was his late mother's sister. He had five other aunts, all of them alive, though in various stages of decrepitude. Lady Grylls was his favourite and, despite failing eyesight and a bad smoking habit, the one who was in the best of health and displayed the liveliest of spirits. He directed an affectionate glance at her across the tea table. Seventy-three if a day, pug-faced, compact and stocky, though with remarkably elegant ankles, she was clad in a tweed two-piece that was a bit too tight for her and bulged in unexpected places, a fact that didn't seem to bother her in the least. She wore a single string of pearls around her neck. Her hair was bluish-grey and carefully coiffed and she wore thick bifocal glasses, which kept sliding down her nose.

There had been only the slightest hesitation on his and Antonia's part when Lady Grylls had suggested that they spend the last leg of their honeymoon at Chalfont Park. After the faded glitter of Monte Carlo and Cap Ferrat – which hadn't been as louche as they'd expected – Shropshire was just what they needed.

Chalfont Park was a moderately large house and in average working order, seventeenth-century in origin, eighteenth-century in atmosphere, gently Gothicized at the turn of the nineteenth by a Grylls who, one imagined, had got bored with the Palladian decorum around him, or found it too overpowering. After visiting the house in the thawing slush of 2nd March 1942 James Lees-Milne had described it in his diary as 'pleasantly unstuffy – something tongue-in-cheek about it – not really suitable for the National Trust, due to the various alterations'.

Major Payne looked round the spacious drawing room with its shabby chintz sofas and chairs, occasional tables, 1930s cocktail cabinets and pictures in gilded frames on the walls, a Moorish Riff knife with an ornate handle and a long slender blade casually lying on the blood-red speckled marble mantelpiece, its point pressed against one of the two photographs of Corinne Coreille, his aunt's French god-daughter. Payne smiled. It did seem the perfect setting for some old-fashioned detective drama. He

13

knew Antonia didn't like him saying things like that, so he didn't.

'Back to *l'affaire* CC,' he went on. 'Why aren't the police involved?'

'Good question. They should be, shouldn't they? Well, when I asked Corinne, she got worked up. Said it would be bad for her career, the wrong kind of publicity, couldn't I see? I don't know what to make of it.' Lady Grylls shook her head. 'It's so *unreal*, if you know what I mean. First Corinne's call from Paris. Out of the blue. Her first call in years, saying someone wants to kill her! I had to pinch myself. Then, only a couple of minutes later, another phone call, would you believe it? This time from some private detective agency acting on Corinne's behalf.'

'French detectives?'

'English. The call came from London. Corinne hadn't so much as mentioned them! An elderly duffer's voice. A Mr Jonson. Droning away. Mademoiselle Coreille had employed their services before. Mademoiselle Coreille was a highly valued client. By that,' Lady Grylls added with a sardonic curl of her lip, 'he must mean that the silly gel paid him a fortune in fees.'

How many people still said 'gel' instead of 'girl'? Antonia wondered about the vagaries of upper-class pronunciation. 'Could the whole thing be some elaborate hoax?' she suggested. 'Today is 1st April after all.'

'April Fool, eh? Of course it is. That's the kind of thing Peverel would do.' Peverel was Lady Grylls's other nephew, the one, she had told Antonia, of whom she was *not* fond. 'Oh well, I'd be only too glad if it turned out to be a hoax. But somehow I don't think it was. The poor gel sounded genuinely frightened.'

'Hardly a gel,' Major Payne said. 'She is fifty-five. I am only two and a half years younger than her. Am I a boy to you?'

'Of course you are, darling. You'll always be a boy to me. Though I must admit it is easier with Corinne. You do look grown-up, you see, while she – I mean, look at her.' Lady Grylls waved her hand towards the mantelpiece. 'In one of

14

those photos she is twenty-five, in the other forty-six. Can you tell which is which? *I* can't. Not without looking at the dates on the back.'

'She looks the same age in both,' Antonia said. 'No more than twenty-something.'

'Precisely my point, my dear. Twenty-something. Extraordinary, isn't it?'

'Perhaps she's had plastic surgery.'

'I wouldn't be in the least surprised. She might even have had it several times. They do, don't they? Show business people. Entertainers. Singers and actors and suchlike. Especially those with trademark faces. Corinne's trademark is her fringe, of course. She's had her fringe since she was thirteen.'

'When was the last time you saw her?' Antonia asked.

'The week after Rory's funeral. Goodness, how time flies. We met in Paris. At a café overlooking the Jardin du Luxembourg. Thirteen years ago, that's it. People stared at her the moment she entered. Started nudging each other. They recognized her at once, despite the fact she had enormous dark glasses on. Corinne had a minder tagging along after her – is that what you call them? Some pasty-faced woman in a trouser suit and a cloche hat, who sat discreetly at another table, ordered a brioche and coffee, and pretended she was on her own. It was a lovely day. Paris is at its best in spring. I needed to take my mind off things, you see. Rory had left his affairs in a mess. You couldn't come, darling, could you?' She turned to her nephew. 'Or could you? I don't mean Paris – your uncle's funeral.'

'I couldn't. I was in Kabul.'

'Oh yes. One of those hush-hush jobs. Tracking down drug traffickers, I suppose. Now of course it would be terrorists.' Lady Grylls took a sip of tea. 'Corinne nibbled at a meringue. What did we talk about? I think I moaned about Chalfont and servants. I told her about Rory's funeral and she was sympathetic, but what she wanted to know – what she *really* wanted to know about were the floral tributes. She kept asking a lot of rather odd questions. Had there been delphiniums? Had there been orchids? What about tiger lilies?'

'Is Corinne – odd?' asked Antonia after a little pause.

'Well, when she was a child she sniffed at a cat and nearly died of it. Came out in the most dreadful red blotches. And when she became famous she put two portraits of Napoleon on her bedroom wall, apparently. No one would have thought she had an authoritarian bone in her body! Well, she's had an illustrious career and made pots of money – but that was all thanks to her clever impresario, I think. Mr Lark. All Corinne's ever done is sing. She's never had to do anything else. What was that cliché that's always used to describe somebody like Corinne?'

'She's led a hothouse kind of existence?' Payne suggested.

'Completely out of touch with reality . . . People say that about the upper classes, don't they, so tiresome – the Queen never using credit cards and wearing such ludicrous hats –' Lady Grylls's hands sketched an improbable shape above her head – 'but heaven knows it's *performers*, actors and singers and suchlike, that are the real oddballs. I mean, who's more peculiar, tell me quickly – poor old Prince Charles or that very strange boy who can't make up his mind whether he wants to be black or –' Lady Grylls broke off. 'You know the one. He's had an awful lot of trouble. He denies it all of course.'

'We know the one,' Payne said. 'Well, darling, I'd say both are equally peculiar . . . So, what's happening exactly? Corinne's coming to England in her jet and landing on your croquet lawn –'

'They wouldn't be able to find my croquet lawn even if they tried, it's so terribly overgrown. Gardeners cost the earth. She didn't mention a jet. She might have one, mind. She's terribly rich. I wish I were as rich. Her sales in South Korea alone have made her a millionaire twice over – and that was back in 1981, I read somewhere . . . She proposes to stay with me, yes. She seems to believe that Chalfont will make a good bolt-hole for her. She's coming the day after tomorrow, 3rd April.'

'For how long?'

'She didn't say! Till this thing blows over, I suppose, if that's the right way of putting it. She didn't even ask whether it would be *convenient*.' Lady Grylls gave a mirthless guffaw. 'She seems to be taking it for granted that it will be all right. She's got houses all over the place – Florida, Geneva, a villa in Antibes, and I don't know where else – yet she's coming to Chalfont.'

Antonia murmured, 'She clearly believes she will be safest here. A haven of peace in the midst of turmoil.'

Payne nodded. *'Pax in bello.'*

*'Pax in bello* be blowed! Why should she believe any such thing? Yes, yes, she's been here before, but she was only three or four then – her mamma brought her. She's seen photographs of Chalfont, of course. What I mean is, the house is jolly isolated,' Lady Grylls went on. 'There's no moat or wall – no barbed wire – nothing to deter intruders – no armed sentinels. If someone wanted to cut her throat or shoot her, there'd be no way of stopping them, would there?'

'Perhaps she'll bring her own bodyguards.'

Lady Grylls groaned. 'Her entourage. What *am* I going to do about her entourage? She mentioned a Maître Maginot. I am sure there will be others.' Lady Grylls counted on her fingers. 'Her personal maid, her make-up artist, her masseuse – um, what else is there?'

'Fitness instructor – nutritionist?' Antonia suggested.

'Yes . . . Her personal chiropodist too, as likely as not – these people are so spoilt – or do I mean chiromancer?' Lady Grylls frowned.

'She probably has one of each.'

'You are *such* a comfort, Hughie . . . Yes, the likes of Corinne usually travel with a retinue. I'm sure they'll be an extremely disagreeable bunch . . . She never said how many!'

'I don't see why you should let that worry you, Aunt Nellie. Plenty of room here.'

17

'Servants, darling. Servants.' Lady Grylls shook her head. 'The bane of my life. I have the most awful struggle, keeping this place together.'

'There's old Hortense. And Provost. And Nicholas.'

Hortense was the cook, Provost the butler, while Nicholas, Provost's teenage son, was learning to be a footman.

Lady Grylls stared at her nephew owlishly. 'As you say, Hughie, there's old Hortense, Provost *and* Nicholas. *Precisely* my point. Chalfont's getting more and more uncomfortable and harder to manage – I don't suppose it's only me entering a particularly morose and acrid dotage, is it? I find the draughts are getting worse, the hot-water system less reliable, the dogs less clean –'

Major Payne put down his cup. 'You haven't had dogs for ages, darling.'

'Kept chewing the carpets, that's why I had to get rid of them. Chalfont will be the end of me. We might have been able to pull it round while Rory was alive – there was still money in the kitty then – but he got this apoplectic look whenever I suggested renovation! I might have been saying, what a pity the *jacquerie* didn't succeed, or do let's join the Labour Party, or some such thing. Rory seemed to equate shabbiness with "good form" . . . You aren't warm enough, are you?' She cast a jaundiced glance at the ancient two-bar electric heater that hissed and crackled in front of the fireplace, giving off a slight odour of burning dust. Pointing towards the high ceiling with her forefinger, she observed that *that* was where all the heat went.

'No doubt most country house owners are similarly handicapped,' said Payne soothingly.

'Don't I know it! Why d'you think I avoid Adela de Quesne and that old stick Bobo Markham like the plague? All they do when they manage to get hold of me on the blower is moan about damp and dry rot and trespassing ramblers claiming the right to long-forgotten footpaths and how *everything* is at near-perdition point.'

Trying to catch her husband's eye and failing, Antonia

said they could always leave, if indeed there were going to be a lot of people coming.

'Leave? Is that some sort of a joke, Antonia?' Lady Grylls said sternly. 'You can't leave now. I need you here! Goodness. Peverel isn't any good in a crisis . . . I don't think such a thing as "trend-spotting" exists, do you? I am sure he made it up. The way he went on about it last night. Gave me a headache. Too bloody fond of the sound of his own voice.'

'He promised he'd set his net scouts the task of finding out as much as possible about Corinne –'

'Ha – net scouts! All bosh, if you ask me, my dear. I wouldn't believe a word of what Peverel says. He can't possibly issue commands to anybody simply by sitting in his room and pressing the buttons of his laptop, or whatever that thing's called – can he?'

'He probably can, darling,' Payne said. 'He can even find you a cheap gardener on the net –'

'But you must try to be nice to him first,' Antonia added with a smile.

Lady Grylls suddenly looked fascinated. 'Goodness – *you actually finish each other's sentences*. That doesn't happen often, you know, that kind of affinity between husband and wife.'

'How tedious that makes us sound.'

'Not at all, my dear. A good marriage is not to be sneezed at, especially in this day and age. Yours is clearly one of those that's been made in heaven. Second marriages are more successful than first ones, or so they say.'

'We like it.' Payne poured himself more tea. 'Maître Maginot – is that spelled like the line? Who is he anyway?'

'It's a she. Some terrible dragon of a woman, by the sound of it. A legal adviser-cum-mentor to Corinne. She seems to have taken over after Mr Lark died. I get the impression she hasn't been with Corinne that long. She was there as Corinne talked to me, breathing down her neck. I could hear her hissing in the background, prompting. Corinne kept referring to her . . . Maître Maginot considered Chalfont Park as a place of refuge *une bonne*

19

*idée.* Maître Maginot doubted whether the death threats were really serious, but wanted to avoid any unnecessary risks. Poor Corinne sounded like a schoolgirl – all timid and halting. Well, I suspect Maître Maginot of monumental control-freakery. I've got to smoke. Where are my cigarettes?' Lady Grylls peered round the table. 'It doesn't help that I am as blind as a bat.'

'Your hearing should be exceptionally sharp then.'

'It isn't. That's a popular myth . . . Thank you,' she said as her nephew struck a match for her. 'So glad you are a smoker, Hughie. Makes *such* a difference. Can't stand it when Peverel looks down his nose each time I light up. What a self-righteous bore he is. Won't you join me? Where's that fragrant pipe of yours?'

Payne obligingly produced his pipe and started filling it out of his pouch. His aunt nodded in an approving manner. 'Now the idea of Maître Maginot doesn't seem so repellent. I can see how people turn to drugs – can you?' She blew smoke out of her nostrils. 'Mr Jonson described Maître Maginot as a *femme formidable.* Don't you think it tiresome when people pepper their speech with frog?'

'Terribly tiresome,' Payne agreed. 'Apart from being *de trop.* Unless they are French, that is. Then they can't help it.'

'From the way he pontificated, Jonson put me in mind of some sort of superior public schoolmaster – or a family solicitor. You know the type. Dry as a biscuit – omniscient godlike manner – the most annoying little cough. Absolute utter drears. I hope he won't overstay his welcome. He said he wanted to look around. Does he imagine he might find Corinne's madman at Chalfont, skulking behind an arras, clutching a knife? D'you think he suspects me of some sort of collusion?'

'Well, he might have got it into his head the madman is your secret lover,' Payne said. 'Gentlewomen of a certain age are notorious for that sort of thing.'

'Are they?' Antonia frowned. Hugh did talk awful rot sometimes. 'Do you mean gentlewomen of a certain age keep secret lovers or that they have a predilection for madmen?' She was amazed to see Lady Grylls nod.

'Apparently madmen make jolly good lovers. No inhibitions and oodles of untapped energy.' Lady Grylls held her cigarette at what in her youth must have been considered a modish angle. 'I did read about it somewhere.'

'Might be a madwoman,' Antonia said. 'I mean the person behind the death threats.' Madwomen were always greater fun than madmen – in books and films at least. More terrifying, for some reason . . . *A Single White Male* wouldn't be quite the same thing as *A Single White Female*. The madwoman in the attic . . . The female of the species deadlier than the male –

'More tea?' Lady Grylls said and she rang for Provost.

Provost was a faded, sandy-haired man in his mid-forties. In the normal course of things he appeared wearing a comfortable cardigan but, presumably on account of Mr Jonson's visit, he had changed into a black alpaca coat, stiff shirt, winged collar, black tie and striped trousers and looked every inch the stage butler. He was rather a gloomy individual; however, his face lit up the moment Lady Grylls spoke to him. A look of complicity passed between them. She murmured something that to Antonia's ears sounded like, 'On with the show!' – causing Provost actually to smile. It was clear he adored her. Who said the feudal spirit was dead?

'The Prince of Wales has Debo Devonshire. Provost has me. I am his confidante,' Lady Grylls declared after he left the room. 'He says only I understand him. Something in that.'

The tea was brought by Provost's son Nicholas, a deadly pale, truculent-looking boy of sixteen, with spiked-up hair and a 'sleeper' in his right ear. He had left school the year before and come to live with his father. He had been caught sniffing glue and, apparently, was interested in magic. 'Pull up your trousers, Nicholas,' Lady Grylls ordered in a stentorian voice. '*Not* at half mast when I am around, I've told you hundreds of times . . . How's the invisible hat doing?'

'It's an invisibility cloak, actually,' he said with a hurt air.

'He's mad about those ridiculous children's books *every-body* seems to be reading on overcrowded trains,' she explained later. '*And* he talks of something called "wacky-baccy" . . . Poor souls. Is that some sort of spell?' Payne cleared his throat. 'Not quite.'

Provost, it turned out, was what was known as a 'single parent'. Lady Grylls pronounced the phrase slowly and doubtfully as though it belonged to some foreign tongue. She went on to explain that Mrs Provost – Shirley – had also been in her employment, but she had left her husband six months earlier – for a black man, a bouncer called C.C.J. Hawkshaw, with whom she now lived in London's Docklands.

'They came on a visit last month. They meant well, no hard feelings and all that, but it was a mistake. Provost has clearly neither forgotten nor forgiven. He walked about handing round drinks, saying nothing, looking shell-shocked – acted as though he had no idea who they were. The boy ran off and shut himself in the potting shed and wouldn't come out. I think I smelled pot, but I may be wrong. Nicholas did behave oddly *afterwards*. Poor souls,' Lady Grylls said again.

'Why don't you raise their wages, if you pity them so much?' Major Payne said as he stirred his tea.

'Can't afford to. Shirley was unrecognizable. She's shaved her head and she and C.C.J. sported identical tattoos on their arms. It was fairly obvious she was preggers as well,' Lady Grylls went on. 'We always got on well – sex-mad, of course – and I thought her new consort a pet. His full name is Clive Junior, but for some reason he hates being called that. He wouldn't say what the second C stands for either. He's terribly sensitive about it.'

Antonia asked, 'Hasn't Corinne got any idea as to who might be sending her the death threats?'

'If she has, she didn't tell me. All she said was "anonymous notes" . . . So annoying, isn't it? Who do you think it is, my dear? You are the expert.'

'I am nothing of the sort.' Antonia said.

'Poor Corinne reminds me of the man who walks on a lonesome road in fear and dread,' Lady Grylls said.

*'Because he knows a frightful fiend doth close behind him tread . . .'* Payne murmured.

'Is that *The Ancient Mariner*? Awfully gruesome . . . Hate poetical effusions.' Lady Grylls paused. 'Who *could* it be?'

Major Payne stroked his jaw with a thoughtful forefinger. 'It could be someone from Corinne's past.'

'Corinne hasn't got a past! Not in the sense I think you mean. All she's ever done is sing. *La chanson, c'est moi.* That's Corinne's motto. She's had it embroidered on her sofa cushions and handkerchiefs and things. I don't think Corinne's ever had time for a private life.'

'Could the death threats have something to do with Corinne's singing then?' Antonia frowned. 'No – that's silly.' We must talk about something else, she thought.

'Shall we explore possibilities?' Lady Grylls looked round. 'Such fun. Do let's.'

## 2

# Look to the Lady

'Well, the whole thing might turn out to be something silly and trivial,' Antonia said after a pause. 'The death threats may have been written by a fan whose request for an autograph Corinne ignored.'

'Or it might be something really twisted and diabolical,' said Payne. 'The Machiavellian Maginot may have done it in order to tighten the screws on Corinne – to increase Corinne's dependence on her?'

'The Machiavellian Maginot, that's right.' Lady Grylls nodded approvingly over her cup of tea. 'I like it when an unsympathetic character turns out to have done it. Maginot strikes me as exactly the type . . . Have you ever hated someone without ever having clapped eyes on them?'

'Corinne might have written the letters herself,' Antonia went on. 'She might be obsessed with death, as her interest in funeral wreaths suggests . . . Some kind of death-wish. Or the death threats might be a publicity stunt – aimed to revive public interest in her – an ageing, self-dramatizing diva's attention-seeking ploy.'

'What a splendid idea,' Lady Grylls said. 'I adore ploys. Such fun, having you here. I don't know what I'd have done if you hadn't come. I really don't. I would have been bored to sobs.'

'The death threats might turn out to be the work of a rival diva. Somebody who's still jealous of Corinne,' Payne suggested. 'One of those legendary cat-fights that go back a long way?'

'The dilemma . . . of the deadly diva?' Lady Grylls shot a sly look at Antonia.

Antonia bit her lip. We are being damned insensitive, she thought, treating this as though it were some sort of parlour game. We are providing entertainment for a bored baroness – like the court jesters of old . . . Corinne Coreille, despite all her oddities and great riches, was a human being, at the moment no doubt a terribly frightened one. Were they so incapable of understanding, empathy and simple compassion?

'The death threats might turn out to be what is known as a "cry for help",' Major Payne was saying. 'Corinne may be mired in misery – on the verge of a nervous breakdown. She may feel her career is on the skids – she may be convinced that she has reached the end of the line.'

Lady Grylls said she was sure Antonia could make any of these theories work if she were writing Corinne's story up in a book – the plot would be one of those complicated clockwork affairs with a hundred moving parts and inter-dependence absolute – she could, couldn't she? Lady Grylls had always maintained that detective story writers were terribly clever.

'Not necessarily. Anyone with basic writing skills, a devious mind and amateur knowledge of psychology can do it.' Antonia hoped she didn't sound too terse. She knew there was more to detective story writing than that but she was annoyed. They should talk about something else, really. 'Who is Bobo Markham?' she asked.

Lady Grylls laughed. It was Major Payne who enlightened her.

'Sir Robert Markham is a widowed baronet who considers himself a good catch. Markham Manor is on the other side of Chalfont Parva,' he explained. 'Old Markham's been trying to get Aunt Nellie to marry him. He's been after you for a long time, hasn't he, darling?'

'Oh dear, yes . . . Heart of gold, but such an old bore. He's nearly eighty,' Lady Grylls said. 'A man who continually asks a woman to marry him and can't make her change her mind, is a man who secretly enjoys devotion to lost causes.'

'He had a good war, apparently,' Payne said. 'He told me he excelled at Dunkirk.'

'I daresay the Charge of the Light Brigade would have suited Bobo much better! I know I am being awfully unkind. I am *not* a good person. Bobo's a splendid old boy, actually, but if I ever married again at my age, it would be to a younger man. Somebody of, say, sixty-four.'

'Darling – a toy-boy,' Payne murmured.

'And he must on no account breed pigs.'

'Does Sir Robert Markham breed pigs?' Antonia was not in the least interested, but she was glad to have managed to steer the conversation in a different direction.

'Listen to this. Corinne might be planning to get rid of the overbearing Maginot who has some hold over her.' Payne paused thoughtfully. 'It is Maginot who will die violently. Corinne is the killer and she has been making it appear as though she is the intended victim . . . It's going to be one of those cases where it looks but only *looks* as though the killer has made a mistake.'

'And I'd lay you long odds it's Jonson who's behind the death threats,' Lady Grylls wheezed. 'Jonson's agency is going bankrupt. He needs money desperately.' Lady Grylls pushed her glasses up her nose. 'The first time Corinne employed him, she paid him a fortune in fees, so he sees her as the goose that lays golden eggs. He conceives of a scheme – he sends her threatening letters in the hope that she'll employ his services – which she does!'

There was a pause. Well, we seem to have exhausted all possibilities, Antonia reflected – and felt cheered by the thought. Whatever happened now, there'd be no surprises . . .

'Do you and Corinne speak in French?' she asked.

'No – English. Corinne speaks English like one of us, on account of Ruse – I mean her mamma. Her mamma was English. *Le falcon* – her father – was French. That's

26

Franglais.' Lady Grylls fumbled with the pack and lit another cigarette. '*Le falcon*,' she repeated.

There was another pause. An unaccountable change had come over Lady Grylls, Antonia noticed with surprise. Lady Grylls had ceased looking jolly. There was a faraway expression on her face. Her eyes had narrowed – her lips trembled slightly. Antonia was visited by an idea –

There was one fantastical possibility they hadn't considered. Had they perhaps been persuaded to look at the case . . . the wrong way up?

Lady Grylls sat smoking in silence. Her eyes seemed to be fixed on the mantelpiece – was she looking at the photos of Corinne – or at the Riff knife whose point was pressed against one of them? Hugh said something, but she didn't seem to hear.

Antonia tried to arrange her ideas logically. They had been told that Corinne Coreille was coming because she believed Chalfont would provide her with a safe haven from an unknown enemy – but they only had Lady Grylls's word for it. They hadn't been there when Lady Grylls took the phone call from Paris. What if that story was a fabrication? What if it was Lady Grylls who had phoned Corinne Coreille and invited her to Chalfont? What if Lady Grylls had made up the story of the death threats? What if Corinne were to die *before the truth came out*?

Was it possible that Lady Grylls was . . . laying a trap? Her eyesight might not be as bad as she claimed . . . Lady Grylls, by her own admission and contrary to all appearances, was *not* a nice person. She could be ruthless all right. Antonia remembered Hugh telling her how at some shooting party his aunt had gone round with one of those sticks with a hammer at the end, clouting half-dead pheasants on the head, finishing them off . . . Lady Grylls adored ploys . . . She must be acting in cahoots with Maître Maginot, whom she professed to detest without ever having seen her . . . Extravagant animosity between two characters was always suspect . . . That might be a mere charade, an essential part of the deadly deception that was being played out . . . Antonia nodded to herself. What about Mr Jonson, the private detective? Well, he would simply . . . fail to materialize. Yes . . . *Mr Jonson did not exist.* They hadn't witnessed that phone call either. Mr Jonson was a figment of Lady Grylls's imagination – the kind of corroborative detail that gives verisimilitude to an otherwise bald and unconvincing narrative . . . Lady Grylls had prepared the ground and was now getting ready to go for the kill.

What reason could Lady Grylls possibly have to want to kill her god-daughter, though? Well, the reason went back a long way . . . It was something to do with Corinne's parents . . . Yes. Corinne's death would be the price for something absolutely terrible her parents had done to Lady Grylls – or to a member of Lady Grylls's family . . . Corinne's father in particular seemed to be implicated. That was when the change had come over Lady Grylls. *Le falcon*, she had reiterated. Corinne's father had been French. A nation of dashing lovers, the French – reputed to be the best lovers in the world. A popular myth, no doubt, but Antonia found herself changing tack . . . Lady Grylls and *le falcon* had had an affair. More than that – they had been secretly married. Corinne was . . . not Lady Grylls's god-daughter, but her *daughter* . . . That was quite an ingenious theory, actually, though it needed to be thought through carefully . . . Lady Grylls kept complaining of a lack of funds. Corinne, on the other hand, was as rich as Croesus. When Corinne died, Lady Grylls – as her mother – would inherit Corinne's millions – and then she would be in a position to have Chalfont Park renovated!

This is *not* a detective story, Antonia reminded herself. Really, I should be ashamed of myself.

# The Secret Adversary

Eleanor Merchant sat in the dining car of the Eurostar, bound for London. They had left Paris some forty-five minutes before. She had taken the letters out of her bag, she couldn't say exactly why, and arranged them fan-like on the little table in front of her. She had kept copies of every single letter – *two* copies – she was most particular about that kind of thing. She had written three times to Corinne Coreille and now six letters lay on the table. Although things had moved on and a confrontation was to take place soon, indeed seemed imminent, she was still curious as to why she had not received any answers. Corinne Coreille's silence had hurt her. It was after all common courtesy to reply to personal messages.

Earlier on Eleanor had had an argument with the waiter. He had brought her a *tarte au citron*, but she had asked for a *tarte au chocolat*! He had had the temerity to suggest that she had made a mistake, the arrogant puppy – that her memory might be failing her. A mistake! Her memory was of the fly-paper variety – she had told him as much. He had appeared unconvinced. He looked the kind Griff might have taken a fancy to, so she refrained from display-ing the froideur and sharp edges of the iceberg that had sunk the *Titanic*. (Why did they have *only* French waiters on the Eurostar? There should have been English ones as well. They wouldn't have been that good-looking for one thing, and then she'd have been able to speak her mind.)

The reason for taking out the letters came to her. She wanted to prove that she had the phenomenal ability to recite extended texts from memory – without taking one little peek. Yes. Eleanor had re-read her letters a great number of times and she knew them by heart, word for word . . . Placing both her hands across the first letter, palms down, rather in the manner of one attending a spiritualist séance, she stared out of the window at the rapidly shifting landscape and started speaking.

'Dear Miss Coreille – it was your voice my son was listening to as he lay dying. His blood had turned the translucent water in his bath scarlet.' Since she had no travelling companion whom she might have been addressing, people passing by her table shot her startled glances. 'You were the only one there. He had chosen you and you alone to share his last moments on earth. It was I who discovered him, you see.'

Eleanor felt like calling the waiter and asking him to check and see for himself that she hadn't made a single mistake, but decided against it. He might get the wrong idea. The common herd, she had noticed, was wont to jump to conclusions. She sighed and shook her head. Perhaps she should do it *sotto voce* – or, better, in her head? I will be my own witness, Eleanor thought with a sad little smile. That, alas, was often the way these days.

She had flown over from Boston to New York. Alma, her niece, was getting married and it might have been the society wedding of the year, but Griff's death spoilt things somewhat. Alma was extremely sore about it. Alma believed that Griff (short for Griffiths) had timed his suicide very carefully, out of sheer spite. That, she told Eleanor, was the kind of thing he would do, in keeping with the immature, theatrical, rather exhibitionistic side of his character. Griff was what Corinne Coreille would no doubt call *un enfant terrible*. Alma seemed to be equally cross with Eleanor, insinuating that somehow it had been her fault, the way Griff had turned out; Alma had implied that Griff had had an unhealthy upbringing, that Eleanor had been a terrible parent – the mother from hell.

The press had been quick to pick up the family connection and that was *not* the kind of publicity her niece craved. Eleanor's sister and brother-in-law, who was the governor's right-hand man, had been more restrained, respecting her grief, or rather observing the decencies. They hadn't said a word about Griff – but Eleanor was sure they shared their daughter's views on the subject.

Eleanor felt a sudden urge to rise to her feet and speak out – recite aloud – make the dining car ring with the sound of her voice – command everybody's attention with her tragic tale. She fought the urge down. Her tale would be quite wasted. The common herd would think her unbalanced. Pity, really, because she had *such* a good voice. It was of the 'cultured' American variety – without a trace of a nasal twang. She sounded like the late British actress Margaret Leighton, she always imagined. In Paris, on several occasions, she had been taken for an Englishwoman of irreproachable birth and breeding. Well, she cut a most elegant and unusual figure. She had been aware of people actually *staring* at her, simple souls – in admiration, awe and wonder, she had no doubt – and she had brought joy into their drab lives by giving them the little see-saw of a royal wave. (The hand going up and down, up and down, the wrist held rigid.)

'All my relatives disapproved of Griff and his lifestyle,' Eleanor said with a sigh. Fury came over her in waves as she thought of her relatives' low, narrow, bestial minds. 'They wouldn't have condemned him if they'd had the slightest understanding of the world and its tricks.'

Her relatives had considered Griff an embarrassment – no, an abomination. *Not* the kind of person you'd care to acknowledge as cousin or nephew. Her relatives would rather Griff had never existed at all . . . None of them came to the funeral. Nor did Griff's father for that matter. Eleanor had no idea where her former husband was. Perhaps he was abroad – he might be dead – or in jail. Lyndon had left her when Griff was seven. That, her shrink had

31

told her, was when the trouble started. Absentee fathers had a lot to answer for.

It was nonsense to suggest that she was in any way to blame for the way Griff had 'turned out' . . . A mean, unpleasant creature, Alma. Her name should have been 'Alice' – then it would have rhymed with 'malice' . . . Well, current rumour had it that her marriage wasn't going at all satisfactorily – it was even suggested that Alma had been driving her husband to drink! Eleanor wasn't the type to gloat, but she couldn't help a little smile at the thought.

A terrible parent indeed! Eleanor hadn't been a terrible parent. Quite the reverse. She had been a marvellous mother. She and Griff had got on extremely well. No, they had got on *stupendously.* Griff had been her companion, her confidant, her playmate. Why, they had adored each other!

Eleanor told Griff things she wouldn't have dreamt of telling anyone else. She never bought a dress or a hat without asking his opinion first. (How many mothers did that?) She introduced Griff to great literature – to the very best of popular fiction as well. She made life for both of them exclusive and amusing. She took him to the Hamptons and Palm Beach for the vacations, and to Broadway every other week – together they had seen *Oedipus Rex* and *Rent, The Boyfriend* and *Dorothy After Kansas.* She let him read her copies of *Vanity Fair* and *Harper's Bazaar.* They had pillow fights to the accompaniment of Leroy Anderson tunes. Eleanor had the most fantastical costumes ordered for their dressing-up sessions. They had played games unknown anywhere else on the planet Earth! They had applied the principle of those bizarre multiple-choice teenage books ('If you want to venture into the Lair of the Giant Dragonfly, go to page 23') to the works of Proust and had come up with entries like, 'If you wish to slip into bed with Marcel, go to page 6. If, however, you want to attend the Germantes' dinner party, go at once to page 546.'

Eleanor remembered another rather complicated game, which they had called 'Abominating Abraxas', Abraxas being an unpredictable pagan deity with a chanticleer's head and a serpent's tail. Griff had done the most wonderfully scary drawing of Abraxas. The interesting – the really *remarkable* – thing was that Abraxas had since acquired a life *outside the game* – he had managed to break through its confines somehow – Eleanor kept seeing him!

Why was the waiter looking at her again? What did he want? Hadn't his mother taught him it was extremely rude to stare at strangers? Eleanor stuck out her tongue at him, then looked out of the window once more.

She had been so happy that day . . . She had spent three hours shopping at Bloomingdale's, had coffee and the most delicious chocolate cheesecake, then went for a stroll in Central Park. She fed the ducks, then sat on a bench, basking in the warm sunshine. It was the first day of spring. She had been full of hope. She had decided to look Griff up and try to reach some kind of reconciliation.

They hadn't been in touch for a couple of months, there had been an estrangement of sorts, the silliest of spats, really. She thought it was ridiculous that they should have fallen out and still be at loggerheads over a remark she had made concerning one of his friends. Griff was morbidly sensitive about his friends, but then he was sensitive about most things. She had bought him two sugared doughnuts, which she carried in a paper bag by way of a peace offering. (Griff adored doughnuts.)

Griff had a flat on the tenth floor of an art deco building in the fashionable district of West Chelsea. Eleanor believed she was humming a tune – 'Top of the World'? – as she let herself in with the key Griff had given her while they had still been on good terms. She stood in the hall, admiring the wonderful matt red walls painted with Muslim-style arches supported by slender columns of dull gold – Griff had always had such good taste. She called out Griff's name. Her hands felt a bit sticky, so she went to the bathroom to wash them –

'Sticky,' Eleanor said. 'It's so hard to keep the line between past and present.'

The next moment she had to bite her lip to stop herself from crying out. A flashback – she'd had a flashback! She had seen it all again. The redness. The stickiness. You mustn't do it, the doctor had told her.

'It is at that point that my life stops and the nightmare takes over,' Eleanor said, her voice soft and hushed as if she were talking in church. 'I haven't been the same since.'

The face that stared back at her from the mirror these days was a face she no longer recognized as her own. (She had never been a great beauty, but she had been attractive in an unconventional kind of way. Griff always said she had the face of an expensive cat.) Her skin was not too lined, but it was shockingly sallow and it had a 'battered' appearance. The despoiling power of grief! Eleanor spent ages making herself up and the effect was frequently disconcerting. Her eyes had lost their lustre; they looked empty and dull. Her mind kept getting into binds. She blamed the medication she had been prescribed for that – anti-depressants, stimulants, sleeping pills, painkillers, energy-boosters and she didn't know what else. She was far from sure they did her any good but she continued taking them in bucketfuls. *Sans souci, but I need to get my mouth round the Xanax – it helps me with my panics –*

Covering her face with her hands, Eleanor began to rock backward and forward. She shook her head and moaned. She expected tears to start flowing from her eyes in unstoppable streams, but that didn't happen. *She had run out of tears.* She had reached the most dreadful part of her letter – she knew what was coming and she dreaded it – she wanted to cut the scene out, the way scenes that were considered too shocking were edited out of films – but of course she couldn't.

'The razor, an old-fashioned one, with an ornate mother-of-pearl handle, the stateliest of objects, lay on the floor beside the bath,' Eleanor whispered. 'It had belonged to Griff's grandfather. It was covered in blood. There was blood everywhere, bespattering the walls, on the floor, even on the ceiling – the small cassette player that stood on the little table beside the bath was sticky with blood. I keep seeing that bath – I only need to shut my eyes. There it is now – and again – and again.'

There had been no religious consolations for her in the aftermath of the appalling catastrophe. Eleanor had had a 'God' once, but after her husband had left her, she ceased to believe. She had been overcome by grief. She had imagined at first that she could draw on reserves of stoicism and imagination, on her sense of the absurd, but she had been wrong – she couldn't. That was why she had 'cracked up' so fast. She'd gone *right* under. She had had a nervous breakdown. Her shrink had diagnosed something called 'florid behaviour'. Eleanor had spent a month at a 'rest home', undergoing various therapies. She had only the haziest recollection of the things they did to her there. After she had come out, she had developed an interest in spiritualism. She had been keeping a psychic journal, in which she regularly recorded her attempts to reach her dead son.

'Sticky,' she said again.

The bath was full of Griff's blood, only his head and part of his shoulders showed above it. It was all appallingly, indescribably, grotesquely Grand Guignol. A scene straight out of one of those old British Hammer horror films she and Griff had always found hilarious – they had revelled in anything high camp – only now it was for real. Eleanor knew at once that Griff had been drained of all his blood; that was why his face was so pale, bluish pale, painfully thin and haggard. His eyes had remained open . . .

Eleanor still did not remember going up to the cassette player, but she must have done. (There had been blood on her hands, as she had discovered afterwards.) She had rewound the tape and pressed the play button. She had expected to hear a final message from Griff, his last words, an explanation, an apologia, the sound of him sobbing or screaming or telling her that he had forgiven her, but what she heard instead was Corinne Coreille's voice.

'It came as a shock. Another shock. As though I hadn't had enough! How I hated you at that moment,' Eleanor recited from the letter. 'There is something about your voice – a certain haunting quality. It's like no other I have ever heard. Griff had played your songs all the time, that was what the neighbours said. They imagined he was French because of his taste in music, also on account of his "flamboyantly European lifestyle", whatever that may mean. They sounded as though they too disapproved. I would have expected people living in that part of Manhattan to display a greater degree of sophistication, but there it is.'

She rubbed her hands together, Lady Macbeth fashion. 'Sticky,' she said. 'After all this time.'


It was eight years earlier that Griff had fallen under Corinne Coreille's spell. He was fourteen at the time. They had been watching television together. They had been lolling on a sofa upholstered in mauve velvet that was big enough for eight, under the Sargent portrait of Eleanor's English great grandmother. They had been eating Hershey's fudge ice-cream and drinking vanilla soda. It was high summer – late afternoon – Eleanor remembered clearly the golden glow that filtered into the room. All the windows were wide open and the filmy curtains fluttered in the delicate breeze. Earlier on they had had a cushion fight . . .

Eleanor had been wearing a tea-gown decorated with emeralds as big as quail eggs, 1920s style, and knee socks. Griff had a frilly Byronic shirt on, gleaming white. They had been watching an old Marx Brothers comedy, but got bored with it. Eleanor had started flicking idly through the channels, complaining how drab and tedious and passé everything looked. (That, as it happened, had been their catch phrase of the moment – passé.) 'Wait, what was that, Eleanor? Go back,' Griff said. (He always called her 'Eleanor', never 'Mother'.)

That had been his first glimpse of Corinne Coreille. It had been Corinne Coreille's Palais de Congrès concert of 1989.

Eleanor remembered her exact words. 'Good heavens, is she still around? Just look at her. So passé, don't you think? Orchids and absinthe and Shocking by Schiaparelli.' She knew that was the kind of remark that amused Griff, but now he remained serious. He asked what the singer's name was. Eleanor told him.

If only they had continued watching the Marx Brothers going on causing havoc and large-scale destruction in their habitual manic manner, the catastrophe would have been averted – or perhaps it wouldn't have? Not for the first time Eleanor Merchant asked herself the question and pondered on the role of chance in one's life and whether everything that happened to people hadn't in fact been pre-ordained.

Corinne Coreille had been singing something heart-wrenchingly sad. So sad, it had made Eleanor laugh. It was one of those ridiculously melodramatic songs. ('C'est toi qui partirait'?) She had asked Griff if he wanted another scoop of ice-cream but Griff hadn't answered. Griff's eyes had remained fixed on the TV screen. Griff had been entranced by the image of the small figure with the dark fringe, smudgy eyes and little black dress . . . When the song was over, Griff held out his hand, palm upwards, as though pleading with a departing lover, which was an exact replica of what Corinne Coreille was doing at that very moment.

'I think you are a witch,' Eleanor said slowly. 'You cast a spell on Griff that day. How else can one explain the fact that you have stayed young? Your appearance hasn't changed one bit over the years. You are four years older than me, but you look like a girl. *Une fille éternelle.* As my grandmother used to say, to look that good at fifty-five, you must have been sleeping with Satan.'

Eleanor's thoughts turned to the Corinne doll she had found in Griff's bedroom. The doll was fashioned in Corinne Coreille's exact image and bore a 'Made in Japan' tag. Eleanor had found herself sticking pins in it – at first casually, but then she had got angry and become quite frantic with it.

She had given an account of what she had done in her first letter to Corinne Coreille.

'You may call it my one attempt at "counter-magic". The first pin went into your dainty little nose, the next two into your beautiful eyes, the third and fourth into your shell-like ears, the fifth into your smooth forehead. I went on till the doll was transformed into a pincushion – no, into a porcupine! It made me laugh and for a couple of moments I felt better. (I don't suppose it hurt?)'

It occurred to Eleanor that that was the way she had recited poems at school – fluently, expressively, without stumbling over words, pausing at all the right places. Anyone listening to her could tell the parentheses from the commas, the semicolons from the full stops. At school her favourite poem had been Browning's *The Laboratory*. (*Not that I bid you spare her the pain – Let death be felt and the proof remain!*) She was particularly good at 'doing' highly strung women in the grip of uncontrollable emotions.

'I was there when Griff was born,' Eleanor said in a tragic voice, placing her hand at her bosom. 'You were with him when he died. There is a fearsome symmetry about this. I would very much like to meet you. Maybe I am being too hard on you? Perhaps I am doing you a grave injustice? You don't seem real on TV or in photographs. Too perfect for one, not a hair out of place, always immaculately groomed, always glowing.' Eleanor touched her own face and hair with an ironic gesture. 'I would like to see with my own eyes what you are really like.'

The waiter had silently beckoned to one of his colleagues and the two young men stood further down the aisle and watched Eleanor's performance furtively but with the liveliest interest.

'I never used to consider myself a "maternal woman", despised the type rather,' Eleanor went on, 'but all I can think of now is my dead son. I don't expect you to know what goes on in a mother's heart because you have never had any children, but perhaps you could try? I hope you write back. For Griff's sake. Your songs clearly meant a lot to him. It is a complete mystery to me why that should have been so, but then I am not exactly one of your aficionados . . . You may at least have the decency to apologize, you fucking crazy bitch. I don't know exactly why I wrote that last sentence, but it seems right somehow, so I will leave it –'

Eleanor Merchant's throat felt dry and a bit sore, so she took a sip of tea. The tea was cold now, tasteless and quite revolting. She glanced down at the second letter through the spread fingers of her right hand, then she covered the letter with both her hands. She had written the second letter a month after the first and again she had sent it by airmail as well as registered, c/o Fabiola, Corinne Coreille's record company in Paris. Corinne Coreille had not deigned to reply to either letter, though Eleanor was absolutely certain that she had received them.

'Fucking crazy bitch,' Eleanor repeated.

4

## Les Parents Terribles

'Have you ever seen her in concert – I mean live?' Antonia asked.

'As a matter of fact, we have,' Payne said. 'At the Royal Albert Hall. Aunt Nellie took us. My sister and me. Corinne Coreille's first concert in England. She gave two concerts, I think?' He turned to his aunt.

'Goodness, yes . . . That was ages ago.' Lady Grylls spoke distractedly. '*Ages* ago . . .'

'Darling, is anything the matter?'

'Why can't one revisit the past, the way one does a foreign country? Of course I remember Corinne's concert.' Lady Grylls sat up. 'Sorry – lost in a brown study . . . I remember it vividly. What d'you want to know about it?'

'I believe the French ambassador was in the audience or did I dream it?'

'No, you did not dream it. He was. Madame de Gaulle was there too, with Lady Soames, the wife of our ambassador in Paris.' Lady Grylls flicked cigarette ash recklessly on to the carpet. 'Corinne was big in France in the late '60s. Everybody was talking of *la nouvelle Piaf*. Corinne was said to be a particular favourite of General de Gaulle. Her first English concert was a glittering gala devised to revive the flagging Entente Cordiale. It has always been in trouble, hasn't it? There were other French singers – Maurice Chevalier, no less. Sacha Distel. On the English side there was Vera Lynn and – what was the name of the chap who sang about wanting to be released?'

'Engelbert Humperdinck.'

'Oh yes. Ghastly name. He also wrote operas, didn't he? No, that was the other one.'

'It must have been 1969 . . . It was 5th May. I was on leave from Sandhurst.'

Antonia smiled. 'You remember the exact date? Did you find Corinne that attractive then?'

Payne started relighting his pipe. Antonia was visited by the unworthy suspicion that he was doing it to gain time. Eventually he spoke. Corinne hadn't been conventionally beautiful, but rather sweet in a *jolie laide* kind of way. ('Sorry, Aunt Nellie, I know we said no frog, but there's no English expression that means quite the same, is there?' – 'Can't you say, her looks were no great shakes, strictly speaking, but *such* charm and sweetness, and that's always half the battle?') Although she had been twenty-one, Corinne had had the air of a little girl about her . . . *Not* his type.

'As for the date,' he went on slowly, between puffs, 'I remember it because it was my sister's birthday. Amanda was passing through a Francophile as well as Francophone phase. She adored all things French. Amanda enjoyed the show so much that she asked me to take her to the second concert, but I had to go back to Sandhurst. I believe she went with someone else.'

'Corinne sang a couple of winsomely wistful waltzes,' his aunt said. 'Extraordinary, how things come back to one.'

'Amanda's favourite was a song called "Adieu, Joli Matelot", for which Corinne donned a sailor's uniform and cap and played the harmonica with great *élan* – or do I mean *esprit*?' Payne frowned. 'Sorry, we said no frog . . . All the songs were terribly French. Either tear-jerkingly melancholy, or saccharinely sentimental – or crazily can-cannish.'

'There was a fourth kind, the military march-like song.' Lady Grylls waved an imaginary banner.

'Gosh yes. She sang "La Marseillaise", didn't she? Lest it

41

be forgotten that the French are a nation of barricade-building Gavroches and Cosettes . . . She wound up with "The Trolley Song". I think it was at that point that Maurice Chevalier joined her on stage?'

'He did! The old fraud! He had his arm around Corinne's shoulders and he kept pinching her cheek. He looked avuncular and brimmed over with bonhomie, yet I couldn't help thinking there was something of the dirty old man about him.' Lady Grylls sniffed. 'It didn't help that he sang "Thank Heaven for Little Girls". I believe he had the idea of staging *Gigi* with Corinne in the title role, but then he died or something.'

'I suppose the show could be called an extravaganza. With hindsight, it was of considerable curiosity value,' Payne said. 'Jolly old-fashioned, even then. I mean, it took place between the swinging '60s and the raucous '70s. It was a rather self-conscious throwback to a previous age – *la belle époque*, no less. The Beatles or the Rolling Stones might not have existed – or for that matter Johnny Halliday. 1968 Paris might never have happened.'

'After the concert we went to see Corinne in her dressing room,' Lady Grylls said. 'It was filled with flowers, remember, Hughie? Some of the bouquets were as tall as Corinne!'

Payne nodded. 'There was a highly charismatic friendly giant sitting there with her, smoking a big black cigar. He gave us champagne. He couldn't have been anything but American. That was the great Mr Lark.'

'It was Mr Lark who groomed Corinne for stardom,' Lady Grylls explained. 'The urchin hairstyle by Elrhodes, which became her trademark, was his idea – the tricolour dresses too. He organized all Corinne's domestic and foreign tours and, generally, took charge of her life.'

'Corinne drank nothing but camomile tea sweetened with honey. She was eating caramelized almonds out of a cellophane bag,' Major Payne went on. 'She ate like a little bird . . .'

'I think you must have fancied her,' Antonia said.

'She was wearing a high-collared blue dress with white

cuffs and a red bow at the throat. She was bourgeois respectability and wholesomeness personified. She was perfectly polite, in a monosyllabic kind of way. Extremely shy. She kept leafing through a book called *The Language of Flowers*. No coquettish toss of the fringe, no calling eye, no provocative laugh. In fact there was more than a whiff of the convent girl about her. I keep telling you, my love – not my type.'

'*Quite* unlike her mamma,' Lady Grylls said with a frown. 'Ruse, you see, couldn't have been more different.'

There was a pause. Again, Antonia was aware of a tension.


'Aunt Nellie and Corinne's mamma went to school together,' Payne explained chattily. 'They were the greatest of chums.'

Lady Grylls said that they had been to *two* schools together. Lady Eden's, then St Mary's Ascot. At one time they had been inseparable. 'Heaven knows why. We had so little in common. A case of opposites attracting, I suppose. Consider. I was pink, podgy, plain and placid. Ruse – her real name was Rosamund – was strikingly beautiful, wildly temperamental and extravagantly romantic. She had almond-shaped eyes and a touch of the tar-brush about her. I believe I had a crush on her for a bit.'

'Something of a rebel, weren't you, darling?'

'St Mary's was a terrible place – impossibly moralistic and repressive – consequently I rebelled, yes. One of my schoolmistresses, I remember, called me a force for anarchy. Nobody would have thought it, looking at me.' Lady Grylls paused. 'I stole sulphur from the chemistry lab to make stink bombs. I read *The Virgin and the Gypsy* at night, by torchlight, under the sheets . . . You know the scene where Yvette meets the gypsy and he knows at once that she is a virgin?'

'I know the scene.' Antonia nodded. Her husband shot her a startled look.

'Oh, I used to get such a kick out of it! I knew several

Mae West songs by heart – some unspeakably dirty ones. I used to spread rumours concerning the proclivities of our gym mistress. Well, we were all sex-mad and impossibly knowing. Ruse was particularly keen on the chaps and she used to tell everybody she was having a tempestuous affair with a guardsman. She also claimed she had Ethiopian blood in her. She was an incorrigible fantasist – a terrible liar, in fact. But she almost always managed to be extremely convincing.' Lady Grylls stubbed out her cigarette.

'Is that why you called her Ruse?' Payne asked. 'Because of her penchant for porkies?'

'I suppose so. She got the Ethiopian idea from a book – some legendary Ethiopian saga. Had a snake in the title. What was it? *Cobra* something?'

'*Kebra Nagast*. The legendary Ethiopian saga.'

'Yes. Goodness, Hughie, how do you find the time? You mustn't allow him to read so much. Saps a man's energy,' Lady Grylls told Antonia. 'That's what Hughie's uncle used to say. Rory never read a novel in his life. He started a Dornford Yates once and it nearly killed him . . . Incidentally, has Hughie taught you to ride yet?'

Antonia answered that he had – but she had been hopeless.

'You weren't too bad.' Payne kissed her. He turned towards his aunt. 'Tell us more about Ruse, darling.'

'Well, her people were frightfully conventional. Her father was a stockbroker, her mother played bridge. They lived in a mock-Tudor house in Kettering. Extremely well off – her father had made a fortune on the Stock Exchange – but frightfully conventional. Ruse despised them, rather. I became Ruse's confidante when she fell in love with *le falcon noir*. That was the name we had for the Frenchman who was eventually to become Corinne's father. Franglais, you know.'

Lady Grylls paused and her eyes narrowed. 'His name was François-Enrique. He was much older than us, at least twenty years older. Tall, terribly good-looking, in a dark, brooding way. Yellow-grey eyes. His nose did resemble a beak and he wore a long, black coat with a scarlet silk lining. He was a prosperous French businessman who had divorced his English wife. I was there when Ruse first met him, you see.'

'Where did you meet?'

'At an Ascot tea shop. He chatted her up. Started talking about the difference between French pâtisserie, English cakes and American cookies – of all the unpromising chat-up lines! Ruse was smitten. She went very white. They started meeting regularly and she dragged me along with her, as some sort of chaperone. We used to play truant, so that we could go and meet him. One weekend, I remember – light, Hughie.' Lady Grylls had taken another cigarette from the pack. Her cheeks had turned pink. 'One weekend he got us on a plane and flew us to Paris where he gave us dinner at Maxim's and took us back later that same night. It was a magical experience.' She inhaled deeply and shut her eyes. 'Extraordinary man.'

Payne gave her a sly look. 'You were in love with him too, weren't you?'

Lady Grylls's eyes remained inscrutable behind the thick lenses. 'As a matter of fact I was. I too was smitten . . . *Le falcon* carried a whiff of danger about him. There was something indefinably *wrong* about him. The kind of man my father called "a bad hat" and warned me against. That only added to his attraction. I remember being consumed with jealousy for quite a bit, resenting Ruse's success, really hating her. Anyhow. He courted her and we were snapped by photographers at all sorts of places. I mean *they –*' Lady Grylls corrected herself with a laugh. 'Wishful thinking! *They* were snapped by photographers. Ruse and *le falcon* were so glamorous, so photogenic. The photos appeared in the *Illustrated London News* – in the *Tatler* and so on. I used to cut them out and paste them in my scrapbooks.'

'Golly. I used to *love* Aunt Nellie's scrapbooks.' Payne smiled reminiscently. 'The Aga Khan and a mystery blonde. Princess Margaret and Peter Townsend. The

Duchess of Argyll and a mystery man. The young Queen and a horse.'

'Ruse and *le falcon* got married and went to live in Paris,' Lady Grylls went on. 'They had Corinne in 1948. They discovered common ground in gambling. Both were inveterate gamblers. They went to places like Monte Carlo. They became regulars at the casinos. They played roulette, blackjack and *chemin de fer*. They made pots of money, but the tide turned and they lost what amounted to a fortune. *Le falcon* then landed in the soup – had a brush with the law, a pretty serious one, I dare say. He was suspected of what they call financial impropriety – of embezzlement on a large scale – of having cheated his firm's clients out of millions and millions of francs. Something on those lines – though they could prove nothing. Ruse adored him and she stuck with him. They were made for one another.'

'Did they love Corinne?'

'Hard to say. Well, they didn't make any fuss over her. They went picnicking *en famille* at the Bois de Boulogne, though I suspect their hearts weren't in it. They were infinitely happier inventing systems for winning at roulette. I didn't mind a flutter now and then myself, but with them it was an obsession. They talked about little else at dinner.' Lady Grylls paused. 'Lethal gamblers – the term might have been coined with them in mind. I found that quite tedious, eventually. Still, I was quite shocked when they died . . . They died together, you know.'

Antonia looked at her. 'They . . . died together? What happened?'

5

# Cat and Mouse

Eleanor Merchant put away the letters. She had suddenly lost interest. She had a copy of the *International Herald Tribune* on her lap now, but wasn't reading it. She had finished her *tarte au citron* and her tea. She couldn't say she had enjoyed her tea, but then she couldn't say she hadn't enjoyed it either. Food no longer interested her. *Citron – chocolat –* as a matter of fact it was all the same to her. She went through the motions, though. She knew she had to eat in order to be able to go on, that was all. To go on, so that she could carry out what she had come all this way for. Her mission.

All the way to Europe. From Boston to Paris and now from Paris to London. By plane, cab and, on one dreadful occasion, the Métro. She hated trains. A long journey – a torture, really. Well, travel *was* derived from the word 'travail', which did mean 'painful effort' – it came from the Latin *trepalium*, a three-pronged instrument of torture! (Eleanor had taken full advantage of her superior education. She had thrived in the rarefied atmosphere of tricky conjunctives and ablative absolutes.)

She was glad she had left Paris. She had found Paris extremely disappointing. Nothing like the lush and colourful romantic image projected by films and photographs. (*An American in Paris* – the famous dance scene beside the Seine!) The great Eiffel Tower was little more than a rusting monstrosity. The celebrated *haute cuisine* had given her

47

indigestion. Then there was the incredible rudeness and arrogance of some Parisians. Parisians seemed to hate Americans.

That tune they were playing on the intercom at the moment . . . 'Paris Is For Lovers' . . . The kind of song Corinne Coreille would sing; perhaps she did sing it. Songs and travel agents made Paris sound like some sort of geographical Viagra. The aphrodisiac city. The city of love. The city *for* love. Love of course meant . . . sex. Eleanor's lips pursed squeamishly – she had never liked sex much . . . Griff had been to Paris several times, each time with a different inamorato, or so she had gathered. (Griff, for some reason, had objected to her use of the word 'inamorato'.) Including the one about whom she had made that disparaging remark. Owen.

Eleanor had had dinner with Griff and Owen once, at New York's Algonquin hotel and famed watering hole. Griff had worn claret-coloured lipstick . . . She hadn't cared much for Owen, in fact not at all. Too aggressively butch, too 'jock' for words. She could remember little about their conversation, apart from it being puerile, suggestive and incredibly silly.

'I love Jesus,' Owen had said. 'No, I love Jesus more than you,' Griff had said. 'You are not worthy of kissing Jesus' feet,' Owen had said. 'I *would* like to kiss Jesus' feet,' Griff had said. 'As a matter of fact,' Owen had said rather complacently, 'I kissed Jesus the other day.'

Jesus, it turned out, was actually the name of a Brazilian boy they were both in love with.

They had then talked about their intention of joining a sect known as Lykaion, whose members seemed to believe in 'unleashing erotic energy' and achieving unparalleled pleasure through pain and violence – self-mutilation came into it – some such pernicious nonsense. At one point Owen had smilingly started to twist Griff's little finger – slowly, backwards. Eleanor had feared it might snap and had nearly shouted to him to stop, but Griff seemed to enjoy the experience. Griff had made a little moaning sound and tilted back his head. Eleanor had always considered herself a woman of the world and yet she had felt shocked and sickened by the spectacle. That kind of thing, she had reflected, has little to do with love. Griff and Owen had been very drunk by then. They had started arguing about the ingredients that went into the making of a drink called kyon. They seemed entirely oblivious of her presence.

Griff had mentioned a Paris club called Le Chevalier d'Eon situated on the Rue des Anglais. It was one of his haunts. He had boasted of meeting an English composer there, someone who had been so taken with him that he had made him the central character of his next, so far unperformed, opera. *Buenas Dias, Bello Diablo*. Eleanor had found the libretto as she had been sorting through Griff's possessions, among the silk dressing gowns, Chervet ties, the Max Factor make-up, Maria Callas CDs, Pierre and Gille posters, black-and-white photos of the improbably named Lya de Putti. (A silent movie actress of the demented diva type, as she had discovered.)

Eleanor had gone to take a look at Le Chevalier d'Eon on her first evening in Paris; it had been a pilgrimage of sorts. She had discovered the place swarming with gendarmes. It had looked like a raid. She had stood not far from the club's garish façade, listening to some of the conversations. There had been a *partouze* – an all-male orgy. Well, it was that sort of place.

She glanced out of the train window once more. The contrast couldn't have been greater. Green meadows, cows and sheep, neat farmhouses, red post boxes, a pub called the Severed Head, overcast skies, a steady drizzle . . . A pastoral picture. Not cheerful exactly, but it had a reassuring effect on her. 'England, England,' Eleanor sang out. 'Green and pleasant land!'

People's eyes fixed on her curiously as they passed her table. Even when silent, she attracted attention. Her face was over-made-up. Her lipstick was the brightest of cyclamen and every couple of minutes she reapplied it to her lips. There were lipstick smudges on her nose and chin. She was wearing a beige picture hat in the mid-1930s fashion, set at a slant to cover one side of her face. Her wispy hair showed from underneath the hat. She had had her hair dyed strawberry blonde the day before, at the hairdresser's at her hotel. She was wearing a pair of egg-yolk yellow gloves. She had a white fur stole draped round her shoulders. It was rather grubby after the fall she had had outside the Gare du Nord. Eleanor had suddenly felt light-headed. Those pills, she supposed.

(Le Chevalier d'Eon, she now remembered reading somewhere, was a historical figure – an eighteenth-century French nobleman who sometimes wore a dress and a cap as a challenge to 'traditional gender roles'. He had given the name to the condition known as 'eonism'.)

The table in front of her was covered with a great number of objects, the whole contents of her handbag, in fact. There were the letters, her lipstick, her passport, receipts from her hotel, wads and wads of dollar bank-notes held together by rubber bands, two handkerchiefs, her psychic journal, two unlabelled jars full of various multi-coloured pills and capsules, a paperback of Henry James's ghost stories, her purse containing euros as well as silver dollars and a book of travellers' cheques.

She had been looking for something, she couldn't say what. It had been a frantic search and it had gone on for some ten minutes, but in the end she had given up. The surge of manic energy having subsided, Eleanor was over-come by fatigue. She was filled with sadness and apathy. Leaning back in her seat, she closed her eyes and thought of her mission.

She was going to England to meet Corinne Coreille. Corinne Coreille didn't know it, not yet. Eleanor felt it imperative that the two of them should meet. Corinne Coreille provided the last existing link with Griff. The link of death. Eleanor thought again of those last terrible moments when the dark red plumes of blood had started spiralling from Griff's open wrists and spreading about the pale blue bath water like so many clouds of crimson smoke . . . She wanted to see with her own eyes what kind of a person Corinne Coreille was. This woman who had exercised such power over her son! There was no one else whom she could talk to about Griff. No one who would *understand*.

None of his boyfriends had been in touch – not one of them had come to the funeral. Certainly not Owen . . . It was the wrong crowd that had turned up. People she hardly knew. Sanctimonious fools, prurient ghouls – some dubious-looking middle-aged men with moustaches – the English composer, tall, majestic, almost Lear-like with his snow-white beard and locks, weeping extravagantly – he had left a china wreath with a black ribbon that said, *Buenas Noches, Bello Diablo* – some distant cousin of Eleanor's, a woman in a purple hat with a veil, shouting, 'Why cremation? What's wrong with a funeral? Now you'll never know where he's going!' It had all been too much . . . Small wonder Eleanor had had a nervous breakdown!

It might be said that Corinne Coreille had sung Griff to death . . . A lethal lullaby . . . *Will it ever cloy? This odd diversity of misery and joy* . . . Eleanor found herself humming under her breath and checked herself. Had there been one particular boy? Somebody who had broken Griff's heart? (More so than any of his predecessors, that was.) Was that why Griff did it? Or had Griff simply decided that he had had enough, that an existence like his was simply not worth living? Had he chosen that particular song as some ironic final statement, as his high camp coda, a silly requiem emblematic of the pursuits of a silly misspent life? *I am feeling young again and quite insane – all because –* Or did his death have anything to do with the Lykaion sect and its teachings?

*A pampered pansy playboy.* That was what her niece had called Griff. Eleanor dabbed at her eyes with her handkerchief. 'I have had a tragic life,' she said. 'I have remained unfulfilled as a woman *and* as a mother.' She found herself thinking back to the day Griff was born. Lyndon – her wayward husband – had not been there. Of course not. Other husbands sat beside their wives' beds in the maternity ward and held and caressed their hands –

but not Lyndon. Lyndon had never been there for her. It had been an incredibly difficult birth. Eleanor had been in labour for forty-eight hours and she had become convinced that Griff didn't really want to be born. She wondered now whether Griff had struck some sort of a deal, so that he wouldn't have to stay long on this earth.

But perhaps Griff hadn't meant to kill himself? That haunting invidious voice might have induced a particularly hopeless mood in him . . . Eleanor wondered what Corinne Coreille would have to say in her defence.

She opened her eyes. 'Chalfont Park, Chalfont Parva, Shropshire, England,' she said aloud. She was going to Chalfont Park. Some grand house, by the sound of it, what in England they called a manor house. It shouldn't be too hard to find. Did it belong to Corinne? Or was Corinne going there on a visit? A thought struck her. Could Corinne be *running away from her*? That suggested not only guilty conscience but fear of retribution! Well, she won't be able to run away from *me*, Eleanor thought, and she nodded to herself grimly.

The widow Saverini, she thought. I am the widow Saverini.


It had been quite incredible, the way she had obtained the Chalfont Park address.

She had arrived in Paris, intent on tracking down Corinne Coreille. Of course Corinne Coreille wasn't listed in the phone book. Eleanor hadn't expected her to be, really, but an idea had already formed itself in her mind. Sitting in her overheated room at the overpriced Hotel Constantinople, she reached out for the telephone and called Corinne's record company, Fabiola, whose number *was* in the book. Substituting her genteel English accent for a brasher American one – not that it would have mattered either way – she asked to speak to somebody in the publicity department. A young man – he had sounded like a young man, extremely pleasant as well as flustered, clearly inexperienced – answered and yes, he spoke English.

(Most French people operating in the excessive and reality-detached world of *le showbiz* did.) In the most casual manner imaginable Eleanor had introduced herself as Tricia Swindon, an American chat-show hostess, and had asked for Corinne Coreille's contact number. For good measure, she had been chewing gum. She had made herself sound ingenuous to the point of naivety – wasn't that how the French imagined Americans to be?

She had explained that it was a matter of great urgency. She needed to speak to Corinne Coreille in person. She had her own TV show in the USA and she wanted to invite Corinne to appear on it. Corinne Coreille had a great following in the USA. Americans still remembered Corinne Coreille's concerts at Carnegie Hall in 1974 and 1982. People still talked about her duets with Danny Kaye and Dean Martin. Ah – 'Amore'! She had babbled on.

She had expected to be referred to Corinne's agent or somebody, and she couldn't believe her ears when the young man started dictating Corinne's home phone number to her. Just like that. Eleanor had been flabbergasted – she had suspected some kind of chicanery, some trick, or indeed a trap . . . Could the police be monitoring her movements? Had she been given the number of the Sûreté perhaps?

After some hesitation, Eleanor had rung the number and almost at once a woman's voice had answered. A maid of some sort, speaking in a very loud voice and with an accent that wasn't French . . . Tipsy, by the sound of it . . . *Yes, I speak Ee-nglish. Yes, this is Mademoiselle Coreille's residence. You want to speak to Mademoiselle Coreille? Oh, but she is away, madame! Mademoisellle Coreille and Maître Maginot, they leave together for the airport. They leave for England. A contact address? Mademoiselle Coreille, she stays at French embassy in London tonight and tomorrow, then she arrives at Chalfont Park on the evening of 3rd April. Chalfont Park, that is correct. Eet eez a big house in England . . . Chalfont Park, Chalfont Parva, Shropshire, England. That is correct. And there was a phone number also, yes.*

The phone number followed.

There must be something wrong, surely? It was a trick –
must be! Or perhaps not. Oversights did happen. Deliberate misunderstandings, too. Eleanor had suffered at the
hands of unreliable – as well as of vengeful – maids, so she
knew how it could be. Maids with a grudge were the devil
. . . Yes, the maid might have done just the *opposite* to what
she had been instructed.

Who *was* Maître Maginot? Eleanor's eyelids flickered –
closed. For some reason she felt exhausted. She hadn't yet
managed to recover from the jet lag, and now she was on
a train, which had never happened before – she *hated* trains
– but she wouldn't have had it any other way. She
wouldn't have wanted to be like the sage who said, *Re
imperfecte mortuus sum*. Eleanor frowned, suddenly struck
by a thought. I died with my purpose unachieved? How
*could* he have said it if he was dead? Was he speaking from
the nether world perhaps?

It would be no good going to the French embassy in
London and asking to see Corinne Coreille, but Chalfont
Park would be a different thing. An isolated manor house
. . . perfect. If she could get there first and see how the land
lay . . . She felt an odd thrill, at the thought of the isolated
house. She remembered the tales her uncle, the General,
had told her about his experiences in the Korean war, and
an image promptly grew in her mind.

Eleanor saw herself in combat gear, a grenade in her
hand, a slim army knife held between her teeth, her face
smeared in mud, her body close to the ground as she
crawled towards the house . . . She'd need to find out
where exactly Chalfont Parva was situated. Some small
village, by the sound of it, in the county of Shropshire . . .
A map. She would need to get a map . . . She would arrive
at Waterloo. Then a cab. No, not another train, thank
you very much – a cab. She hated trains. Money was no
object –

Eleanor could hear the raindrops tapping on the
window-pane, like so many fingers telling her something
in Morse . . . Why, it *was* Morse! As it happened, Eleanor
knew the Morse alphabet. She inclined her head towards

the window and listened . . . Sounded like a message of some sort. The . . . third . . . of . . . April? That was the date of Corinne Coreille's arrival at Chalfont Park – of course!

*The third of April. Do not forget. The third of April. Do not forget. The third of –*

Who was sending the coded message? Was it . . . Griff?

# 6

# Murder on Safari

'Good lord,' Major Payne said, remembering. 'Corinne's parents died some horrid death, didn't they?'

Lady Grylls agreed that indeed it had been horrid. It wasn't the kind of end one would have wished to one's bitterest enemies. Too horrid for words.

'What happened?' Antonia asked again.

Lady Grylls started lighting another cigarette. Her hand shook a little and her face became mottled. Well, Ruse and *le falcon* had been killed in Africa . . . Killed, yes . . . Killed *and* mutilated. They had gone to Kenya on a safari. That had been surprising since neither of them was a great traveller, Ruse always said she was no good in the heat, and it wasn't as though Africa was famous for its casinos, was it? Lady Grylls would have understood it, if they'd gone to Las Vegas or some such place . . . Thank God they hadn't taken Corinne with them. They had ignored the warnings about the notorious criminal gang operating in the area where they had chosen to stay. In their second or third week they had left the hotel in a hired jeep.

'They were never seen alive again. There was a search and their bodies were found, or rather what was left of them. It seems wild beasts had devoured most of them. They had been terribly mangled, unrecognizable, or so they said . . . Don't let's talk about it.'

There was a pause. *Neither of them was a great traveller . . . Ruse always said she was no good in the heat . . .* Curious,

Antonia thought. Or am I being ridiculously fanciful? Why do I always notice things like that? 'Who identified them?' she asked.

'Who identified them? Goodness, my dear – you don't think –' Lady Grylls shook her head. 'They were identified by Madame Coreille. *Le falcon*'s mother. She flew over to Kenya. She was a tough old bird, one of the leading psychoanalysts in France at the time, but what she saw shook her up. She told me about it later. She decided to have the mortal remains buried there, in Kenya. I do hope it was a bullet or a knife that killed them first.' Lady Grylls paused. 'The news found its way into the British press. I believe I collected every scrap of information there was about the case.'

Antonia asked, 'Have you kept your scrapbooks?'

Lady Grylls pushed her glasses up her nose and said she was not sure. 'I may have thrown them away. I burnt an awful lot of stuff over Christmas. Had a big bonfire made . . . So much rubbish everywhere . . . Or they are lying somewhere, gathering dust. I don't know. At the bottom of some trunk most likely. By the way, Hughie – that stool Peverel wants so much – it's not a real Pugin, is it?'

'They used to be in the library,' Payne said.

'I *mustn't* drop ash in the saucer – why doesn't someone tell me off? Provost hates it when I do. Where's the damned ashtray?' Lady Grylls peered round in an abstracted manner.

She seemed reluctant to divulge the true whereabouts of her scrapbooks. Emphatically vague, Antonia decided – and she wondered as to the reason.

Payne said, 'Corinne was badly affected by her parents' death, wasn't she?'

'She was . . . terribly affected. Poor thing. She was twelve when it happened. They tried to keep her in the dark but it slipped out somehow. She'd gone to live with her grandmother. Madame Coreille came into a lot of money about that time and she opened her own clinic. I don't think *she* gambled. Some kind of inheritance. Rory was of the opinion that the bloody Frenchwoman would only succeed in messing the gel up completely.'

'How bad was the trauma?' Antonia asked – though what she really wanted to know was the exact provenance of Madame Coreille's good fortune.

'Bad enough . . . Corinne read the story of her parents' death in some ghastly gossip rag – *Ici Paris*, I think. A magazine. Isn't it odd that the French have no tabloid papers, only gossip magazines? *Eaten Alive.* Some such ghastly headline. The shock was so severe that Corinne lost her power of speech. She stopped eating – became extremely withdrawn. That went on for some time. Corinne didn't seem to respond to *any* kind of treatment. Madame Coreille had tried analysis – she was at her wits' end. Then, one day, something very strange happened. Can you –'

'Corinne started singing?'

'You are a dangerous woman, Antonia – nothing ever escapes you! Yes. *Corinne started singing.* Madame Coreille thought at first it was somebody on the wireless. She imagined it was Piaf or somebody. You see, Corinne had *never* sung before. She'd never shown any particular interest in music either. It was an extraordinary voice. Pure and light – like a bell. *Puissant*, I think was the word Madame Coreille used. She phoned me that same evening. A couple of days later I flew to Paris. I knew what she meant the moment Corinne opened her mouth. It was quite extraordinary.'

'I believe I've heard the story before,' Payne said. 'You thought she sang like an angel. It made you blub.'

'Don't scoff, Hughie. You sound like Peverel when you do. Corinne did sing like an angel. And I did blub. Yes. It was a very special kind of voice . . . The more she sang the more her health improved. Madame Coreille hired a private music tutor for her, who was astounded and predicted that before long Corinne would have *toute la France* at her feet. Well, it happened seven years later. I was in Paris, sitting in the TV studio, next to Madame Coreille, watching Corinne appear on *Jeu de la Chance*.'

'What game of chance is that?' Antonia asked.

'The show that discovers and promotes new singing talent. I think they still have it. I am sure you are familiar with the kind of thing? *Fame Academy – Pop Idol*. Don't you watch them?' Lady Grylls breathed incredulously as Antonia's face remained blank.

'My wife's viewing habits are uncompromisingly intellectual,' Payne said. 'She rarely watches the box and when she does, it's only carefully selected programmes.'

'Really? How very interesting. My dear Antonia, you don't know what you've been missing. I wonder if it's to do with you –' Lady Grylls broke off. 'What they have on *Pop Idol* is a lot of singularly talentless young people wearing extraordinary clothes, posturing and squawking in the most incredible manner. When they lose, they start crying. Such fun!'

Antonia found herself puzzling over what her aunt by marriage had been going to say. *I wonder if it's to do with you –* What? Being middle class?

'Of course Corinne was a completely different kettle of fish. There was a collective gasp the moment she opened her mouth,' Lady Grylls went on. 'She sang two little-known Piaf songs. "La Fille de Joie" and "L'Homme Qui . . ." something or other. The man who – no, can't remember.'

'*Qui m'aime?*' Payne suggested. '*Qui m'assassine?*'

'Don't be silly, Hughie. Anyhow. That launched her singing career. She was an instant hit. Never looked back. The whole of France voted for her. *She got every single vote.* They said General de Gaulle was one of the callers. Mr Lark took the next plane from America. He had watched the show on TV. He offered his services, was accepted and took control of Corinne's career. He made sure Corinne was showered with offers. Olympia – Carnegie Hall. The rest, as they say, is history.'

There was a pause. 'Was there ever a man in her life?' Antonia asked.

'No. I don't think so. I don't think she's ever had a romance.' Lady Grylls sighed. 'Poor gel.'

'No boyfriends?'

'No. Nothing serious at any rate. She was too busy singing.'

'Mr Lark. I seem to remember a rumour,' Payne said. 'Wasn't there something between them?'

'I may be wrong,' Lady Grylls said, 'but I don't think she's ever had an intimate relationship with a man. No, no girlfriends either. Out of the question. One simply doesn't think of Corinne in those terms. Isn't that extraordinary?'

'Oh, but you are wrong. A lot of people *do* think of Corinne in those terms,' a man's voice said. 'You'd be amazed.'

# 7

# Sleep and His Brother

Eleanor didn't know how much time had passed. She was sure she hadn't been asleep, not quite, only floating in some self-induced trance-like daze.

She had been thinking of that golden September day twelve years previously, when Griff and she had taken a leisurely drive up the coast from Los Angeles to Santa Barbara. It had been extremely hot to start with but then, just south of Ventura, there came that magical instant when the air cooled and the ocean appeared without warning in a blaze of reflected sunlight, a sudden flash of infinite sky and dazzling cobalt blue, waves breaking on reefs like lace on a glass table. The beauty had been so great, so overpowering, it rendered them speechless. It had felt like receiving an unexpected draught of some clarifying narcotic. 'If only we could stay here for ever,' Griff had said.

Eleanor felt confused and disoriented. Her heart was beating like a drum. For a couple of moments she had no idea where she was. Was this a train? She never travelled by train – never! She'd always had a beautiful chauffeur-driven car at her disposal – her 1954 Rolls-Royce Silver Wraith Six Light Saloon. Trains made her feel ill. She needed to get out – she felt a panic attack approaching – where was the emergency button? Gasping, she half rose from her seat.

'Would you like more tea, madame?' The waiter had

come up to her. She saw him look at the heap on the table as though he disapproved, then back at her.

'I don't want anything, thank you very much,' Eleanor managed to say.

'Is there anything wrong?'

'No – nothing wrong!' Eleanor snapped. She felt annoyed, which was a good sign for it meant that she had recovered. She resumed her seat. The waiter lingered and stared . . . Arrogant puppy! Sleek raven-black hair. Beetle brows. Melodramatically flaring nostrils. Buffed up through regular workouts. Very male, impossibly macho – oh so full of himself!

'Not long until we arrive at Waterloo,' the waiter said.

'Have you heard of Corinne Coreille?' Eleanor asked on an impulse, making it sound like an insult.

'*Who?*' He appeared startled. He was no more than twenty-eight or nine.

'Corinne Coreille.'

'Oh. She was a singer, no? *Very* old?'

'She is not very old,' Eleanor bristled.

'No? She is dead?'

'She is not dead. She is in England.'

'In England? I thought she was dead.'

Eleanor watched him swagger down the aisle. Why couldn't she have had a son like him? Somebody who thought Corinne Coreille was dead and shrugged his shoulders with eloquent indifference when told she wasn't.

Then the thought came into her head again. *Without Corinne Coreille's lachrymose French songs Griff wouldn't have killed himself.* Eleanor was now convinced of it. Corinne Coreille's voice had been the catalyst. Yes. It had – tipped the balance. Corinne Coreille's songs were bad for sensitive, vulnerable boys of Griff's kind.

Eleanor's research had revealed that Corinne Coreille sang the French version of 'The Little White Cloud That Cried', which, she had gathered, was what was known as a 'gay anthem'; it was played regularly at Le Chevalier d'Eon.

She held out her hand before her in an eloquent gesture.

'You must stop at once. Wasn't it enough that you killed my only son? This is a matter of life and death, can you not see that?'

She broke off. She had had the sudden sensation of being whirled round in one of those revolving wheels at the circus. She felt giddy, nauseous, completely powerless . . . What she experienced next was a terrifying fragmentation – a total dissolution of her identity. Who *am* I? Eleanor moaned. She longed for peace, for deep, dreamless sleep – for oblivion – for death even . . . Sleep and Death. They were brothers, weren't they, according to the ancient Greek proverb?

My emotional repertoire is not up to tragedy, Eleanor had once wittily said at a party in New York – to Gore Vidal, as it happened. But it was true – she was not equipped for dealing with tragedy . . . Pull yourself up, girl, she murmured. Perhaps she could take a sedative? She picked up a bottle of pills and capsules and unscrewed the top. Now which was which? Were the orange capsules sedatives and the blue ones stimulants, or was it the other way round? What were the *yellow* ones for? It was *so* unlike her to forget! She took one of each. Three capsules in total. Then, on an impulse, she took a fourth – a yellow one. The same colour as her gloves. She closed her eyes.

Eleanor used to enjoy sleeping. The ancient god Sleep – whom she always saw as a gracious host resplendent in Byzantine robes and a crown – used to conduct her into what she privately thought of as her true dimension, in which she became a vivid player, weightless and some-times skittish, embroiled in obscure adventures, some risky, some very odd indeed, most of them delightful, which puzzled her only when she woke up – but since Griff's death, sleep had become something of a burden. She regularly had nightmares, from which she woke screaming, sweating and gasping for breath, with skin-crawling recollections of being pursued, buried alive, mutilated or infected with hideous diseases.

The dream she had had the night before had not been as terrible as that, but it had been harrowing enough. After a long journey, having walked down endless dark corridors, stumbled through a swamp, in which something had swirled and hissed, and inched her way across a narrow bridge slung high above a dark abyss, she had at long last managed to confront Corinne Coreille. She had felt angry – furious. She had spoken in a choked voice – *My boy, what did you do to my boy?*

She was clutching a knife in her hand, the army knife that had been between her teeth earlier on, its blade flashing in the bright light, blinding her. She had worked herself into an unbridled frenzy and kept thrusting the knife forward in the direction of Corinne's face. In response Corinne only gave a sad smile and held out her hand gently, in an imploring manner, palm upward, as though saying adieu to a parting lover. *You crazy bitch.* Infuriated, Eleanor slashed at Corinne's neck several times, but the odd thing was . . . there was no blood. Not a drop of it. And the knife met with no resistance at all!

Sinking into sleep once more, Eleanor heard a voice whisper in her ear.

*She is a false creation. She is just a name and a voice. She does not exist.*

8

# That Obscure Object of Desire

Peverel de Broke, Lady Grylls's other nephew, the son of her late brother Lionel, was a year younger than his cousin Hugh. He was very tall and managed to look at once languid, athletic and rather distinguished. But for a weakish chin, he might have been thought handsome. Lady Grylls had observed that his was the kind of face that sixty-five years ago would have been considered incomplete without one of those silly toothbrush moustaches and a rimless eyeglass. The kind of man who would be equally comfortable in a dinner jacket and an old Barbour, thought Antonia. Peverel was clever, Hugh had observed, in that whimsical English way that disconcerts and misleads foreign diplomats. Lady Grylls resented what she called 'Peverel's tiresome propensity for meaningless badinage'. (She had been particularly annoyed by a joke Peverel had told in which somebody confuses Eton with Eden.)

Peverel's sun-bleached hair and eyebrows in conjunction with his deep tan suggested an explorer who spent half the year in hot climes, which was not too far from the truth. He had returned from Shanghai a couple of days earlier. Peverel travelled round the globe in the capacity of a trend spotter, an unusual and, he had hinted, highly lucrative occupation, which his aunt for one refused to take seriously.

The night before, Peverel had sat explaining exactly what it was he did. He collected information for brands like Volvo, Intel, British Airways and Nestlé. He diagnosed and explored trends in everyday life. (Antonia thought it all a bit obscure.) He went to supermarkets where he stopped people, pointed to items in their shopping basket and asked why they had bought them. ('Infernal cheek,' Lady Grylls had said.) He eavesdropped on conversations on trains, planes, buses, beaches and boats. ('Not at all surprised,' Lady Grylls had said.) He and his colleagues never knew when a snippet of information might prove useful. They took what was happening 'out there' and translated it into 'stuff our clients could use'.

Everybody knew that Helen Fielding had dreamt up Bridget Jones, but apparently it was a trend spotter who diagnosed the single white professional syndrome first. It wasn't a trend spotter who invented the term 'wigger', to describe white youths copying blacks, but it was again one of Peverel's colleagues who introduced it to the media.

Peverel had entered the drawing room and was looking down at what appeared to be internet downloads.

'You'd be amazed to hear that from the very start of her career Corinne Coreille's been the object of intense prurient speculation,' he said. 'According to a website called Rumour Has It, Corinne Coreille had simultaneous affairs with the octogenarian Charlie Chaplin and Sophia Loren during the making of *A Countess from Hong Kong*, though oddly enough she rebuffed Marlon Brando's attentions. That was in 1967. A roll-call of her alleged lovers includes Maurice Chevalier, Brigitte Bardot, Mr Lark, Alain Delon, General de Gaulle –'

Lady Grylls gave her vast explosive snort. 'Stuff and nonsense!'

'– Peter Sellers, Simone de Beauvoir, a defrocked Italian priest and the teenage Prince Albert of Monaco, whose later inability to marry some have attributed to the effect Corinne Coreille had on him.'

'This is not Corinne Coreille's official website, is it?' Antonia said.

'No. Corinne's official website is maintained by a Belgian called Bruno Van den Brande and it is bland and somewhat boring. Want to know what it says? Corinne Coreille's career was at its zenith between 1967 and 1989. She started as a Piaf clone and a variety *vedette*, but evolved into an international star, part pop, part diva. She became an iconic and later a cultish figure in Latin and Germanic countries and in Russia – also, in Japan, where a Corinne doll was produced last year. In 1972 Corinne's face became the model for Marianne, the symbol of France. She was painted by Warhol and photographed by Cecil Beaton, Horst and Norman Parkinson –'

'Wasn't she in some film?' Payne interrupted. 'Or did they only *consider* her for one?'

'Well, Alfred Hitchcock told François Truffaut that he wanted to shoot a murder scene in a cabaret where Corinne Coreille sits and watches her doppelgänger perform on stage. Buñuel did give her a walk-on part in his film *That Obscure Object of Desire*. She isn't credited. She appears for about two seconds.'

'From such trivia is fanatical cinephilia born . . .'

Lady Grylls rolled her eyes at Antonia as though to say, Heaven preserve me from clever nephews.

'Quite . . . An independent Swiss director intended to shoot a Gallic version of *The Wizard of Oz*, with Corinne as Dorothy, but plans were abandoned when the L.M. Baum estate objected strongly to the script on account of the "great number of inappropriate scenes" . . . The proposed title was *L'Histoire d'Oz* . . . What else do you want to know?' The sheets rustled in Peverel's hands. 'In her prime Corinne modelled for Yves St Laurent and Chanel, but she has a particular weakness for Lacroix. She won the Eurovision song contest in 1970. She performed songs from *The King and I* in French for the Duke and Duchess of Windsor at a soirée at their villa in the Bois de Boulogne on 4th July 1971.'

'*Le Roi et Moi*?' Payne murmured. 'Doesn't sound right somehow.'

'She sang Russian gypsy songs at the Kremlin for the Brezhnevs, "Hands Across the Sea" at the White House, for the Nixons and later for the Reagans, and "C'est Si

Bon" for the whole Communist Politburo of China. In one single year she gave three hundred performances on German television. She is a member of the controversial Kabbalah movement, which promotes an ancient brand of Judaism and promises immortality. She appears on a triangular San Marino stamp and an orchid in Liechtenstein was named after her.'

'There seem to be the devil of a lot of websites devoted to her.'

'A reasonable number – nothing like Madonna. Most are perfectly innocent but some are unwholesome . . . A little *too* esoteric even for my understanding . . . We are talking fetish.' Peverel cleared his throat. 'Mule, Octopus, Pendragon, Elf, Pigsnout, Oedipus R, Killerbitch, Flasher, Weasel . . . Some of these men – I assume they are men – are interested in Corinne's hair, others in her hands. I bet you didn't know that the little finger of Corinne's left hand is as long as her index finger, did you?'

'D'you mean there are people who get a kick out of that sort of thing?' Lady Grylls suddenly guffawed.

'They do seem to, yes. One chap calling himself Chirophile – Greek for "lover of hands" – has written several erotic poems on the subject of Corinne's hands. He wants to "lay a little lick" on each individual knuckle . . . Another website – maintained by Sniffer – focuses on Corinne Coreille's favourite scent.'

'What *is* her favourite scent?' Antonia asked.

'Old-fashioned violets . . . Footspy, on the other hand, is intensely curious about the kind of shoes she wears. There are at least – let me see – twenty pages of photos of shoes. High heels, boots, sandals . . . It is alleged that these are all the shoes Corinne has worn over the last thirty years. Look.'

'Goodness. Poor child. She does seem to attract oddballs.'

'As usual, darling, you've hit the nail on the head . . . Now, *must* you smoke?' Peverel sighed as his aunt lit a cigarette. 'You know very well what Dr Morgan said.'

'Spoilsport,' Lady Grylls said somewhat childishly. 'Or wet blanket, if you prefer.'

'D'you mean me or Morgan?'

'*You*. Morgan too. But you are worse than him.'

'Well, wet blanket would be the more appropriate expression,' Peverel pointed out after a moment's consideration. 'Given your dangerous habit of leaving smouldering fags about.'

'I do nothing of the sort.' Lady Grylls blew out a smoke ring provocatively. She seemed to have decided not to lose her temper with him. 'You are what the French call *un empêcheur de danser en rond*.'

'Somebody who prevents others from dancing in a ring?' Payne translated dubiously.

'Dr Morgan said I should smoke *less*. A rule with which I have complied.' Lady Grylls scowled at Peverel. 'I used to smoke ten a day, now I am down to eight, so yah-boo sucks to you.'

'Corinne's kissing the Pope's hand!' Antonia exclaimed as she stood peering over Peverel's shoulder. 'Is that really the Pope or a look-alike?'

It was the Pope himself, Peverel said. Corinne had sung 'Ave Maria' at the Vatican in 1985. (It was Peverel's Italian scout who had provided the information.) Catholics regarded Corinne as some sort of a holy *vierge* figure and a candidate for sainthood. She was reputed to have healed a little girl of a particularly disfiguring birthmark by merely touching her. Once her singing career came to an end, she'd go into a nunnery, or so it was alleged. Corinne Coreille had made a much-publicized vow to serve God. An aunt of Corinne's, her father's sister, had been a Mother Superior at a convent near Lourdes. That must have fuelled the speculation.

'And now, ladies and gentlemen – from the sublime to the ridiculous –' Peverel held up another sheet for their inspection – 'I Want To Be Corinne . . . A trannies' website.'

Antonia smiled. She could see how Corinne Coreille's fringe, dramatic mascara-ed eyes, elaborate frocks, demure nun-like manner and stylized gestures made her an impersonator's delight.

'Corinne has become something of a gay icon,' Peverel went on. 'The reason, I suppose, is obvious. She never married – she's led a reclusive and rather enigmatic existence – her appearance has never changed – she has stayed young and beautiful. Her speciality is the melodramatic, tear-drenched *chanson* on the subject of hopeless love. She's been dubbed the French Judy Garland.'

Corinne Coreille's songs – one of Peverel's four gay scouts had reported – were currently favoured listening in Old Compton Street in London, at some particularly flamboyant locales in Berlin, in certain Tangier tavernas, as well as on the beaches of Mykonos. On a more elevated note, Corinne Coreille was said to have inspired Tennessee Williams' last unfinished play, in which an alcoholic baseball player can make love to his wife only when listening to the songs of a mysterious French *chanteuse* whose parents have been devoured by African lions.

'One young American apparently slashed his wrists as he lay in a hot bath while listening to Corinne sing "Mad About the Boy" in French,' Peverel went on. 'The dead boy's mother – incidentally, his name was Griff – seems to have gone mad with grief.'

'Really?' Antonia looked up.

'French farce meets Greek tragedy,' Payne murmured. 'Or am I being too awfully callous? Agamemnon did die in his bath, didn't he?'

'Lesbians admire Corinne for being sensual, pure and discreet,' Peverel continued. 'They insist she is one of them – a vanilla.'

'I haven't heard so much nonsense in my life,' Lady Grylls said.

'The suicide story – how did your scout get hold of it?' Antonia asked.

'There is a website that's been constructed by the dead boy's mother. It's she who tells the gruesome tale in some detail. She writes under the *nom de guerre* of Saverini. She appears to be some super-rich heiress and quite demented to boot.'

'Saverini?' Major Payne frowned thoughtfully.

'Saverini appears in several photos in which she is seen posing with her son. It is impossible to say what either of them really looks like since in each photo they wear some kind of elaborate fancy dress. They appear as mustachioed grenadiers, as eighteenth-century madams wearing powdered perukes and covered in patches, as little Lord Fauntleroy and the Earl of Dorincourt, as a pair of jolly sailors, as sinister nurses and as kneeling nuns.'

'How perfectly ghastly,' Lady Grylls said.

'A fearful Freudian nightmare, I entirely agree. Saverini explains that she often has dinner *à deux* with the marble urn containing her dead son's ashes. She expresses the opinion that Corinne Coreille's CDs should be boycotted and that Corinne herself should be despatched to Devil's Island. She also reports that her son has made attempts at contacting her . . . My cartridge was running out of ink, so I didn't print any of it.'

Lady Grylls shook her head. 'Don't tell me that anyone can put idiocies like that on the internet.'

'Anyone can – and they do it all the time. Why don't you try it sometime, darling? We are already connected. Who knows, you may even be able to get a good price for Chalfont on eBay.' Peverel winked at his cousin. He reached out, took a piece of cake from the cake stand and started munching lazily. 'Do you think I might have a cup of tea? *Thank* you, Antonia. You are the only one here who cares about me . . . Incidentally, Corinne Coreille also plays a part in the metrosexuality phenomenon.'

'What *is* metrosexuality?' Lady Grylls asked.

'That, darling, is a subject you could introduce when you preside over the next session of your local Women's Institute. Metrosexuality,' Peverel explained, 'is where straight men do things that are decidedly gay, like wearing salmon-pink shirts, putting on fake tan, having their eyebrows "done" and their nails buffed – as well as listening to songs from musicals and to Corinne Coreille. This last applies mostly, though not exclusively, to the Continent.'

There was a pause. 'That all?' Payne said.

Peverel took a sip of tea. 'You want the extreme trivia as well? Corinne is allergic to cats. Detective stories frighten her. When she was a girl, she was passionate about playing poker with her grandmother. She displayed a distinct gambling streak, though in later life she was too busy to ever visit a casino. Her favourite toy was a glove puppet called Miss Mountjoy, a rather bossy governess-y character in a turban. Miss Mountjoy was forever telling people what to do or not to do.'

'I remember Miss Mountjoy.' Lady Grylls nodded. 'I was staying with them in Paris once and Corinne followed me around the house with that damned puppet on her hand, saying, "You smoke too much. Smoking is bad for you. You must stop at once." Earlier on Miss Mountjoy had told Ruse off for putting too much make-up on! Corinne was driving everybody potty. She was seven or eight. Long time ago.'

So Corinne *does* have an authoritarian streak, Antonia thought. 'What about her more recent activities?' she asked.

'Well, in 1990 Corinne Coreille started slowing down and then there was a sudden five-year hiatus, when she simply disappeared from view,' Peverel said. 'That was in 1997, a month after she had the *Légion d'honneur* bestowed on her.'

'I imagine her disappearance unleashed more rumours?' Payne said.

'It did. Hope this is not getting too tedious. That she'd become a lay nun in Jerusalem, that she'd got married to a lion tamer, that she'd died and been buried secretly, that she'd opened a florist's shop in Dieppe, that she'd married a transsexual illusionist, that she was paralysed after a car crash and could only breathe with an oxygen mask, that she'd renounced all her wealth and become a nurse in a leper colony in Zanzibar.' Peverel paused. 'Well, Corinne Coreille resurfaced with a triumphant concert in Osaka,

Japan, last November. Here are some pictures from the concert.'

'What did I tell you? Unchanged,' Lady Grylls wheezed.

'And she's wearing a Chanel dress.'

'Are you sure this is a recent picture?' Major Payne asked his cousin.

'Well, yes.' Peverel tapped the sheet. 'Telephoto 2002.'

'She looks no more than twenty-eight, thirty at the most. Look at her jaw-line,' Antonia said.

'One of my scouts does believe she's had something major done at a Swiss clinic, though there's been no confirmation of plastic surgery.'

'Excuse me, m'lady.' Provost's voice was heard from the doorway.

'I'm running out of cigarettes,' Lady Grylls said. 'Provost, would you be good enough to tell that boy of yours to hop on his bike, pedal to the village and get me the usual?'

'Very good, m'lady.' Provost lingered. 'Excuse me, m'lady. Mr Jonson has arrived.'

# 9

# Towards Zero

Having checked for any text messages from Griff, Eleanor Merchant switched off her mobile phone. It is only a question of time, she murmured.

So Chalfont Park belonged to Lady Grylls . . . Eleanor slowly ran her tongue across her upper lip. She was thinking about the call she had made minutes before the train had arrived at Waterloo. It was Lady Grylls's butler who had answered. It was good to know the exact set-up. *Lady Grylls*. Fancy Corinne having such grand friends. *Wrong number*, Eleanor had said and rung off. Well, the more she knew about Chalfont Park, the better. *Forewarned is forearmed*. She had heard her uncle, the General, say that on a great number of occasions. Eleanor had decided to conduct the whole thing like a military operation in a manner that would have made her uncle proud . . . Dear Uncle Nat. Ninety-six last fall but still going strong at his luxurious nursing home in Palm Beach.

Suddenly Eleanor Merchant had the feeling of having lived that moment before. She experienced a strong sense of déjà vu . . . She was standing outside W.H. Smith's at Waterloo, the grubby stole around her shoulders, her picture hat set at an even sharper angle, her yellow gloves on her hands, her brocade overnight bag at her side. She felt sure there was something *French* about her appearance. Well, when she had spoken to the butler earlier on, she nearly introduced herself as Madame la Duchesse de

Saverini, an intimate friend of *la chanteuse* Corinne. That would have suggested that Corinne Coreille was on familiar terms with the highest echelons of French society, with personages whose ancestors went back to the halcyon pre-revolutionary days – to the *ancien régime*, no less! (Wasn't *The Laboratory*'s subtitle *L'ancien régime*? Of course it was!)

Eleanor had no doubt she'd have been terribly convincing as a French noblewoman, but she had had second thoughts about it. She needed to be careful. The library at Chalfont Park almost certainly contained a copy of the *Almanach de Gotha*, and they might have wanted to check on her. They would have seen it was a bogus title and then they would have called the police. Eleanor nodded to herself in a satisfied manner. What a fine logical mind she had! How could anyone have ever suggested there was anything *wrong* with her?

Eleanor had a headache and just a touch of vertigo. Some twenty-five minutes before they had reached London, she had started counting telegraph posts and got to fifty-six. If I make it to sixty, Corinne will die, she had said to herself. As it happened, she failed to make it to sixty, but the physical effort of pinning her eyes on an object from a moving carriage, of swivelling her body round each time, had made her giddy.

What was that in her hand? A plastic cup filled with something the English called coffee. Eleanor had no recollection of buying the coffee and she wondered whether she might have picked up somebody else's abandoned cup. This is a risk I am going to take, she thought solemnly as she placed four Solpadols on her tongue and washed them down with the coffee. She must have bought the Solpadol at the pharmacy called Boots, though again she couldn't remember doing so. *Boots, boots, boots,* she recited. Old Kipling, of course. She had always preferred English poetry to American, Master Poe and Miss Emily Dickinson being the only exception . . .

There was something else she had to do. A map, yes. She was going to buy a map. She needed a map. She couldn't proceed without a map. Then – a hotel. A hot bath followed by a little drink – a malt – no, nothing to eat – then a four-poster bed. A four-poster, Griff had said once, was the only bed worth sleeping in. Her original idea had been to get a room for the night at some unostentatious place in Bloomsbury, where she wouldn't be noticed, but now that she had become la Duchesse de Saverini, nothing but the London Ritz would be good enough for her.

I am a woman of many parts, Eleanor thought. As she entered W.H. Smith's, she imagined she saw Griff standing beside one of the magazine racks, engrossed in a copy of *Newsweek*, but she was mistaken. It was somebody else – a stranger, but his hair, like Griff's, was the colour of autumn leaves. How the poor boy started when she impulsively went up to him, placed her hand on his neck and tried to give him a kiss! Eleanor apologized at once and said she had taken him for her son.

I am not a mad woman, I am a wounded woman, she thought. 'The Ritz Hotel,' she told the cab driver. She sounded like one of those stuffy English dowagers now. It was some half an hour later and a map of Shropshire lay on her lap. She held up an imaginary lorgnette to her eyes. That was how she would set off in search of Chalfont Parva tomorrow morning, after some toast and a refreshing cup of Earl Grey tea. It all felt like a real adventure! 'Soon at King's, a mere lozenge to give – and Corinne should have just thirty minutes to live,' Eleanor quoted from *The Laboratory*, substituting 'Corinne' for 'Pauline'.

'I don't suppose you know your Browning, my good man?' Eleanor said to the cab driver. The portly beturbanned Sikh looked at her in his mirror but said nothing. She clicked her tongue. 'I thought not. I am so sorry I do not speak your beautiful language. I'd have *loved* to be able to recite Omar Khayyam in the original.'

If only Griff could have been with her now – how much he'd have enjoyed himself! The mixture of histrionics and high society jinks, a night at the Ritz, the trawl through Merrie England, plus the whiff of danger and the prospect of a police chase would have been to his taste. She could

76

hear Griff say something on the lines of, 'I do admire the English police. So stern and hardboiled. Quite a thrill, the whole business.'

Eleanor had a mental picture of the two of them, walking arm in arm in the formal gardens that surrounded Chalfont Park. She knew *exactly* what they would see. She thought she might be a bit psychic . . . Labyrinthine paths covered in sand as fine as gold dust that went courteously around and about. Geometric lawns that might have been designed by Pythagoras. Emerald-green bushes trimmed with clinical precision into cones, globes and pyramids. Maroon-veined marble balustrades. Slightly sinister statues in indecipherably enigmatic poses on colossal cubic plinths . . .

As the cab paused at traffic lights, she saw the god Abraxas, with his evil chanticleer's head, the arms and torso of a man and the tail of an entwined serpent, cross the road slowly. He turned round and looked at her fixedly. She pretended she hadn't seen him. That, she had discovered, was the right way to act. The last thing she wanted was to encourage Abraxas!

At least she'd had Griff cremated, not buried. She hadn't been able to bear the thought of worms ravaging – *feasting* – on his poor body . . . Once more she saw the polished coffin sliding theatrically into the furnace . . . She missed Griff . . . If it had been possible, she'd have brought the urn with his ashes with her. On second thoughts, no, that would have been quite unnecessary.

Griff, after all, was coming back soon. It was only a question of time.

# 10

# Those Who Walk Away

It was now five in the afternoon. Antonia had walked over to the french window and was standing there, looking out. The last week of March had been warm and sunny and the gardens at Chalfont were glowing squares of rich embroidery. She recalled Mrs Miniver's extravagant words: *a lavishly lovely spring*. The ancient trees were rounded, cushiony and mustard-gold, the grass under the fruit trees was already scattered with petals. The chestnuts were still in tight bud, but were about to burst open. Underneath them on the ground she saw powdery-blue patches – dead beech leaves from last year, Antonia imagined – the sort of speckle an Impressionist painter would have made hay with. Clumps of pale orange crocuses and tiny scillas sparkling like blue gems were clustered around the base of the trees. As she glanced across the lawn, she saw an octagonal structure with glass panel walls – a greenhouse? Antonia felt like going out for a walk and picking some flowers for their bedroom, only she didn't want to miss the private detective.

'Where is he? I heard no car,' Lady Grylls was saying. 'I am not going deaf as well as blind, am I?'

'Ah, the indignities of old age,' Peverel murmured. 'Blindness, deafness, muddle, fuddle.' He turned to Payne. 'D'you know what Aunt Nellie did last Christmas? Sent out-of-date printed cards that said, *Season's Greetings from*

*Lord and Lady Grylls.* Uncle Rory's been dead these last thirteen years! I am sure you got one?'

'I didn't,' Payne lied loyally.

'Needed to get rid of the blasted things,' Lady Grylls said, unperturbed. 'Hate waste.'

Provost cleared his throat. 'Mr Jonson is aware that he is a bit early and he was phoning on the off chance that you may agree to see him, m'lady, so he's parked his car outside the gates. He called on his mobile phone, m'lady. He doesn't mind waiting, he said.'

'Who is this man Jonson?' Peverel asked. 'Not from the National Trust, is he? Have the National Trust reconsidered their decision?'

'Tell him to come in, Provost. We might as well see him now. The sooner he comes, the sooner he'll go. I suppose we'll have to give him tea.' Lady Grylls sighed gustily. 'Put the kettle on, will you?'

'Yes, m'lady.'

'Aunt Nellie, I forgot to tell you that I'm leaving for London early tomorrow morning,' Peverel said.

'Good,' she said.

'I am glad I'll be spared the gross usurpation of Chalfont. I imagine Corinne Coreille will be the guest from hell . . . It will be like having Norma Desmond, Dorian Gray and the Phoenix bird rolled in one staying.'

'Is that supposed to be clever? And must you eat all the cake?' She regarded him balefully. 'I don't think there'll be any left for Jonson.'

'There's a whole Madeira cake in the pantry.'

'We can't have a new one cut just for Jonson.'

'Just for Jonson! Really, darling,' Peverel said. 'Listening to you, one might think you were some suburban housewife and not the relict of the tenth Baron Grylls.'

Lady Grylls said that sometimes she wished she *were* a suburban housewife. Life would have been *so* much easier. For one thing she wouldn't have had an eccentric super-rich *chanteuse* for a god-daughter who'd want to hide in her house. 'Do you know, Antonia, I am fed up with this whole business before it's even started. Do tell me that I am being selfish. Do tell me.'

'In the circumstances I'd feel pretty much the same myself. I'd be absolutely terrified. But then,' Antonia smiled, 'I've been a suburban housewife for quite a while.'

*'Just for Jonson,'* Major Payne murmured. 'Sounds like the title of a '30s musical comedy.'

Lady Grylls slumped down in an armchair, making it creak. She took the last cigarette from the pack. 'Age asks ease, as the poet put it. I don't feel like seeing anyone. What I'd like to do is put my feet up, ask Provost to mix me a gin-and-tonic and watch the box. I hope I won't have to miss *EastEnders* again. What happened last night?' She shook her head. 'Neither of you watches it, I keep forgetting. I don't suppose Jonson watches it either. Private detectives are always busy following clues.'

'Is Jonson a private detective? You can't be serious.' Peverel picked up a napkin and wiped his fingers. 'Well, I hope he manages to rumble the author of the death threats *before* he carries them out.'

'It may be a she,' Antonia said, casting a covert glance at Lady Grylls and hating herself for it.

Peverel halted by the door. 'Indeed it may . . . I don't know why, but I have always had a weakness for the least likely suspect idea. Who *is* the least likely suspect in this affair? Do we know?'

'We do . . . *You,*' said Lady Grylls promptly. 'The fact that you are going away just when the detective is about to appear and you don't want to meet Corinne is damned suspicious.'

'I am taking the Gothic prayer stool with me to London. You said I could, didn't you, darling? The one with the unicorns?'

'I did say you could, but I've changed my mind,' Lady Grylls said. 'You can't take it with you. I need it here.'

'Now be reasonable,' Peverel drawled. 'What do you need it for? It's not as though you pray.'

'I do pray.'

'Not on a *stool* . . . Ridiculous.'

'I need it to lean my rheumatic knee,' Lady Grylls said firmly.

'Since Peverel hasn't ever met Corinne Coreille,' Payne pointed out, 'it would be a bit far-fetched to imagine that he should have any reason to want to send her death threats.'

Lady Grylls held her cigarette away from her eyes. 'Wait a minute. Who said he didn't meet her? He *did* meet her. In 1969 . . . You did meet her. I'm sure Amanda said you did.' She turned towards Peverel. 'I remember now. It was you who took Amanda to Corinne's second concert!'

His hand on the doorknob, Peverel gave an indulgent smile. 'What second concert, darling? You must have dreamt it.'

'I didn't dream it. It's all coming back now. Hugh's leave was over, so he had to go back to Sandhurst and that very same day you came down from Eton. Amanda wanted to go to Corinne's second concert and I do remember her begging you to go with her. I was there. I heard her.'

There was a little pause, then Peverel drawled, 'Well, she did beg me, but I didn't feel like going. I thought it would be a bore. So I didn't go.' He left the room.

A moment later the door opened once more. 'Mr Jonson,' Provost announced.

# 11

# Sleuth

Much to Antonia's surprise, Jonson was not at all like the portrait painted of him by Lady Grylls. She had described him as a dry-as-a-biscuit elderly duffer of the retired public schoolmaster or family solicitor variety – but he was nothing of the sort. He was most certainly not of retirement age – no more than thirty-eight, if that, Antonia decided. He had the physique of a rugby player who had started going to pot somewhat. He was wearing a grey sports jacket of goodish quality, a blue open-neck polo shirt and black corduroy trousers. Driving gloves stuck out of his pocket and he was carrying a briefcase. He had short fair hair, and that, combined with his fresh unlined face, gave him a boyish look. Despite the fact that his nose had been broken, in a scrum, one assumed, he wasn't bad-looking. He gave the impression of toughness, yet there was something curiously gentle and vulnerable about him – as well as an air of reliability.

His voice, when he spoke, was well modulated, precise and hesitant, but there was nothing elderly or 'dry' about it either. Whatever had given Lady Grylls that impression?

'Good afternoon.' He stood looking round at each of them and focusing unmistakably on Antonia's aunt by marriage. 'Lady Grylls?'

Leaning back in her chair, she pushed her glasses up her nose and subjected him to one of her owlish stares. 'Who are you?'

Disconcerted, he blinked. 'Jonson . . . Andrew Jonson. I –'

'You aren't. You can't be.'

'I phoned you earlier on –'

'You didn't. Wrong voice.'

He turned a little pink – smiled – it was a particularly sweet smile, Antonia thought. 'That was my telephone voice, Lady Grylls.'

'What telephone voice?'

He cleared his throat and said again. '*That was my telephone voice, Lady Grylls.*' This time he sounded quite different – strangulated and clipped. '*I am calling on behalf of Mademoiselle Corinne Coreille, your god-daughter.*' It was an uncanny performance.

Lady Grylls gasped. 'Goodness. What kind of ventriloquism is that? You make yourself sound perfectly ghastly, a cross between Mr Chips and – Perfectly ghastly. Why do you do it? Don't tell me you believe that speaking like that inspires greater confidence in your clients?'

'Well, that was the idea. It seems to go down well with the French. I – I don't do it every time –'

'I should hope not! Aren't people filled with mistrust and suspicion the moment they clap eyes on you and see you are actually jolly nice and normal?'

'It has happened. Then I show them my licence and everything's fine.'

'Well, I am glad to hear it,' Lady Grylls said doubtfully. 'I must say you are good.'

His smile was half sheepish, half pleased. He looked like a schoolboy who had pulled off a successful prank. He was an extremely likeable young man, Antonia decided. 'My licence,' he said. Taking a folded paper from an inside pocket, he handed it to Lady Grylls.

She glanced at it in a cursory manner, shrugged her shoulders and tossed it over for Antonia and Payne to inspect. 'My nephew Hugh Payne and his wife Antonia,' she introduced them with a wave of the hand. 'Like you, they are detectives, so beware. They are terribly clever. They're planning to open their own detective agency. Perhaps you could give them some tips?'

'My aunt's joking. This looks all right,' Major Payne said. 'It's just a piece of paper . . . Jonson. Anyone can call themselves Jonson,' Lady Grylls said sternly, but her eyes twinkled. She seemed to have taken to him, Antonia thought. 'Do sit down. Ah, there you are, Provost. Do help yourself to some tea, Mr Jonson.'

Provost had wheeled in a trolley with a steaming pot of freshly brewed tea, a cake on a stand, a cup and a jug of milk.

'The man I saw coming out of this room,' Jonson said over his cup. 'I think I've seen him before. In Paris.'

'Really? That was my nephew Peverel. Paris, did you say? He travels a lot, so I wouldn't be at all surprised if someone said they'd bumped him off in Acapulco – I mean bumped *into* him – wishful thinking!' Lady Grylls laughed. 'Now then. The job you did for Corinne. I mean your previous commission. Last December, was it? Tell us about it. '

It had been Maître Maginot, Mademoiselllle Coreille's legal adviser, who had contacted his London office. Maître Maginot had been very concerned about leaks to the press, to a gossipy illustrated magazine called *Voici*, of sensational stories concerning Corinne Coreille's private life. Maître Maginot suspected one of the staff they employed. In fact she was *sure* it was one of the staff – only she couldn't tell which. She had wanted Jonson to find the person, so that she could dismiss them and sue them for breach of confidentiality.

Lady Grylls wanted to know more about the story which had been leaked to the press. Nothing about Corinne's love life, she hoped? She had heard enough bosh about Corinne's love life already.

Jonson shook his head. No – it hadn't been that. (Antonia imagined there was a slight change in his expression at the mention of 'love life'.) It was something completely different. The leak concerned Mademoiselle Coreille's appearance – her hair, in particular.

'Ah, the trademark fringe.'

The story that had found its way into the magazine was to the effect that Mademoiselle Coreille's fringe was not her own – that she had lost all her hair in a fire – that she was completely bald and wore a wig.

'Like in Ionesco,' Payne murmured. *'La Cantatrice Chauve* . . . Am I right in thinking that the bald prima donna never actually appears?'

'She doesn't . . . Stop showing off,' Antonia whispered.

'I always imagined the famous fringe was insured for millions of francs,' Lady Grylls said and she urged Jonson to eat. He must be famished after his drive. ' Do have some cake. It's awfully good, usually. Shall I cut you a slice?' She picked up the knife. Antonia smiled. Lady Grylls was treating Jonson like a growing boy. He might have been the youngest of her nephews.

'Thank you . . . There was also the more serious claim that Corinne Coreille had lost not only her hair, but her voice as well,' Jonson went on. 'It was alleged that she had only mimed to playback during her Osaka concert last November.'

Lady Grylls continued firing more questions at him. It was funny that it was *she* who was conducting an inquiry and not the other way round, Antonia thought, amused. Why had Corinne employed the services of an English private detective? Weren't French detectives good enough?

'Mademoiselle Coreille's view was that the less her compatriots knew about her private life the better. Besides she did have the idea that English detectives were more efficient than French ones.'

'Reading too many Sherlock Holmes stories, I expect.' Lady Grylls went on to ask Jonson if he had known who Corinne Coreille was before she had employed his services.

'No. I'd never heard about her before.'

Lady Grylls shook her head in a perplexed manner. 'She is my god-daughter but she's a bloody enigma. I can't take the measure of her, really. Rather a strange character. The more I hear about her, the less I feel I know her . . . What did *you* make of her?'

Jonson's face remained blank. He hadn't had the chance to form an opinion, he said. He had seen Mademoiselle Coreille only twice. On both occasions she had been very pleasant to him. Very polite. His dealings had been mainly with Maître Maginot.

'And did you find Maître Maginot "pleasant"?' Lady Grylls boomed. 'Would you say that she was a nice woman? Who is she anyway?'

'Well, I can't pretend I liked her, but, on the whole, she was perfectly civil to me . . . She is a former barrister of considerable standing. I believe she studied law at the Sorbonne as well as at Columbia University. She has all sorts of diplomas on her study walls. Accolades from various societies. Framed letters of thanks from Henry Kissinger, Elizabeth Taylor and the Sultan of Brunei.'

'Ha!' Lady Grylls said derisively.

There had been an odd flatness in Jonson's voice, which puzzled Antonia; it hadn't been there earlier on. Did he know something discreditable about Maître Maginot? Antonia wondered what it might be. Were Maître Maginot's exalted diplomas perhaps forgeries? Could Maître Maginot be an impostor?

'She holds Mademoiselle Coreille's power of attorney and the right to act as her spokesperson,' Jonson went on. 'She has complete control of Corinne Coreille's estate, or so I gathered.'

'How old is she?'

'I don't know. Um. Fifty-five –'

'The same age as Corinne?'

'No – I mean, she must be in her sixties – maybe older. I don't know . . . I believe she's had a stroke sometime in the past and suffered some kind of paralysis.' Suddenly Jonson looked confused and very worried. 'She has almost completely recovered – I don't think her brain is at all affected – but she tends to lose her temper. Her face is an odd shape – her mouth is slightly twisted to one side.'

Lady Grylls smiled and she clapped her hands. 'A gorgon – in more ways than one! She bullies Corinne, doesn't she? '

'Really, Lady Grylls, I can't possibly –'

'You don't think she imposes Nazi-style diktats on my god-daughter? Oh very well – you are being tiresome. Do

86

go on with your story. Wait – let me give you another slice of cake. So. Did you rumble the scumbag who'd been feeding canards to the press?'

'I did. It was one of the chambermaids. A girl from Normandy named Emilie,' Jonson explained as he munched. 'I discovered a photograph she'd taken of Mademoiselle Coreille hidden under another, larger, photograph, of some young heart-throb of an actor. The two photos were pinned inside Emilie's locker.'

'What does Corinne do in the photo?' Lady Grylls leant back in her chair. 'Details, please. I love details. Unless it's a compromising photo – I don't want to hear if it's anything salacious!'

'No, nothing like that . . . Well, Mademoiselle Coreille is sitting at her dressing table, putting on her make-up. The way the light falls on her head, it does make her look as though she has no hair. It is only a trick of the light. Her face is covered in make-up and she is admiring the effect.'

His voice was softer now, Antonia noticed – gentler. She was struck by a thought: had Jonson fallen in love with Corinne Coreille? She must be – what? Twenty years older than him – still, these things did happen.

'There is a ki –' He broke off. 'There is a *kipper* – um – on a plate on the dressing table.'

He had flushed deep red. Had he been about to say something else? Antonia wondered.

'A kipper! Goodness. Is Corinne fond of kippers?' Lady Grylls exclaimed. 'Are you sure? Must remember to order some for her breakfast . . . What else?'

'A wig *can* be seen on a dummy's head on the table beside her. Maître Maginot explained that Mademoiselle Coreille did not lose her hair, merely had it cropped very short for a while as part of some special treatment aimed at strengthening her scalp. Mademoiselle Coreille apparently has two wigs, both of them identical, which she uses in emergencies.'

'Did that gel – the maid – make a clean breast of how she'd taken the photo, or did she put up a fight?'

'Emilie denied taking the photograph at first, but I pointed out that actually her reflection could be seen in the photo – that it had been caught in the lower left corner of the mirror. I said she could be seen with the camera held up to her face.' He grinned. 'I bluffed – but it did the trick. Emilie broke down and admitted she had taken the picture through the bedroom door, which had been left ajar. Maître Maginot then dismissed her and that was where the matter rested. Maître Maginot didn't carry out her threat to take the girl to court, no. She explained she did it out of consideration for Corinne. She felt that a court case would have brought a great deal of unwelcome, lurid and inaccurate publicity at a time Corinne Coreille was making a come-back.'

Major Payne cleared his throat. 'About this business of the death threats, Jonson. Your present commission. Have you any ideas as to who might have been sending them?'

'There's nothing conclusive but at this stage, sir, there is one person who seems to be – indicated. An American woman called Eleanor Merchant. It's a very peculiar story –'

'Her son committed suicide as he listened to a recording of a Corinne Coreille song?'

He stared at Antonia. 'Yes. How – how did you know about it?'

'I told you they were terribly good!' Lady Grylls cried.

'Eleanor Merchant has written three letters to Corinne Coreille. She seems to believe that her son wouldn't have killed himself, if he hadn't been listening to Corinne Coreille singing. It looks as if she's got quite a bee in her bonnet about it. She implies that it was Corinne Coreille's voice that "killed" Griff.'

'Have you got the letters with you?' Lady Grylls asked.

'Yes. Maître Maginot faxed them to me together with the death threats. The letters are handwritten and signed with Eleanor Merchant's name . . . The death threats are unsigned. I established that each one of them was constructed with letters cut out of the *International Herald Tribune.'*

'The favoured reading of Americans in Europe,' Antonia said with a smile.

'Eleanor Merchant has created a website devoted to the memory of her son,' Payne said. 'An internet shrine of sorts.'

'Really?'

'I told you they were good,' Lady Grylls said again.

'I had no idea . . . Are there any photos of Eleanor Merchant?' Jonson asked.

'Yes – several, apparently – we haven't seen anything, actually,' Payne admitted. 'My cousin told us about it. I don't suppose the photos will be much good to you since in all of them Eleanor Merchant is in some kind of outrageous fancy dress. Her son as well.'

'Why do queers always have neurotic mothers?' Lady Grylls said. 'Have you noticed?'

'Would you be able to show us Eleanor Merchant's letters?' Antonia turned to Jonson. 'Or would that be a breach of confidentiality?'

'It would be nothing of the sort,' Lady Grylls said firmly. 'It's not as though any one of us is going to spill the beans to Maginot, is it? Besides, this is *my* house. Can we see the death threats first? I've never seen death threats in my life.'

After a moment's hesitation, Jonson picked up his briefcase and placed it across his knees.

# 12

# In the Teeth of the Evidence

'Nothing special,' Lady Grylls declared several moments later, when he had obligingly spread the photocopies of the anonymous messages on the table before her. '*You crazy bitch. Prepare to die.* She wrote the same thing three times. *You crazy bitch. Prepare to die. You crazy –*' Lady Grylls tapped her lips with her fingers in a feigned yawn. 'Goodness, how tedious . . . Are these the letters?'

'Yes. First – second – third,' Jonson said, arranging them in order.

There was a pause as they read the first letter. 'She clearly felt the overwhelming need to unburden herself . . . Her shrink couldn't have been doing his job very well,' Major Payne murmured after a while.

'Very interesting,' Antonia said. 'Sad too, in a way.'

'Do you think so? I don't lack compassion, but I find it hard to be sympathetic to the Mrs Venableses of this world.'

'Totally potty,' Lady Grylls said. 'She calls Corinne a witch but it is she who sticks pins in the doll and asks Corinne if it hurts! Who is Mrs Venables, Hughie?'

'A monstrous matriarch whose son Sebastian dies an outlandish death. It's a play.'

'She calls Corinne a crazy bitch, but it is more than clear she is the crazy one. I believe there is a word for it . . . Transference? When you attribute your demons to somebody else? I say, that's the same phrase as in the death threats!' Lady Grylls cried with an air of discovery. '*Crazy bitch*. You do see – don't you?' She pushed her glasses up her nose.

'We do, darling.'

'It's certainly suggestive,' Jonson said non-committally.

'Suggestive? My good man – it's what they call a clincher! It proves beyond doubt that the blasted American woman wrote the death threats as well. You need look no further. She's your pigeon.'

'That would be the obvious conclusion, yes.'

*What is the matter, Corinne? Why don't you answer?* (The second letter began.) *It is now more than a month since I wrote to you. Airmail letters take no more than four days to get to Europe. I did check. I sent the letter to Fabiola, your record company in France, by registered mail, same as my first. You must have received it, so why don't you answer? I wouldn't have minded a postcard, with just a few words of acknowledgement and some expression of sympathy, perhaps? Is that too much to ask?*

*You couldn't have been busy. If you had been, it would have said so on your official website. (I check your Agenda every day, twice.) You have had only one concert and that was last November. It is January now. You can't pretend you never received my letters. I wouldn't believe you if you said you didn't.*

*Last night after I went to bed and turned off the light, I heard a voice whispering in my ear. I'd been expecting to hear from Griff, but it wasn't his voice. It was a woman's voice. (It sounded uncannily like mine!) It was very interesting, what the voice said. 'Remember the singing mermaids that lured poor Odysseus' sailors to their doom?'*

The letter ended abruptly, with a squiggle and the initials E.M.

'Why isn't this person in a loony bin?' Lady Grylls scowled at Jonson as though expecting him to provide an immediate answer.

The third letter in contrast was startlingly amiable – cheerful and girlish. To Antonia's way of thinking it was the spookiest of the three. Eleanor Merchant appeared to have been on some kind of a 'high' when she wrote it.

*Dear Corinne, I haven't heard from you yet, but I want you to know that I am not in the least mad at you. I am not! I am sorry I lost my temper last time. Perhaps it wasn't your fault. Perhaps you didn't receive any of my letters. Well, letters do get lost in the post – even registered ones!! In fact I think I know what must have happened: the person at Fabiola didn't pass them on to you! They simply forgot!! You should have them sacked!*

*I have a surprise for you. I am flying to Paris next week. Yes! I have already booked my plane ticket, a week from today. I have started brushing up my French by re-reading Maupassant's short 'contes' in the original, though of course your English is perfect.*

*There have been developments. They have changed my medication and I feel much more positive about things. More importantly, most importantly, Griff has been trying to get through to me. I heard his voice this morning, only it was so muffled, it was hard to make out what he was saying. He sounded as though he were speaking through a cushion, or had filled his mouth with cotton wool. I am sure it is only a question of time before we manage to establish proper contact. In the manner of a demanding film director, I keep rehearsing our reunion in my mind, striving to make it more moving, more triumphant. I am full of hope. I await my reunion with Griff with a girl's ardour. This world has its impossible limitations but the idea no longer troubles me. A whole new dimension has opened up! The realization has put a smile on my face. It felt as though I had been watching a conjuror make dozens of gaudy umbrellas explode out of a small box!*

*You and I shall meet soon. There are all sorts of questions I would like to put to you. I know that what you did was very, very wrong, but I am prepared to give you a chance, so that you could explain yourself. Au revoir. A bientôt!*

'Prozac?' Antonia said thoughtfully. 'Morphine?'

Payne pointed to the dates. 'Eleanor Merchant's last letter from America was written on 25th February. She said she'd be flying to Paris in a week's time . . . 4th March? All the envelopes that contained the death threats have Paris stamps – 5th March, 8th March, 11th March . . . They've been written at three-day intervals.'

'That's what they call irrefutable evidence. It's her. Eleanor Merchant.' Lady Grylls leant towards Jonson and tapped his arm. 'You'd be a fool if you went looking for anybody else. You'd be wasting your time.'

'You are probably right, Lady Grylls, but I do need to collate the evidence, sequence it and assess it properly.'

'You'd be wasting your time,' she repeated.

'How did the death threats reach Corinne?' Major Payne asked.

'Through Fabiola, that's Mademoiselle Coreille's record company – same as the letters.'

'It's her,' Lady Grylls said. 'Eleanor. What do you think, my dear? She compares Corinne to the singing mermaids and so on. Hasn't it been said that obvious solutions are usually the correct ones?'

Antonia agreed that that was so. The other, also rather obvious possibility – she went on after a moment's hesitation, rather apologetically – was that somebody was using Eleanor Merchant as a scapegoat. Eleanor had written the letters all right, but she might be no more than a harmless lunatic while it was another person – the *real* killer – who had sent the death threats to Corinne. Eleanor Merchant was being set up – as the killer prepared to strike.

'I wouldn't call Eleanor Merchant harmless,' Lady Grylls said. 'But if you are right, then it's got to be somebody who is familiar with Eleanor Merchant's letters!'

'Someone who's close to Corinne – who has had access to her private papers – who knows about Eleanor Merchant's letters.' Major Payne paused. 'A member of Corinne's coterie – of her inner circle?'

'I don't think there's such a thing as an inner circle,' Jonson said. 'There's only Maître Maginot.'

'Ah. The ruthless, manipulative, cunning, power-mad Maître.' Lady Grylls gave a portentous nod. 'I completely forgot about her.'

'Darling, you are attributing to her qualities normally associated with the conclaves of the Mafia *capi* . . . Well, it might be the chambermaid who was so unceremoniously sacked for selling stories to the press,' Payne went on.

'Emilie. Emilie, you must agree, has a goodish reason for seeking revenge, wouldn't you say?'

'Emilie left in December. Eleanor Merchant's first letter arrived a month later, in January,' Antonia pointed out.

'Does Corinne employ a large staff?' Payne turned to Jonson.

'No, not that large. Two maids, a secretary, a gardener, two security guards. They have very little contact with Mademoiselle Coreille . . . As it happens, they are all rather young. In their twenties. I understand some of them hadn't even heard of Corinne Coreille when they went for their interviews. It is Maître Maginot who does the interviewing. She deals with references, conducts all the character checks, draws up the contracts and so on.'

There was a pause. 'Why only young people?' Antonia said.

'Fear of age? The cult of youth?' Payne stroked his jaw with a thoughtful forefinger. 'All in keeping with Corinne's unchanging appearance? Perhaps they don't want people who are old enough to remember Corinne in her prime?'

'I think you just said something very interesting –' Antonia broke off and frowned. 'I don't know in what way exactly it is interesting . . .'

'I am sure it will come to you in due course. The little grey cells, they will not fail you.' Lady Grylls tapped her forehead significantly.

Antonia saw Jonson run his hand across his face. She remembered how deeply he had flushed earlier on. Once more she wondered about what it was he knew.

# 13

# Vendetta

The library, Major Payne reflected, was as he remembered
it. It hadn't changed one little bit. The oak panelling, the
Gothic fan tracery ceiling by Wyatville, the sagging leather
armchairs, the pictures of horses and dogs. Talking of the
pictures, his aunt had said that there was nothing there she
could not sell to a wandering sheikh for something as
pathetic as a fifty-pound note. If a wandering sheikh had
anything as pitiful as fifty-pound notes on his person,
Major Payne had riposted – but he knew that that was a
fanciful exaggeration. Some of the pictures were genuine
Stubbses and Landseers. They all hung as they had done
for some hundred and fifty years, on chains, from original
gold lion masks.

Payne recalled the fascination the lion masks had held
for him when, as a boy, he had been left to stay with his
aunt and uncle. The smell hadn't changed either. Ancient
paper, dust, stale cigar smoke, musty pot pourri, leather.
The windows were wet with rain and the wind howled in
the Adam fireplace. The mantelpiece was decorated by a
bronze of a hawkish Wellington on horseback and a bowl
of chrysanthemums that had been defunct for quite some
time – not from last autumn surely?

It was getting dark. He turned on two table lamps and
stood looking at the rows and rows of books in dark
mahogany cases built into the walls, the leather and vellum of their bindings cracked and scarred by age or neg-

lect. Some books, on the other hand, looked as good as new. The *Encyclopaedia Britannica* – two sets of it, an Edwardian one and a 1960 edition, neither of them showing signs of ever having been opened. There were some uncut first editions, which must be valuable . . . *Black Beauty, The Country House in our Heritage, Greyfriars Bobby, Where's Master?* by Caesar. Caesar was a dog, of course, one that had belonged to Edward VII. Caesar had walked immediately behind the gun carriage at the King's funeral in 1910 and every now and then he had raised his head and howled disconsolately. That poignant passage, Payne remembered, had reduced him to tears when he had read the book as a boy. He had actually believed that it was Caesar who had written the book!

Detective novels: ancient green Penguins from the late '40s and early '50s. Ronald Knox, John Wade, E.C. Bentley. Did anyone read them nowadays? Forgotten biographies. *The Regent and his Daughter* by Dormer Creston. A very prettily bound almanac of poems, circa 1835, with a lyre engraved on the cover. Maupassant's complete short stories –

That was the book he had been looking for. A bee in my bonnet, he thought. 'Oh hello,' he said as Antonia entered.

'Perhaps I could help your aunt tidy up the library. I don't think I have yet lost my expertise,' she said. Until a couple of months before, Antonia had worked as a librarian at the Military Club in St James's Street in London, but after the success of her second detective novel she had given up her job to write full time.

'You mean cataloguing and dusting and things?' He went on to say it would be the kind of labour Hercules would have bridled at.

'It would be a shame to allow all these books to go to rack and ruin.' She was standing beside the huge round table. From among the piles of ancient communications from various wine societies and an assortment of seed and plant catalogues, she picked up a book and started leafing through it. 'Listen to this . . . *Nothing can be more unfair or more unjustifiable than a doubtful answer given under the plea of sparing the suitor's feelings. It raises false hopes. It renders a man restless and unsettled –'*

'Golly. That's *exactly* how I felt after I proposed to you and you said you'd have to think about it!' Payne cried. 'Restless and unsettled sums it up nicely. What book is that?'

'A Victorian book on etiquette . . . Constable, 1895. I thought I might find Jonson and your aunt here. They are going round the house.'

'Ah, the security checks . . . He looks as though he's taking it all extremely seriously, doesn't he?'

'He does. What do you make of him?' Antonia asked.

'Of Jonson? Seems a decent enough chap.' Payne cocked an eyebrow. 'You disagree? What is it?'

'I don't know.' Antonia paused. 'He is immensely likeable, but I do believe there is something he isn't telling. Several things, perhaps. It's the way he talks about Corinne and Maître Maginot – the way his voice and expression change.'

'You don't think it's anything to do with Peverel?'

Antonia stared. 'Peverel?'

'Jonson said he'd met him in Paris. Which is where Corinne Coreille lives.'

'Yes . . . Your aunt is convinced it was Peverel who took your sister to Corinne's second concert. He denied it point blank.'

'That was odd, wasn't it?'

'*Very* odd . . . What's that book?'

'Maupassant's short stories.' Payne was running his finger down the contents page. 'The Merchant uses the name Saverini on her website.'

Antonia frowned. 'What's that got to do with Maupassant?'

'In her third letter the Merchant writes that she's been reading Maupassant's *contes*. Well, the name Saverini struck a chord the moment I heard it.' Payne started leafing through the book. 'I remembered a short story by Maupassant with a character called Saverini in it. The

widow Saverini . . . Here it is! It's called "Vendetta".
I knew I was right!'

'"Vendetta"?'

'"Vendetta". Rather suggestive, isn't it? It did occur to
me that the Merchant might be identifying with the widow
Saverini. The widow Saverini's son is murdered and she
plots an elaborate revenge on the killer. She is single-
minded, ruthless, methodical and, although it's never
spelled out for us, more than a little crazy. Maupassant
clearly wants us to sympathize with her, which is jolly
unsettling . . . Listen to this. *Don't worry, my boy, my poor
child. I will avenge you. Do you hear me? It's your mother's
promise, and your mother always keeps her word. You know
that.*'

'Why are you putting on an Italian accent? I believe I've
read it . . . A dog comes into it, doesn't it?'

'It does. The widow Saverini proceeds to train her dog to
attack an effigy made in the likeness of the killer, who is a
local man. She roasts a sausage and sews it inside the
effigy. She goads the dog into ripping the effigy apart.
Then she does it all over again – another effigy, another
sausage and so on – then again. Months pass . . . She
starves the dog . . . The whole thing's impossibly contrived
and wildly improbable – but in a funny way, it's also
rather frightening.'

'Obsession is always frightening.'

'The story ends with the dog jumping on the killer and
chewing open his throat. The widow Saverini then goes
back home and for the first time since her son's death, she
has a good night's sleep.' Payne paused. 'It does suggest
that the Merchant has revenge on her mind. Why else call
herself Saverini?'

'Why indeed . . . Yes. She is a driven woman. I don't
quite see how she could possibly find out that Corinne was
coming to England.'

'I don't see either. You heard what Jonson said – everybody's been sworn to secrecy by Maître Maginot and
so on.'

'That's what Jonson said . . . What if –' She broke off.
'Just imagine . . .'

'Imagine what?'

She shook her head. 'No, nothing . . . Let's stick to the known facts. Nothing's happened yet and I hope it stays that way!'

'I think I know what you mean,' he said slowly.

'No, you don't. You can't read my mind.'

'I can –'

'Where does your aunt keep her scrapbooks?' Antonia had started looking around the library.

'If memory serves me right, they used to be in that mahogany cabinet, over there, by the potted palm. That palm needs watering . . . What do you want the scrapbooks for?'

Antonia went up to the cabinet and opened it. There were two scrapbooks inside. She took them out. They were bound in faded maroon leather and had the dates stamped in gold on their spines, 1943–1949 and 1950–1960.

'I want to check something,' she said. 'It's nothing to do with any of this. At least I don't see how it could be. Just an idea.'

'A bee in your bonnet.' Payne nodded in a gratified fashion. 'Aunt Nellie was right. We are terribly alike. That's why we got married. We'd have remained incomplete if we hadn't.'

Antonia looked at him. 'We don't really finish each other's sentences, do we? It's been bothering me.' Blowing the dust off its surface, she opened the first scrapbook and started leafing through it.

It wasn't really surprising that Lady Grylls's youthful tastes should be revealed as a mixture of high society gossip, scandal, matrimony – and crime.

# 14

# The Secret History

*Lord Redesdale denies being a fascist . . . King Farouk's young daughter sends chocolates to Princess Elizabeth and Princess Margaret . . . Mrs Charles Sweeney falls forty feet down empty lift-shaft . . . Was Mr Somerset Maugham a spy? . . . The Hon. Jessica Gerrad's Lagonda stolen . . . Lady Mosley released from Holloway prison.*

There were pictures cut from the *Illustrated London News*. They were brittle, crinkly and yellow with age. *Dashing debs: Miss Rosamund Cadogan and best friend the Hon. Anelie de Broke presented at court.* Well, Corinne's mother was exactly as Lady Grylls had described her: a proud beauty, head held high, almond-shaped eyes, dark and long-legged, wearing a most revealing dress. Lady Grylls had denigrated her own appearance, but she wasn't bad-looking either. Somewhat on the plump side, true, but not unattractively so – she might have posed for Rubens. Lots of men liked that type, Antonia reflected. She had a lovely heart-shaped face, luxuriant blonde hair and a sweet shy smile. She had taken her horn-rimmed glasses off for the picture and was clutching them in her hand. There was something endearing about it.

*Mrs George Keppel buried under cypress trees in Protestant Cemetery in Florence . . . Lady Docker's jewels stolen . . . M. François-Enrique Coreille and Miss Anelie de Broke dining at the Café de Paris in Coventry Street. M. François-Enrique and Miss Rosamund ('Ruse') Cadogan dining at the Savoy.*

*Le falcon* – if one had to call him that – did look devastatingly charming and was, in all probability, utterly rotten. Ruse was gazing at him in an adoring manner. She was wearing a shimmering sleeveless dress. Her arms blazed with diamond bracelets from wrist to elbow and she sported a striking brooch on her bosom: two ostriches attached, back-to-back, Siamese-twin fashion. It was the kind of brooch Mrs Simpson had favoured, Antonia thought.

*Greta Garbo in England: 'Please to leave me alone' . . . Lord Grylls to marry the Hon. Anelie de Broke . . . Where did Mrs Vicary go after the charity ball?*

Antonia opened the second scrapbook. *Sir Winston Churchill and new friend Aristotle Socrates Onassis.* The two famous men were shown wearing yachting caps and smoking monstrously long cigars. Antonia gazed across at her husband. 'I bet you don't know what Onassis's second name was?'

'I do. Socrates. I know all sorts of silly and pointless things, I keep telling you.'

'How many gardeners did it take to paint the roses red in *Alice*?'

'Three.'

'Is there really such a thing as "lion's powder" or did you make that up?'

'There is. You can get it at Harrods. You throw it in the lion's face and the brute sneezes its head off, after which he leaves you alone. The Sardauna of Sokoto has a standing order for it . . . You don't believe me? What *are* you looking for?' Payne went round the table and stood beside Antonia. He took her hand and tried to kiss her on the lips. 'I know that bloodhound look . . .' He glanced down at the open scrapbook. *'Fancy dress party at the Casanova Club: Princess Margrethe of Denmark as Red Riding Hood, Mr Dominic Elwes as American Cowboy . . .* What would *you* look like,' he murmured, 'dressed up as Red Riding Hood?' He put his arms around her waist and nuzzled her neck.

'I'd look ridiculous . . . *Stop* it, Hugh. What would your aunt say if she were to come in now?'

'She would applaud. Aunt Nellie likes her males red-blooded and alpha-amorous . . .'

Antonia managed to turn another page. 'There it is. I've found it! *Couple abducted in Kenya . . . 13th May 1960. Monsieur and Madame Coreille –'*

'Good lord.' Payne relaxed his embrace. *'Affluent Anglo-French couple . . .* Corinne's parents. So that's what you were looking for!'

'Yes . . . *Travelling on their own . . . Ventured into hazardous areas . . . Proliferation of dangerous gangs . . . Several abductions already. A Dutch couple disappeared only the week before . . . Foreign embassies had issued warnings. The Coreilles refused the services of a local guide . . . Last seen leaving the Royal Mombasa hotel in hired jeep. Jeep later discovered abandoned . . . Ransom note delivered at hotel early next morning . . . Half a million dollars requested for their release . . . Ultimatum given – both die if demands not met . . . Police warned not to take action if the Coreilles are to live . . . Police believe threat to be serious. Previous abductions of Western tourists ending in tragedy . . . Coreille relatives in England and France contacted . . . Shocking discovery . . . Bodies found by passing Masai farmer –'*

'Gosh,' Payne said quietly. 'They didn't wait, did they? That's only two days later!'

'Yes . . . *Bodies horribly mangled – unrecognizable – severe mutilations – PM to be held . . . Clothes, personal items and passports in name of Monsieur and Madame Coreille – relatives in England and in France notified . . . The police searching for clues.'*

'What paper is that?'

'The *Evening Post.'* Antonia went on reading, *'The late Monsieur Coreille was in the news recently in connection with an investigation conducted by French police into his affairs. As we reported earlier, large sums of money belonging to clients of the firm where he was one of the trustees had been disappearing. The total sum amounts to four hundred and ninety-five thousand pounds. The investigation continues although it is doubtful whether any of the money will ever be recovered –'*

Antonia looked up as the door opened. 'Gotcha!' Lady

Grylls's triumphant bassoon was heard. As she entered, her eyes fixed on the scrapbook in Antonia's hands.

Lady Grylls's face was extremely flushed and her eyes were bright behind her glasses. She appeared to be in suspiciously high spirits. 'That young man's brilliant, absolutely brilliant. You should have seen the way he put Peverel in his place! I didn't hear what he told him exactly, but it knocked the wind out of Peverel's sails good and proper. He whispered something to him. I was smoking, you see, flicking ash everywhere. As you know, Peverel always has something to say when that happens, but this time he didn't. Dumbstruck!'

'Did he tell you what it was he said to Peverel?' Antonia asked.

'No, but he promised he'd tell me later. We'd gone into Peverel's room – part of the security checks, you know. Such fun, poking under beds and things – raising clouds of dust – we kept sneezing and coughing. I could have died of shame – made me feel like a dirty old woman!' Lady Grylls laughed raucously. 'I do need to have Chalfont spring-cleaned one of these days, but there's never enough money in the kitty!' She laughed again. 'Who was it who said, I don't drink to excess, I drink to *everything*?'

Major Payne raised an eyebrow. 'Are you all right, darling?'

'Of course I am all right. Never felt better. Silly question. You don't seem to understand, Hughie. I smoked in Peverel's room – his very private sanctum – and *he didn't say a word*. Didn't even give me one of his looks. He seemed jolly discomfited by what Andrew said to him.'

'Andrew?'

'You wouldn't believe this, but Peverel ceased to be his usual superior self and became rather meek and mild, like the proverbial lamb. I've never seen him look like that! Never! Extraordinary. I must say I like Andrew enormously. A splendid young man.'

'Do you mean Jonson?'

'We can't go on calling him Jonson. Mr Jonson is even worse. Ridiculous. By the way, I asked him to stay.'

Payne put his head to one side. 'Darling, do correct me if I am wrong, but have you been drinking?'

'The merest drop of Amontillado –'

'Not Uncle Rory's Amontillado!'

'Don't be a bore, Hughie. Of course it was Rory's Amontillado. It's more than a hundred and fifty years old –'

'Precisely!'

'We needed to celebrate the successful completion of the security checks and the fact we found no madman,' Lady Grylls explained calmly. 'Andrew had been planning to get a room at the local hotel. Those had been Corinne's instructions, he said, but as you know the local hotel is a ghastly hole, not the kind of place where splendid young men stay, so I wouldn't hear of it. I gave him a clean toothbrush and a pair of Rory's pyjamas. I am sure he'll be snug as a bug in them.' Lady Grylls pushed her glasses up her nose. 'Now then, Antonia. Have you found what you were looking for?' She crossed to the table and looked down at the open scrapbook.

'*Le falcon* and Ruse . . . Look at that brooch! It's magnificent, isn't it? I gave it to her.' Lady Grylls tapped a page. 'Cost me a pretty penny. Cartier's . . . There's me with *le falcon* at the Café de Paris. Look at my dress – studded with diamonds – see how it glitters? My figure wasn't really bad then. If I wore something like that nowadays, I'd look like a spray-flecked seal . . . The way the falcon's eyeing me!' Suddenly Lady Grylls became serious. 'Wasn't that what you were looking for, Antonia? I did give myself away, didn't I? Well, this is not the only picture of us together. There are others. There's one of him kissing me on the steps of the Savoy.' She started leafing through the scrapbook. 'It's somewhere – I don't think I've thrown anything away.'

There was a stunned pause. 'You don't mean you and him . . .' Major Payne began.

'I do mean me and him, Hughie. *Le falcon* and I saw quite a bit of each other – both before and *after* he'd got engaged to Ruse. There was quite a thing between us. I'd always wanted to know why Linda fell for Fabrice, you see. I mean *The Pursuit of Love*. Or Lady Donna for the Frenchman in the creek. Goodness. My head was full of that kind of romantic bosh . . . Don't stare like that. It was all a long time ago. François-Enrique was double-crossing Ruse with me. I can't say I am sorry. In a way I was glad . . . Wasn't that what you wanted to find out, Antonia?' A defiant note had crept into Lady Grylls's voice.

'No. It was – it was something else,' Antonia faltered.

'Are you sure? You *are* a dangerous woman.'

'Not at all –'

'Well, I might as well tell you the whole story. I was in love with the falcon. No. *I was mad about him*. I've never loved anyone as much as I loved him. The way he looked at me! Ah. I'd got it into my head that I was on my way to becoming a dowdy back number, you see, but he made me feel – goodness, I can't explain – as though he were inspecting one of those jewellers' trays on which famous diamonds are displayed! I'd have done *anything* for him. If he'd told me, here's a gun, go and shoot the Prime Minister, I'd have gone and done it. I honestly would have. Mr Attlee would have been a dead man. So would Mr Churchill.' Lady Grylls sounded disturbingly earnest. 'So, for that matter, would Mr Eden –'

'Darling – not *three* prime ministers. It lasted that long?'

'Well, our affair started while he was courting Ruse. And we continued seeing each other after he and Ruse got married and went to Paris. Rory hadn't an inkling . . . Such a fool!' She guffawed. '*Le falcon* came to London often, on business trips. I lived for those visits. I paid a price of course . . . The usual . . . I don't know why I am telling you any of this. None of your bloody business.'

'You don't mean you got . . .'

'Preggers? I did, Hughie.'

'Corinne is your –'

'Don't be absurd, Antonia.'

'*Not* Cousin Patricia?'

'Well spotted, Hughie. My daughter Patricia. My first-born child was his. I fear so – yes. She's got his eyes – yellow grey. And his fatal passion for gambling, sadly.'

'Did Rosamund know?'

'She didn't know about Patricia, I don't think, but if you mean about her husband having an affair with me, yes. Ruse saw a photograph of us in the *Tatler*. She saw the look on François-Enrique's face. Then she asked me point blank and I confessed . . . I don't think she quite minded.' Lady Grylls scowled. 'You see, she knew that he would never leave her. She knew her power. She was so damnably cocky about it. I did hate her for it. Oh well. It's all in the past now . . . Goodness, I do feel light-headed. I'll go and have a lie-down. Do excuse me.'

The door slammed shut behind her. There was a pause. Payne looked at his wife. 'Well! What do you think of that?'

Antonia shrugged. 'As she said, it's none of our bloody business.'

There was another pause. Payne pointed to the scrapbook. 'You don't think Ruse and François-Enrique really died, do you?'

'It's just an idea . . . In the months leading up to their tragic death, François-Enrique had been under investigation for stealing half a million from his clients. A very, *very* large sum of money in 1960 –'

'They had been mangled by wild beasts. Unrecognizable, that's what it said in the paper, didn't it?' Payne paused. 'The bodies were identified by his mother. She went to Kenya. She then decided to have them buried there. Soon after she opened her own clinic, I remember Aunt Nellie telling me. It costs a pretty penny to open a clinic. Aunt Nellie thinks Madame Coreille got some kind of inheritance – but what if there wasn't an inheritance? The money could have been –'

'Madame Coreille's reward for her cooperation. Exactly. *It all fits in*. There was the falcon and Ruse's fatal love of gambling. They had been losing a lot of money. They ignored warnings about dangerous gangs. They didn't take a local guide with them. A Dutch couple had disappeared in the area a while earlier. Is it too far-fetched to suppose that the falcon and Ruse –'

'– staged their own death? No, not too far-fetched at all.'

'Oh God, we do finish each other's sentences, Hugh. Did you notice?'

'We do it *only* when propounding theories. Now don't interrupt . . . The falcon and Ruse were both wrong 'uns. They could have struck up some sort of deal with one of those criminal gangs,' Major Payne went on. 'The poor Dutch couple might have been kept captive by the gang, pending a ransom or something – it might have been *them* who got killed and substituted for the Coreilles . . . As you say, my love, it is certainly an idea. It's not as though that kind of thing has never happened. People do steal fortunes, fake their deaths, assume new identities and disappear to paradise islands. Only,' Major Payne said, 'I don't quite see how any of this could have any bearing on the death threats received by the Coreilles' daughter forty-three years later . . . Do you?'

'No, I don't . . . Changing the subject,' Antonia said, 'what do you think Jonson told Peverel to make him look uncomfortable?'

# 15

# The Haunting

It was early the following day, 2nd April.

Antonia sat in bed writing her diary, a blanket around her shoulders. Her bedside table lamp was on. It was five thirty in the morning and too early to expect tea. The heating had not come on either.

Antonia was dying for a cup of tea. She wished she had accepted Lady Grylls's offer of an ancient Teasmade. It would have been so nice to have it hissing and spluttering on the bedside table. Beside her Hugh hadn't stirred . . . Should she sneak down to the kitchen in her dressing gown and brew herself a pot of tea? No. Too cold. The wind was in the east. She could hear it roaming about the house like a ranging animal, thrusting its paws into the crannies and holes that had been formed as a result of the late Lord Grylls's reluctance to repair and modernize Chalfont, sniffing under lintels, whining hoarsely the while. Antonia shivered and pulled the blanket round her shoulders. She remembered what Noel Coward had written in his diary after a weekend visit at Chalfont in the mid-1930s: *Woke frozen. Shaving sheer agony. Loo like an icebox. Breakfast a bore.*

She concentrated on her diary.

*Corinne Coreille is not quite real.* (Antonia wrote.) *Her perpetual, unchanging youth for one puzzles me. We have been given so much information, some silly, some downright bizarre, all of it fascinating, and yet, like Aunt Nellie, I feel I know* nothing about her. What is she like as a person? Really like. Has she got a personality at all, like us, ordinary mortals? She must have and yet I keep thinking of her as belonging to an alien species, as of some fabulous monster, an ageless phantom embalmed in her all-devouring myth.

I had a dream last night. I was walking down a labyrinthine yellow road – hints of Oz? – under crepuscular light. Orchids, roses and other exotic flowers whose names I didn't know, grew on either side of the road, Triffid-sized, as tall as trees! I had no idea where I was going but I was aware of a sense of anticipation. Then suddenly, at the end of the road, standing on a raised circular platform and revolving like the ballerina on an old-fashioned music box, I saw Corinne. She was singing. It was a song called 'Vous Qui Passez Sans Me Voir'. (Is there such a song?)

As I went closer, she started vanishing. She took off her hair first, which was just a wig, then peeled off her face, which was a mask, then her hands, the way one removes gloves. Underneath there was nothing. Nothing at all. She never for a moment stopped singing. Eventually her dress fell to the platform and she disappeared completely. It was like H.G. Wells's invisible man. The platform went on turning round and her disembodied voice went on singing. I felt as though I had witnessed some conjuring trick.

I continue to feel uneasy about Jonson – or Andrew, as Aunt Nellie insists on us calling him. Last night he declared the house and the grounds 'clean'. The more I get to know him, the more I like him. And yet, I don't think that he's told us the whole truth about Corinne Coreille. There is something wrong there. What is it he knows? He couldn't be the killer, could he? No, of course not. He might have been able to arrange for the death threats to be sent to Corinne in Paris, but how could he possibly have known about Eleanor Merchant and her letters? Well, he could have seen Eleanor's Saverini website. But why should he want to kill Corinne?

All right – they might have had an affair after she employed his services last year. He might have fallen madly in love with her and become very upset and angry when she broke up the affair. No, that's nonsense – Corinne wouldn't be asking him to *do another job for her if their parting had been in any way acrimonious, would she?*

*NB. I need to learn to curb my imagination. This is NOT a detective story.*


The rain outside continued pouring down and the wind could be heard wailing in the chimney. The dining-room windows creaked and rattled. (Double glazing was one of the things the late Lord Grylls had considered 'vulgar'.) All the lights were on and every now and then they flickered. The house, Lady Grylls said, needed rewiring. 'When I asked Rory to have it done, he told me I knew as much about such matters as your average Masai warrior. He said soda-water siphons knew more about rewiring than I did . . . D'you know what Rory liked doing best?' Lady Grylls looked round the table. 'Getting up at the crack of dawn, putting on an old shooting jacket and pottering out to the woods at the back to "investigate" the habits of badgers. Before the badgers he was engrossed in some drama involving a colony of bats. He wrote endless letters to *The Times* about his "findings".'

So much for my lavishly lovely spring, Antonia thought as the windows rattled again. The picture that was emerging of the Gryllses' marriage was not particularly attractive either. Soda-water siphons! Antonia suddenly felt rather depressed. I am glad Lady Grylls had an affair with a Frenchman, she thought defiantly, to boost her spirits.

It was nine o'clock and they were sitting around the polished Queen Anne table, having breakfast. Two kinds of eggs, scrambled and boiled, somewhat overdone rashers of bacon, glue-like porridge, which proved amazingly tasty, Oxford marmalade, toast, tea and coffee. She couldn't afford kedgeree or devilled kidneys or any such nonsense people staying in country houses seemed to expect, Lady Grylls had declared. Still, the butter pats were pressed with the Grylls baronial coronet, Antonia noticed. Peverel, they were informed by Provost, had left very early in the morning in his car.

'It's a filthy day but these are glad tidings.' Lady Grylls cast an affectionate glance at Jonson who was standing by the sideboard, plate in hand. She seemed to be crediting him as the main contributor to her nephew's departure. She lit a cigarette, then picked up her cup and took a sip of coffee. 'You are not eating much, Antonia. You aren't on a diet, are you?'

'No . . . I don't think I should be on a diet, should I?'

'By no means – but Hugh might have been giving you ideas. Men are funny about that sort of thing. Elizabeth was thin.' Lady Grylls lowered her voice. '*Too* thin, I always thought.' Elizabeth was the name of the first Mrs Payne.

'I didn't like it.' Payne spoke from behind *The Times*. 'I told her but she wouldn't listen.'

Antonia felt absurdly gratified.

Provost had left the dining-room door open and the telephone was heard ringing in the hall. That was the third time since they had started breakfast. Jonson looked up. Lady Grylls leant back in her chair and said, 'I bet it's our friend, the anonymous caller, again.' Payne pulled at his lower lip and shot Antonia a glance. Eventually Provost entered the dining room. He looked across at his mistress, his brows slightly raised.

'The anonymous caller?' Lady Grylls said.

'Yes, m'lady.'

'He means business, clearly. Whatever his business is. Again – not a word – just breathing?'

'Yes, m'lady.'

'Breathing! Wrong time of the day. I mean that's the kind of call one normally receives late at night, *not* during breakfast.' She guffawed.

'The call lasted four and a half seconds exactly. I timed it. I said hello several times and asked who it was, but the person rang off. The same as earlier on.'

'Man or woman, d'you think?'

'Couldn't say, m'lady . . . Woman, I think.'

'Really? How interesting. How could you tell?'

'I don't know, m'lady.'

'Breathing like a woman . . . Breathing like a man . . . Do

111

women breathe differently from men? Oh well. Never mind. The world's full of crackpots,' Lady Grylls declared cheerfully and poured herself more coffee. 'I loved that puzzle you told us last night, Hughie. About the dead man in the middle of the field with the square package beside him. I don't suppose you know any more like that?'

'Oh, no – no more puzzles, please,' Antonia said.

'As a matter of fact I do.' Payne pushed *The Times* to one side. 'Did I tell you the one about the woman kissing a stranger?'

'No – but I rather like the sound of it.'

'Very well. A woman is walking in the street. Suddenly she rushes towards a man and gives him a long kiss on the lips that attracts everybody's attention. She has no idea who the man is. Why should she want to kiss him?'

'And I suppose he is not madly attractive? No. Well, she knows her husband's following her and she wants to make him jealous? That's what I would have done, if Rory had been the least bit jealous, which he wasn't.' Lady Grylls paused wistfully. 'That's not the correct answer, is it?'

'No. The man's had a fit and is lying on the ground. She gives him the kiss of life.'

Lady Grylls looked enchanted. 'A fit! Oh, you are so frightfully clever! A fit!'

A tinkling crash on the terrace betokened the fall of yet another tile from the roof. There was a pause. Major Payne said, 'Could that have been the Merchant? I mean the person who keeps phoning.'

'Don't call her the Merchant, Hugh . . . How could she possibly know this number?' Antonia looked at Jonson.

He shook his head. 'She couldn't. Maître Maginot said nobody knew it, apart from her and Corinne. She couldn't know the address either.'

'Ah, but you are forgetting that people of a lunatic cast of mind like the Merchant are terribly cunning,' Lady Grylls said. 'Method in their madness and all that . . . Does anyone want more toast?'

Antonia looked round the table and asked, 'Is there a song called "Vous Qui Passez Sans Me Voir"?'

'You who pass without seeing me?' Payne translated. 'Not one of Corinne's, is it?'

'I don't know. I believe I dreamt about it.' Antonia smiled. 'It would be very odd if no such song existed.'

Jonson cleared his throat. 'I think it's an old song. One of Jean Sablon's,' he said, going red. 'Jean Sablon was a crooner. France's answer to Bing Crosby –' He broke off, aware of their eyes on him. 'I like French songs. I developed a taste after – um – after I heard Corinne Coreille sing.'

'About that photo you found in Emilie's locker, old boy. The photo of Corinne sitting in front of her mirror, putting on her make-up. With the kipper in front of her and so on. I don't suppose you have it here, have you?' Payne said. The night before he had told Antonia that he found the kipper business damned odd. 'I'd like to take a squint at it, if possible. I've been wondering what Corinne looks like these days.'

Antonia was watching Jonson and she was convinced that there was an infinitesimal pause – a flicker of the eyelids – before he shook his head. No, he didn't have the photo. He had handed it over to Mademoiselle Coreille – together with the negative – and the film.

*He was lying.* This time there was no doubt about it. He wasn't used to telling lies. He was a decent man and, like most decent men, a bad liar. That's why he kept giving himself away. For some reason he had kept the photograph. No – had a copy made. Why had he done that? For his records? She saw him cast his eyes upwards, at the ceiling, and look down at once. His hands were on the table – she saw them clench and unclench . . . Not only did he have a copy of the photograph, but for some reason he had brought it to Chalfont with him! Antonia felt great excitement surge through her. Yes. The photograph was in his room – in his briefcase, most probably. Antonia had caught sight of several files and manila envelopes when Jonson had taken Eleanor Merchant's letters and the death threats out of it . . . For some reason Jonson didn't want them to see the photo.

113

It would be interesting to know why. Extremely interesting . . . Why had he brought the photo with him? That
case was over, finished. Was it to remind himself of his
past triumph? As proof of it? He didn't look the type who
did that sort of thing . . . Why do people carry photos with
them? For sentimental reasons? For blackmailing pur-
poses? Now that was an interesting line of thought . . .
There was something in that photo Jonson didn't want
them to see. What *was* it? She needed to find out. She *must*
find out.

She was going to ask Hugh to keep Jonson occupied
while she went up to his room and looked inside his
briefcase . . . When should she do it? Antonia glanced at
the rain-bespattered windows. Well, no better time than
the present.

The conversation at the breakfast table had turned to
billiards. Jonson was saying that he rather enjoyed playing
whenever he got the chance. As a matter of fact, so did he,
Payne said. There was a billiard room at Chalfont, did
Jonson know? Yes, he had been in it the night before,
briefly, Jonson said, during the 'checks'.

'Rory and I used to have the odd game. He always
accused me of cheating. Why don't you two boys have a
game?' Lady Grylls urged and she offered to keep the
score for them.

'Yes, why don't you?' Antonia said casually. 'The perfect
solution for a wet day.'

# 16

# Rear Window

She should stop doing it, Eleanor Merchant told herself. She was gaining nothing, phoning like that. Nothing at all. It was careless of her. Well, she hadn't been able to help herself. She'd got the idea that Corinne Coreille might have arrived earlier, that she might be at Chalfont Park already. Eleanor had hoped she might hear French speech somewhere in the background. She had even imagined that Corinne Coreille might pick up the phone herself! To hear that voice saying, '*Allo? Allo? Oui, c'est moi, Corinne –*'

Why not? It wasn't impossible. If Corinne happened to be passing by the phone, she might pick it up – what if it wasn't her house? – people did that sort of thing instinctively . . . The thought that she might have heard Corinne Coreille's voice sent shivers down Eleanor's spine.

No more phone calls, Eleanor decided. Why imperil the whole enterprise? Lady Grylls might be put on the alert and call the police! It would be so easy for the police to find Eleanor. She seemed to be the only stranger wandering the two main streets of Chalfont Parva under the falling rain. With her mink stole, badly bespattered with mud, yellow gloves and striped golf umbrella, she must stand out a mile . . . No, she mustn't imperil the enterprise.

(What enterprise? Experiencing a sudden, if short-lived, return of her sanity, Eleanor stood frowning in a puzzled manner. She had absolutely no idea why she had come all this way. What was she doing here, in this dump? What was it she intended to *do*? Pursue and harry an elusive *chanteuse* to the death, as though she were the Quorn and Pytchley and Corinne a fox? The thought made her smile and shake her head. That was the kind of thing only a nutcase would do!)

The few drab village shops had unattractive displays in their dim windows. It was a depressing place. What a *dump*, she said in her best Bette Davis voice. (That had been another of her and Griff's catch-phrases.) What a *dump*. So much for the greatly vaunted charm of the English countryside! Eleanor had been buying things she didn't need. She opened her bag and inspected her purchases. Sweets, rock cakes, a couple of scones and a jar of something rather intriguing called Marmite. She had also bought a local paper – all about some agricultural show, a church fête and a man called Markham who had a sow for sale. She had wanted to get some peanut butter cookies but there weren't any. The locals had been staring at her ghoulishly and she had heard them commenting on her American accent, which was odd considering that she did *not* have an American accent. Eventually she changed her hat to a silk scarf, which had been another of her London purchases, together with the umbrella, an electric torch and a pair of powerful binoculars.

There was one more day to go. *Tomorrow and tomorrow and tomorrow* . . . She had left London quite early in the morning, at half past five. She had been eager to get up and go. She had gulped down her tea and scalded her tongue. It still hurt – felt swollen. The cab, on the other hand, had been fast enough, though the driver, to start with, had had no idea where Chalfont Parva was – he'd had to consult her map. Anyhow, the journey itself had taken less than three hours. Eleanor had booked herself into a motel outside Chalfont Parva and she could have stayed there, in her room, lain in bed, caught up on her sleep or watched television. She had caught a glimpse of *The Haunting* on TNT as she flicked through the channels, but she had felt extremely restless and impatient.

What if Corinne Coreille had arrived and was already

there, at Chalfont Park? What if that woman who'd answered the phone in Paris, the servant, had said the *second* of April, not the third? Eleanor might have got the date wrong. She might have misheard. Sometimes, she had to admit, her brain didn't function properly.

She had found where Chalfont Park was easily enough. It was a property belonging to Lady Grylls who was a baroness, she had been told by the postmistress, who had spoken in tones of hushed reverence. There was a large map in the post office window, which showed the whole of Chalfont Parva. Chalfont Park was only half a mile away. Eleanor stood under her umbrella, tracing very carefully the route from the village to Chalfont Park with a forefinger. Map reading is an art, girlie, Uncle Nat had said.

Moments later she started walking down the street. The wind had dropped but the rain hadn't let up for a second.

A thought popped into her head, like a jack in the box, for no particular reason, out of the void. *The open wounds in Griff's wrists had been like open mouths.* She glanced down at her own wrists. That same second she was aware of a buzzing sound. It felt as though she had bees trapped in her head. Angry bees – was that some kind of warning? Was it wise for her to go anywhere near Chalfont Park? Well, all she wanted to do was take a little peep at the house and study the grounds. If Corinne was already there, she'd know it at once, she felt sure – she'd get one of those special feelings. She *was* a little psychic.

*Buzz, buzz*, Eleanor mouthed. She put her hand into her pocket and her fingers closed round her weapon. *Buzz-buzz.* She felt reassured – for a moment she had thought she might have left it in her hotel room. She had to protect herself, that's why she needed it. In case Corinne Coreille didn't like what she had to say to her and attacked her. Corinne was unpredictable, volatile, emotionally unstable, mad. It was disgraceful – scandalous – that she hadn't been put away yet. They should banish her to Devil's Island.

Uncle Nat's words floated into her head. *Kill or be killed.*

117

*That's what I told the soldiers under my command. There's no third choice, boys.*

'I am really sorry but I had no choice, Inspector,' Eleanor said aloud in her most genteel voice. 'I did it in self-defence. She tried to kill me, you see.'

The end of the street. Now to the right from somewhere nearby came the mournful moo of a cow . . . a field . . . two men . . . farm labourers . . . big and burly. One of them, the younger, looked like Owen. Perhaps it *was* Owen? Could Owen have followed her all the way from the US? Perhaps they had sent him to spy on her and bring her back? He might be acting on orders from Eleanor's brother-in-law, who was a powerful man, or even the FBI. Owen would do anything for money. Griff, despite all his loyalty, had hinted as much. Or would the FBI employ a homosexual? They were very particular about that sort of thing – unlike the British secret service, which at one time had teemed with homosexuals. Perhaps Owen only *pretended* to be a homosexual? Perhaps the FBI used him as their hit-man and his brief was to eliminate homosexuals? Perhaps it was Owen who had killed Griff . . . It would have been so easy – as part of one of their 'games'. He could have cut Griff's wrists. Griff had liked pain.

Spotting a clump of crocuses under a tree, Eleanor was put in mind of a drawing Griff had done. The flower of unforgetting, he'd called it. Owen's name had been traced out in a series of concentric circles, in green and scarlet, so that the whole composition seemed to be of some monstrous blossom in which the petals were still unfolding . . . If Owen got anywhere near her, he'd regret it! Eleanor pushed her hand into her pocket once more. She imagined she heard a branch snapping – the sound of somebody's heavy breathing – and cast a glance over her shoulder. She gave a sigh of relief. No, it wasn't Owen – it wasn't a human being that was following her – only Abraxas. 'Stop following me,' she said in a low authoritative voice and she shook her forefinger at him. At once Abraxas started dissolving.

The grove. It was darker here, much darker. Quieter too.

The only sound she could hear was the swoosh-swoosh murmur of her wet shoes. The trees met at the top and formed a tunnel. Hardly any rain fell here, just the odd drop. She took the torch out of her bag. A torch was *essential* . . . She was walking along a path with trees on both sides. It felt cosy – a pleasant mushroomy smell – like being inside a hollow, or inside a womb. Eleanor felt the irresistible urge to lie on the ground, curl up among the heaps of dry leaves, shut her eyes and have a little sleep . . .

The instant Eleanor emerged from the grove, the rain stopped. She saw that as a sign that all would be well, that her mission would be a great success. 'Thank you,' she said, looking up and blowing a kiss off the palm of her right hand . . . Griff was guiding her . . . And there, no more than ten minutes away, was the house! Chalfont Park. Not as grand as she had expected it to be – quite unlike the way she had seen it in her mind's eye. She took out the binoculars and held them to her eyes. A once graceful residence fallen on hard times – paint peeling – the lawn was shockingly overgrown. No statues. No splashing fountains. No grandiloquent gates either. There had been a wall once, but it was in ruins now. Both house and garden had the dismal condition known as 'reduced circumstances' written all over them. '*The superannuations of sunk realms*,' Eleanor murmured.

She started walking round, crab-like, keeping her distance, and eventually caught sight of the back of the house. Through her binoculars she saw a stone terrace and french windows. She looked in the opposite direction. What was that octagonal building made of wrought iron and glass? A disused air about it . . . A greenhouse?

'The first requisite of any invading army is a base,' she said and, without a moment's hesitation, she made for the greenhouse. She walked carefully, warily, trying to make her feet kiss the ground, no more – she didn't want to broadcast her presence! On reaching the greenhouse, she turned the door handle down. Unlocked – another sign! 'Goody,' she said.

119

She marched into the dim arboreal light, switched on the torch and stood looking round . . . Plants. Some in rather poor condition. They were still recognizable as what they had once been, but just about. Roses in urns on plinths, various creepers climbing up a trellis obelisk, ivy, ferns with curling fronds . . . There was a sweetish putrid smell in the air, but she didn't mind. It was warm enough, dry too . . . Garden furniture. Two wooden chairs and benches painted battleship grey. An old tartan blanket. Some empty sacks on a stand in the corner. A bamboo table with a book and a magazine on it. *Who's Who in EastEnders* and last August's *Vogue*. The latter's cover showed one of those super-thin female models, her golden hair matching her golden tan, cuddling an over-bred, absolutely vile-looking Siamese cat with a diamond choker around its neck. 'Miaow,' Eleanor said. Then she made an angry hissing noise. Beside the table stood a large glazed pot of a classical design – empty but for a number of cigarette ends. She picked one up – Sullivan Powell. She sniffed at it. Somebody had been smoking good quality cigarettes . . . The baroness? At one time Eleanor had smoked Sullivan Powell cigarettes herself. A rich tarry taste . . .

Eleanor came to a decision. She had no doubt in her mind it was the right decision. *She wouldn't go back to the motel.* She would stay in the greenhouse and watch out for Corinne. She could sleep here tonight – on one of the benches. Those sacks would make a good pillow . . . There was the blanket and her fur stole to cover herself with. It was far from the comfort and luxury she was used to, Sparta rather than the Savoy, but she would survive . . . She took out a scone and bit into it. No jam or cream, and the Marmite proved to taste foul, so some of it stuck in her throat. A frugal Calvinistic feast. She had bought a small bottle of mineral water but she must drink sparingly, she reminded herself.

Standing beside the glass-panelled wall, she held the binoculars to her eyes once more. She saw a fox standing among the laurel and rhododendron on the left of the lawn – tall and grey-coated – what they called a dog-fox,

Eleanor imagined. The fox looked back at her unblinkingly
. . . She wondered if the fox would like a scone . . . The fox
couldn't be Corinne, could it? *Lady into Fox.* Corinne was a
witch and witches could transform themselves into anything they liked. Should she go and cut the fox's throat? It
wasn't against British law to kill foxes, was it – though it
might provoke the ire of the Society of Suppression of
Savage Severances . . . Eleanor giggled . . . They had quaint
things like that in England. Well, they need never know!
As though reading her mind, the fox disappeared into the
shrubbery.

Keeping the binoculars close to her eyes Eleanor gazed
in the direction of the house, at the french windows on the
ground floor. No light, even though it was such a dark
morning. She saw that on the outside the windows were
festooned with climbers . . .

Her attention was suddenly drawn to a window on the
first floor of the house. Somebody had entered the room
and turned on the electric light. The curtains weren't
drawn across that window and she could see perfectly. A
woman. Late forties? An oval face, short brown hair –
olive-green dress – pleasant, intelligent – keen look –
rather a flushed face. The woman stood there, as if on an
illuminated stage. How easy it would have been to take a
shot at her, if one had a gun and felt the inclination. One
couldn't possibly miss. Eleanor twisted her head to one
side, shut her left eye and pretended to take aim. She made
a popping sound with her lips.

The woman had started moving around the room. Something furtive and guilty about her manner. What was it she
felt so guilty about? *It wasn't her room.* Of course. Eleanor's
interest increased greatly with this discovery. The woman
was a stranger but Eleanor could identify with her – she
knew how she must feel. We are both trespassers, she
thought – we'd be in trouble were we to get caught . . . It
felt as though she were in a box at the theatre, watching a
play. She brought the binoculars closer to her eyes. Would
the woman see Eleanor's white blob of a face staring up at
her if she were to glance out of the window? Unlikely . . .

121

At any rate the woman was walking *away* from the window – in the direction of a desk in the corner . . . She was opening the briefcase that lay on top of the desk. She took out a folder, then another one – she seemed to be looking for something.

Quick, *quick*, Eleanor urged her, beating her palm against the glass panel, infected by the woman's frenzy. She trembled with excitement and dread. Make haste, girl, or they'll catch you! Somebody may come in any moment! Eleanor felt the urge to cross over to the house, throw a pebble at the window, draw the woman's attention, talk to her, confide in her, seek her counsel – feminine counsel had its special place in times of turmoil – impossible of course –

The woman seemed to have found what she was looking for. Eleanor saw her lips part. An object inside the case – what *was* it? Some document? A letter? No, a photograph – yes. The woman was looking down at a photograph. Eleanor saw her eyes widen in recognition. (She was sure it was recognition.) What a shame *she* couldn't see what was in the photograph! How frustrating! Eleanor beat the pane with her fist . . .

It must be something quite astonishing.

# 17

# The Fool of Love

Antonia entered the billiard room, doing her best to appear as calm and normal as possible. She watched her husband play a shot and miss rather an easy cannon off the red. Major Payne made an impatient gesture and grumbled that it was too damned hot in the room, didn't they think? Impossible to concentrate. His face was very red and he had an expression like thunder. Antonia guessed that he had been losing game after game to Jonson . . . Hugh was not a particularly gracious loser. The squabbles they had over Scrabble! He seemed bent on revenge. Both men were in their shirtsleeves, facing each other across the billiard table, holding up their cues, scowling – like duellists *en garde*, Antonia thought.

Lady Grylls was sunk in one of the two dark leather button-backed chairs by the fireplace. She had a black silk Chinese shawl embroidered with dragons around her shoulders. She was eating chocolates out of a circular box embellished with mauve orchids and lavender silk ribbons, sipping brandy from a balloon glass and smoking through a long jet-black holder. A gold ribbed cigarette case with *pavé* sapphires lay on the round table beside her chair. She had a stately and somewhat decadent air about her – rather as if she taught etiquette on a pirate ship, Antonia thought.

Lady Grylls had been telling her nephew and Jonson how she could have become Princess Philip of Greece. That was back in 1946, the year before Philip had married the Queen. Lady Grylls hadn't been married either – she'd been a mere Hon. They had met during an extremely dull shooting party. Philip had been jolly keen, but she hadn't reciprocated his ardour. Still, she had been fascinated by his turbulent family history and strange genetic heritage. His grandfather had been assassinated, his father exiled, his mother had become a nun and had then been consigned to a lunatic asylum, at least one of his sisters had married a Nazi. 'When we met again a couple of years ago he thought I was somebody else.' Lady Grylls sighed.

It was quarter past eleven. They had been having coffee – a tray with three ultra-thin porcelain cups, red with gold borders, and a silver pot stood on a side table. Antonia had heard Lady Grylls describe the new brand of coffee her suppliers sent her as 'rich and dark as the Aga Khan', which, she gathered, had been a non-PC advertising slogan from Lady Grylls's youth.

'Hugh, I'd like a word.' Antonia tried to smile. 'I do apologize, but it's important.'

'Ah, the little secrets of the newly-weds . . . A chocolate, my dear? The violet creams are particularly heavenly.' Lady Grylls proffered the box but Antonia declined. 'You *are* on a diet, admit it!' Lady Grylls cried gleefully.

Payne put down his cue. 'I'll be back in a jiffy. I haven't finished with you yet,' he told Jonson. 'What's the matter?' he asked Antonia.

'*Wait*,' she mouthed.

Up in their room she said, 'I found it. The photograph. It was in Jonson's case. He did bring it with him.'

Major Payne looked scandalized. 'You ransacked Jonson's room?'

'I didn't ransack his room. The photo was in his case. You won't believe this –'

'You don't think it's Corinne? Is that why you are so excited?'

'No . . . It's her all right. At least it *looks* like her. She has very short hair and a wig can be seen on her dressing table – it's exactly as Jonson said.' Antonia frowned as though for a moment something bothered her, then waved her hand. 'That's not it. There is a photograph on Corinne's dressing table. A framed photograph –'

'A photograph within the photograph? A double-edged clue, eh? Who's in it?'

She told him. He stared at her. 'Fancy now . . . A framed photograph on Corinne's dressing table suggests a degree of intimacy. Are you sure?'

'I am sure, yes.' Antonia paused. 'He looks younger but it's him all right . . . When *did* they meet?' The next moment she gasped. 'Of course. The second concert. So he did tell a lie!'

'Yes. Let's make assurance doubly sure.' Payne turned round and made for the door.

'Where are you going?'

'Going to phone my sister. She will tell us . . . Amanda's always at home these days – ever since she got divorced and became an agony aunt to the great and the good.'

There was nobody in the hall. Payne walked across the parquet floor that had been recently polished by Nicholas. The portrait of the eighth Baron Grylls stared down at him disapprovingly from its momentous place at the foot of the staircase, as though to say, No scandals in *our* family, but Payne ignored him. His eyes fixed momentarily on the glass case above the massive fireplace, which contained a grotesquely large stuffed salmon that had been caught by the ninth Baron in the Spey in 1920, pinkish but dull, its body's dance and sheen long gone. He walked up to the small table, where the ancient black telephone made of Bakelite stood beside a Waterford bowl filled with rose petals, and dialled his sister's Park Lane number.

'That you, Amanda?'

'*Hugh?* Good lord. Where are you phoning from – Cap Ferrat? Shropshire? At Chalfont – nothing wrong, is there? Is Aunt Nellie all right? She hasn't had her cataract operation yet, has she? I hope Antonia's well – Sorry? Do I remember –? What an odd question! Of course I remember Corinne Coreille and the Albert Hall . . . 1969. We went together, didn't we, me, you and Aunt Nellie . . . What?

125

The *second* concert? Yes, I did go . . . Speak up, would you? Yes, it was with him – he didn't want to go but I persuaded him . . . He had come down from Eton – he was staying with his parents in Kensington . . . Yes, we did go to see Corinne Coreille in her dressing room afterwards . . . Did anything *happen*? What do you mean? What in heaven's name are all these questions for?'

'Did they talk?'

'Of course they talked. It would have been odd if they didn't.' A cautious note had crept into Amanda's voice. 'Why do you want to know?'

'I have my reasons. Did anything happen? Come on, Amanda. As a matter of fact, I know something happened, I only want you to confirm it.'

'How do you know?'

'He told me,' Payne said, giving Antonia a wink. 'I didn't believe him, that's why I am asking you. Thought he was boasting.'

'He *told* you? He swore me to absolute secrecy!'

'Well, he said it no longer mattered – it was all such a long time ago. More than thirty years. We sat drinking last night and he suddenly came out with it. You know the way these things happen – chaps together,' Payne went on improvising.

'Is he at Chalfont too? He's gone now? Oh very well.' Amanda paused. 'He took a wild fancy to Corinne – one of those instant things. I could tell, despite his cool exterior. He asked her out . . . No, Mr Lark wasn't there. It had to be kept secret from him. He was extremely protective of Corinne, yes. I don't know whether Mr Lark too fancied Corinne – he was a great number of years older than her – maybe he did, though it was her career he said he cared about.'

'Did they really start seeing each other?'

'All right. They did. He kept going to Paris. She gave him her grandmother's phone number. She did like him too, obviously. It was so funny – the way they stood looking at each other – he so English, she so French . . . Did

126

they –? All right. Pretty intimate, yes. He told me later – boasted about it. Her very first. His first too.'

'It all came to nothing, apparently?'

'Yes . . . So sad . . . Her career took off and the protective net around her became impenetrable. That's why he joined the diplomatic corps and then the trend-spotting thing – to be able to travel because of her. She was travelling an awful lot, but it was no joy . . . Yes, he did tell me all that himself. I am very good at receiving confidences and giving advice, you know . . . He was devastated when –' Amanda broke off.

'When what?'

'Nothing.'

'Nothing? Come *on*, Amanda.'

There was a pause. 'He didn't tell you that – all right – there were developments – it was all rather distressing –'

Payne listened. His brows went up. Soon after he rang off.

'Not only did they have a relationship,' he told Antonia, 'but Corinne became pregnant by him. Sadly, the child was born prematurely and died. She couldn't have any more children after that, apparently. It was all kept hush-hush. He was extremely cut up about it. You wouldn't have thought it of him, would you? That's why he never married. He always blamed her for having given in to Mr Lark's bullying – for being Mr Lark's puppet. Amanda doesn't think they have been in touch since, but of course she may be wrong.'

'The fact that she still keeps his photo on her dressing table suggests she probably still has feelings for him,' Antonia said thoughtfully. 'Jonson must have recognized him when he bumped into him here. He clearly didn't like to be reminded.'

'Yes.' There was a moment's silence, then Payne continued, 'Must be in the blood. I mean not one but *two* de Brokes succumbing to the fatal charms of the French.'

Antonia said, 'Poor Peverel.'

# 18

# They Came to Chalfont

Corinne Coreille and Maître Maginot arrived the following day, 3rd April, at six o'clock in the afternoon. It was an extremely low-key event, with no pomp or circumstance and not a modicum of showbiz glamour. A non-event, in fact. There had been no jet and, much to Lady Grylls's relief, there was no entourage. The two women, travelling unobtrusively, incognito, entirely on their own, had taken a plane from Charles de Gaulle airport to Heathrow. It was only as the taxi which brought them left London that Maître Maginot phoned Lady Grylls from her mobile and told her to expect them.

'She sounded exhausted,' Lady Grylls commented to Payne and Antonia in gleeful tones. 'Rather subdued too. I expected to be hectored! The first thing she asked was if the central heating at Chalfont was working, then if I kept any cats and I said no. She perked up even more when I told her Andrew was actually staying at the house. She was pleased about it, I could tell. She asked who else was here and didn't like it when I told her that I had my nephew and niece-by-marriage staying with me. Not at all happy. Oh well, she'll have to lump it.' Lady Grylls laughed. 'Showed her true nature then – flared up. I rang off. The battle lines have been drawn, my dears. So, like all good scouts, be prepared.'

\*      \*      \*

As the taxi drove up the alley towards the house in the gloom, under pelting rain that was turning to sleet, Eleanor Merchant stood inside the greenhouse in her mink stole, pressed her nose against the glass panel and watched. Her picture hat was back on her head, but it now resembled a squashed cabbage leaf. It had got colder and her teeth chattered. Her breath came out in swirls, causing the pane to mist over. She wiped it off frantically with her gloved hands. *She had to see.*

The lights were on in the room beyond the terrace – the drawing room, as she had gathered. And this time, luckily, they had omitted to draw the white damask curtains across the french windows. Eleanor held the binoculars to her eyes. She could see that the curtains were still tied with their heavy black loops . . . She had an excellent view of the room . . . Etruscan red walls with a touch of orange. Fireplace of blood-red speckled marble in what, she imagined, was the Directoire Egyptian style. Two rows of pictures in gilded frames . . . Grey chairs with rather faded green stripes . . .

After a wait that seemed interminable, but must have been no more than five minutes, Eleanor saw the two women enter the drawing room, first the older, then the younger, followed by the fat elderly woman with the thick glasses she had seen earlier on – Lady Grylls.

Eleanor's hands were shaking so badly now, she nearly dropped her binoculars, and she found it hard to hold back the tears that kept prickling at her eyes. At long last, she thought – *at long last.*

The older woman was dressed in purple and she was wearing black gloves. She held her torso erect and walked in a regally stiff manner. She looked extremely forbidding. Her face was lopsided, deformed. Her lower lip was longer and jutted out. That, combined with the turban she was wearing, put Eleanor in mind of the Ugly Duchess in *Alice* . . . Brought up as she was in the 'English' tradition, Eleanor started humming under her breath – '*A most unattractive old thing – Tra-la – with a caricature of a face . . .*'

The woman had an air of immense authority about her

129

– she might have been an ambassador representing some prosperous kingdom – but she lacked the serenity one associated with that sort of person. She kept reaching out for Corinne's arm . . . Her eyes darted suspiciously around the room, as though expecting some kind of ambush. Who was she? Was that the Maître Maginot the tipsy *femme de chambre* had mentioned on the phone? Was she – Corinne's minder? 'Well, she'd better mind her own business,' Eleanor uttered in menacing tones. Eleanor's gaze then fixed avidly on Corinne Coreille.

At long last.

Eleanor took in every little detail: the blue high-collared dress with the tiny bows – the cross around her neck – the thick dark fringe – the slightly upturned nose – the large eyes –

AT LONG LAST.

Eleanor experienced a sick feeling at the pit of her stomach. She gasped. She was overcome with dizziness – the circus wheel sensation again – and for a moment feared she might pass out. No, she mustn't – not when she was so close to her goal! She leant forward and pressed her forehead against the glass wall.

Then, recovering, she once more raised the binoculars to her eyes. Corinne Coreille – from that distance at least – looked exactly as she had in the myriads of photographs she had seen of her on those old vinyls she had found in Griff's room – as she had looked at the Palais de Congrès concert she and Griff had watched together seven years before. Not a day older. *Exactly* the same – younger, if that were possible. A fifty-five-year-old woman, looking like a young girl – like a blushing bride – like a virginal bride. It was scandalous – uncanny – wrong – obscene! How dared she remain the same, untouched by time, while – while all that was left of Griff was a handful of grey ashes?

'Whore . . . bitch . . . witch,' Eleanor whispered. '*Witch* . . . Yes. That's what you get when you cross a whore and a bitch. Shameless . . . evil . . . sold her soul . . . sleeping with Satan . . .'

Eleanor pulled her scarf around her shoulders tightly. It

was a Hermès scarf. She had spent some time in London looking for a Hermès scarf. No other scarf would have done. Hermes, after all, was the divinity that conducted the souls of the dead to Hades. Hades . . . That was where Corinne was going.

'If only I had a sniper,' Eleanor said.

Encompassed as the three women were within the french windows, Eleanor had the strange feeling that once more she was watching a television screen – an old-fashioned variety programme, with Corinne Coreille appearing between two eccentric elderly comediennes, one owlish, fat and jolly, not unlike the late Queen Juliana of the Netherlands, the other hideous, severe, displaying the camp stateliness of a drag queen . . . At one point Maître Maginot and Corinne made exactly the same gesture – as though the whole thing had been choreographed and rehearsed! Eleanor nearly expected Corinne to break into song – something outrageous and indescribably silly – something ambiguous and suggestive – 'J'ai Deux Amours'? 'Ladies of Lisbon'? And of course the two elder women would join in – this would be followed by the three of them linking arms and doing the cancan –

(*Où finit le théâtre? Où commence la vie?*)

Eleanor started giggling – her hands clutched at her stomach – she couldn't help herself.

# 19

# The Birds

*We didn't meet them until some time later.* (Antonia wrote in her diary.)

*Maître Maginot came down first. She was clad in a magenta gown that swept the floor and a silk turban with a brooch pinned to one side of it – only part of the brooch was visible, a bird of some kind, made of silver, from what I could see, the rest being hidden within folds of the turban. She also wore pendant ruby earrings and a ruby necklace and a curious red string bracelet on her left wrist. Her hands are veined, her nails long and varnished red, and she wore several large-stoned rings. She looks tall but, as I discovered, that is due to the high-heeled shoes she has on. Her appearance was striking and extremely theatrical. She might have been the high priestess of some esoteric cult.*

*There is something seriously wrong with her face, the result, as Jonson had told us, of a stroke. Her eyes give the impression of having been sewn into slits and consequently have a Chinese-looking slant, which gives her face the cast of an Oriental warrior. They lack mobility and she seems to find it difficult to blink. Her complexion is the colour of raw veal and she tries to improve it, rather unsuccessfully, by applying some very white powder. Her brows have been plucked and pencilled over. Her age is difficult to gauge. Mid-sixties, at a guess – maybe older. The cruel set of her mouth and jutting lip lend a ferocity and a distinctiveness to her expression. Her voice is unpleasant. She speaks with the venomous rasp of a predatory creature.*

*I felt a leaden oppression descend on me the moment I laid eyes* on her. I seem to possess the kind of morbid sensitivity to emotional atmosphere which, according to Hugh, is common to lovers and housewives. Introductions having been made, Maître Maginot hardly spoke to me, didn't so much as glance at me, in fact. Hugh looked rather distinguished in his maroon smoking jacket and she fixed her eyes on him quizzically for a couple of moments.

It was the petrifying gaze of a Medusa, he said later. Unless she wanted a toy-boy for some unspeakable sexual practices and he fitted the bill. He expected her tastes to be shockingly kinky, he said, warming to the fantasy. Clearly, she was the dominatrix type.

Provost handed round pale sherry of exceptional quality. Maître Maginot sat next to Jonson on the sofa and addressed herself to him, exclusively. She berated him for having failed to make sure the field would be clear for their arrival. She spoke in a loud enough voice for me to hear. She and Corinne were not having the privacy they had expected. Corinne was jumpy and tense. Corinne found it impossible to relax in the company of strangers. Maître Maginot looked from me to Hugh, rather pointedly. (Did she really believe Jonson could have shooed us off the premises?)

She went on breathing toxic dragon-fumes at him. Had he checked the house from top to bottom? Every single room? The cellars and the attics? The pantry? The outbuildings? She seemed to doubt whether the search had been thorough. He had conducted a search the day before, but not today? Would he repeat that? Not today? She threw up her hands in dismay. But that was exceedingly remiss of him! What had he been doing with himself? Was that why she had employed his services? To lounge about? To kick his heels? She was so enraged that her turban shook. Suddenly – and rather bizarrely – she reminded me of the glove puppet Corinne had had as a child. The bossy governess – Miss Mountjoy.

A fresh search must be conducted tonight, she said, raising an admonishing forefinger. We shall do it together. We'll check every part of the house and the outbuildings. We shall go over it with a – what was that ridiculous English phrase? – fine-tooth comb? Yes – after dinner. I saw Jonson nod agreement.

Lady Grylls – resplendent in a light green silk dress with trailing sleeves – was clearly determined not to be intimidated or made angry by Maître Maginot. As the latter held forth, Lady Grylls assumed a mock-solemn expression by drawing the corners of her mouth downwards while rolling her eyes. She kept nodding with exaggerated portentousness. Once or twice, when she was sure Maginot was not looking, she gave us a wink.

It was getting late. Provost had come in twice to say that dinner was ready. Maître Maginot turned to Lady Grylls – 'Is that man reliable? Have you checked his credentials? Has he been with you long?' To all three questions Lady Grylls answered placidly in the affirmative. 'I think we should go ahead and eat now,' Maître Maginot said eventually. Corinne was probably on her knees, praying to the Holy Virgin. Corinne had been in a strange, fatalistic mood the last couple of days. Corinne's nerves had been torn to shreds. Maître Maginot blamed that crazy American woman's letters with their wild assertions. And of course the death threats. Nonsense of course, nothing but empty threats, but so terribly unsettling for poor Corinne. (If she thinks they are empty threats, why does she make such great fuss over the security checks? A contradiction, surely?)

It was as we were sitting down to dinner that Corinne Coreille joined us.

No meeting ever matches up to one's prevision of it. In my mind I had consigned her to a third world, one ruled by unreason, miracles and magic; I had imagined her to be as foreign as the sphinx, and now felt startled and disappointed at how normal she seemed. All right, she clearly wore tons of make-up and her glossy chestnut hair was most probably a wig, but apart from that there isn't anything particularly extraordinary about her. She was clad in a high-collared dress of very light blue, with a red bow at the neck, and she had a red string bracelet on her left wrist, the same as Maître Maginot. I smelled her scent – old-fashioned violets.

She doesn't look fifty-five. That of course could only have been achieved through very recent and rather superior plastic surgery, conducted by the most skilful of Swiss surgeons. She might also have had shots of Botox. It's the hands that betray one's real age, but Corinne's were smooth and unpigmented, without a single *liver spot. I marvelled at that until I discovered that she was actually wearing flesh-coloured gloves, with the nails painted in. That was the only real oddity about her.*

*'You remember Hugh of course?' Lady Grylls boomed.*

*Corinne gave a sweet smile. 'Oh yes, ' she said. 'I remember Hugh. The Royal Albert Hall, 1969. You had a little limp, yes? Result of playing "footer"? I hope your foot is better?'*

*'Much better, thank you,' Hugh answered, poker-faced. 'I've had – um – sufficient time to recover.'*

*'Thank you very much for the flowers,' Corinne went on in her shy voice. 'They were lovely . . . How is Amanda? Is she still fond of her dog Bernard?'*

*'I am afraid Bernard died back in 1974, I think.'*

*'Oh, I am extremely sorry!' Corinne looked genuinely distressed.*

*Could she really be so peculiar, I wondered – or had she decided to put on the kind of performance that would confirm the popular perception of her as a person who was completely out of touch with reality?*

*There was a little commotion as we took our seats at the dinner table. Maître Maginot refused to sit with her back to the door, so Aunt Nellie's seating plan underwent a last-minute change. 'We must be able to see who comes in. We all need to be extremely vigilant,' Maître Maginot said, looking round the table.*

*Dinner was superb. Mashed avocado with crisp bacon, prawn pancakes, and these were followed by roast grouse. We had champagne first, then red burgundy, then Sauternes (which I didn't drink, but Hugh hailed as 'first-class'.) Lady Grylls was served first, before any of us, in the ancient feudal manner, the idea being that in the event of the food being poisoned, the hostess would gallantly succumb, and her instant death would be a warning to the rest of the table to abstain.*

*Maître Maginot drank a fair amount of wine. Lady Grylls hadn't stinted herself – she could be a wonderful hostess when she chose to. We were served by Provost and son Nicholas, both clad in black-and-yellow striped waistcoats and white gloves. Like the waiters at Maxim's, Aunt Nellie said vaguely.*

*Conversation was rather strangled and uneasy, at least at the start. It was punctuated by unnerving silences. There are limits* to the kind of small talk people can maintain in the face of mysterious adversity without appearing ridiculous. How could we have pretended that this was an ordinary social visit, when we all knew that it was anything but? Maître Maginot maintained her air of disapproval. Jonson didn't say much. He and Corinne had exchanged nods and smiles, but they didn't communicate in any other way in the course of the evening.

'It is cold here. I am particularly susceptible to colds,' Maître Maginot complained. 'England is a cold country. I do not normally drink much but I need to keep myself warm. These English country houses, they are always the same. I started reading a book on the plane. A detective story, as it happens, set in an English country house. It was quite absurd, but I felt disturbed by it. I can't say why. I left it on the plane. I never finished it. I'd forgotten how much I hate that sort of thing – but you must take my word for it that it was quite absurd.' Maître Maginot was becoming voluble, no doubt mellowed by the wine she was drinking. 'The Hunt for – No, I can't remember what it was called. Some unusual name. For some reason it gave me the creeps.'

'Antonia writes detective stories,' Lady Grylls said, but Maître Maginot grimaced as though she had bitten into a lemon, shook her head vigorously and said that that was not a subject she wished to discuss.

'What are these red bracelets you are wearing?' Hugh asked.

'The red string wards off the evil eye,' Maître Maginot explained. 'We are both daughters of the Kabbalah. When somebody is as famous as Corinne, she needs protection. The red string only looks like red string but in actual fact it carries great powers with it.'

Pudding was served. Delicious crème brûlée, and there was a second choice: frothy chocolate mousse. Corinne had two helpings of the latter, I noticed. Lady Grylls asked about Corinne's Osaka concert last November. It was Maître Maginot who gave us an account of it. (She seems to be taking her duties as Corinne's spokesperson too literally.)

'It was magnificent,' she breathed. 'Truly triumphant. Sublime. Corinne was in superb form.' Warmed by the good wine, Maître Maginot was slipping into the known Parisian tendency of linguistic inflation. Her French accent had become more pronounced. 'There were six encores.'

There had been a pin-drop hush to start with. Every member of the audience had held their heads bowed low, in anticipation. They might have been participating in some act of religious observance. They were strange individuals, the Japanese. The moment Corinne appeared on the stage, they went wild. They screamed so much, they had to be cautioned – some of them had to be physically restrained, otherwise they would have joined Corinne on stage!

The wine sparkled blood-red as Maître Maginot held her glass to the light. The concert hall had teemed with security guards and secret police. There had been a number of policewomen dressed as geishas who had carried stun guns hidden within the folds of their kimonos. Several doctors and nurses from the American hospital, warned of the possibility of incidents, had also been present.

The applause that met each of Corinne's songs had been deafening. At the end, the audience had overcome the ushers and the guards and surged towards the stage. Corinne had found herself under a shower of lotus blossoms, rose petals and star-shaped confetti. The cries had been indescribable, the flash of the cameras blinding. Men as well as women wept and they beat at their faces with their fists. 'For a moment it looked as though things were getting out of hand,' Maître Maginot said. 'Then we heard a sharp crack – someone had let off a gun!'

Maître Maginot had no idea whether it had been a real gun – probably not. It was the last of the encores – an extremely popular Japanese song, which could be roughly translated as 'I Am Nothing Without You' – that had provoked the furore. For that particular song Corinne had changed into the nun-like nurse's uniform of the Dames of Malta.

'I do not exaggerate. I rarely exaggerate. Never before in my life have I observed such a spectacle.' Maître Maginot shook her head. 'Men in a state of exaltation, banging their foreheads before Corinne. Blood streamed down their faces but they didn't seem to care. They looked radiant. It was as though they had been – how do you say? – vouchsafed a glimpse of the godhead.'

One extremely fat Japanese man, wearing a smart light-brown

suit and a yellow waistcoat, his hair en brosse, had managed to climb on to the stage and he got hold of Corinne's ankle. 'He looked extremely prosperous,' Maître Maginot said. The man had attempted to take off one of Corinne's golden slippers – as a souvenir, no doubt – or maybe he was one of those disgusting perverts, Maître Maginot was not sure. 'He wouldn't let go and had to be forcibly dragged away! He bit one of the policemen and kicked another, so they used a stun gun on him. When he collapsed, it took ten people to carry him out of the hall! That made me laugh, I must confess, though of course the whole episode was rather grotesque.'

'I was very frightened,' Corinne whispered.

'I know you were. Ma pauvre petite. You trembled like a little bird.' Maître Maginot reached out for her hand. The way Corinne reacted to MM's touch made me think she was afraid of her. A certain tensing of the shoulders.

'The Japanese were very good to me,' Corinne went on. 'They produced a CD to coincide with the concert.'

'Ah, the new CD.' Tilting her head to one side in an oddly bird-like manner, Maître Maginot regarded Corinne with the kind of pride that could only be described as motherly. 'Perhaps we could listen to it now, yes?'

At a sign from Lady Grylls, Provost inserted the CD and turned on the player.

> J'ai vu son visage tout au long de ma vie
> Comme si je n'avais connu que lui –

It was a song that started as melancholy and became progressively intense and dramatic.

> Va décrocher tes lunes
> Bâtir tes cathédrales
> Dans les matins sans brume
> Mais ne me fais plus mal . . .

When the song was over, Maître Maginot asked for the player to be turned off. She said, 'Corinne, ma chère, would you sing *that last bit for us again?' And Corinne smiled – and did. Although the song wasn't my cup of tea, I have to admit that her voice is as beautiful and powerful as it is fresh. Any suspicions that Corinne might have mimed to playback at her Japanese concert were dispelled in an instant. That, I believe, was Maître Maginot's secret intention – to show us, in case we harboured any doubts.*

*We were having coffee in the drawing room when Provost came in to say that someone had rung, a Miss Tricia Swindon, an American lady. She wanted to speak to Miss Coreille. Corinne didn't stir. Maître Maginot rose to her feet. 'I'll speak to her. I have no idea who she is. It might be the other one, the crazy American woman, don't you think?' Her eyes flashed angrily at Jonson. 'However did she manage to get this number?'*

*As Maître Maginot left the room, I noticed something very strange. Corinne tilted her head to one side, in a movement that was an exact replica of the one made by la Maginot.*

*When Maître Maginot returned, she said, 'It was most peculiar. The woman rang off the moment she heard my voice. Didn't say a word, apart from asking if I was Corinne Coreille. Have you had any other such similar calls?'*

*She cast an inquiring glance at Jonson, who – after a moment's hesitation – told her about the anonymous calls. 'But this is terrible!' Maître Maginot cried. 'It must be that crazy American woman. I am afraid we'll have to inform the police first thing tomorrow morning. We have no option. I am sorry,* ma petite.' *She looked towards Corinne who hadn't stirred but continued sitting passively, blank-faced. 'For the time being we rely on you to protect us, Mr Jonson. I am sure you will do your best to justify your fee.'*

*I saw Lady Grylls pushing up her glasses and squinting at Maître Maginot's turban, at the place where it had been fastened by the silver bird brooch. The turban folds having got a bit loose, more of the brooch was revealed now. I could see that it was in fact not one but two birds standing back to back, linked by their tails, Siamese-twins fashion.*

*Two ostriches.*

*I believe I experienced something of a shock when I realized where I'd seen that very same brooch before. It would be too much of a coincidence if there existed two such brooches.*

*It was Ruse, Corinne's mother, who wore the brooch in one of the photographs pasted in Aunt Nellie's scrapbook.*

# 20

# Put on by Cunning

They discussed the matter later in their bedroom.

'It's a fantastic idea. Not impossible though,' Payne said.

'We were right,' Antonia said.

'Mother and daughter, eh? Well, now that you mention it, their eyes are quite similar, if not identical. Deep-set, light-brown, almond-shaped. That's one of the first things I noticed about la Maginot and I thought that perhaps she had been a good-looking woman once, before her stroke. Then I convinced myself I'd imagined the resemblance since in every other respect they couldn't have been more different, but now that you mention the ostrich brooch –' He broke off. 'We were right!'

'Yes. It makes perfect sense when you think about it,' Antonia said. '*Le falcon* steals half a million from his clients. He is under investigation. He and Ruse think of a way out. They hit on a cunning scheme that combines keeping the money, cheating the law and getting rid of media attention once and for all. A triple whammy. They are gamblers. They are reckless – have ingenious minds. They are ruthless operators. They go to Kenya and contrive to get in touch with the leader of a dangerous local gang. They strike a deal with him – they pay him a handsome sum and in return he provides two dead bodies. Man and woman.'

'The Dutch couple?'

'The Dutch couple. The Coreilles supply the gang with

their clothes, personal effects and passports to plant on the bodies. They themselves disappear. They already have forged passports in different names – possibly in a different nationality. A ransom note is left at the hotel . . . The bodies are abandoned in the open – the lions do the rest.'

Payne stroked his jaw with his forefinger. 'Yes . . . Madame Coreille then "identifies" the bodies. She of course is acting in cahoots with her son and daughter-in-law. Her cooperation is essential. She has been in on it from the start. She too receives money – she needs it for her pet project – the clinic. The Coreilles, in their new identities, disappear – to a part of the world where they do not stand a chance of being recognized. They settle down and live happily for the next forty years.' Payne paused. 'When François-Enrique dies, Ruse returns to France. She contacts her famous daughter – manages to meet her. Ruse tells Corinne who she is and what she has done.'

'Or they might have been in touch already?'

'It's possible. Either way, they must have hit it off. One suspects Ruse is completely amoral while Corinne's moral sense is probably undeveloped. Corinne's career has been showing signs of flagging and Ruse, enterprising as ever, believes she can help. She is unrecognizable after a stroke. She assumes yet another identity – she becomes "Maître Maginot", Corinne's legal adviser and protector. She moves in with Corinne and takes complete control of her affairs. Her intention is to revive her daughter's career and make even more money for her – for both of them – and she manages to do it. The Osaka concert is a spectacular success.'

'However –'

'However, somebody starts sending death threats to Corinne. Ruse decides on England and Chalfont Park as a retreat. Chalfont is pitched very much in a rural solitude. She has no fear of her girlhood friend Nellie recognizing her, not after all these years – besides, she knows that Nellie's eyesight has always been bad . . .'

*     *     *

It had been the old trout who had come to the phone. The Frenchwoman with the Frankenstein face. Corinne's minder.

Eleanor stared dully before her. She couldn't say what she had been hoping to achieve with that phone call. She had had very little sleep the night before. It had been freezing cold, which, together with the wailing wind, the drumming of the raindrops on the greenhouse roof and the hooting of owls, had given her a horrible headache. In the morning there had been the dolorous cooing of doves. To her ears it had sounded like a bored or half-hearted keening for the dead . . . Her head was feeling very funny now. There was again the buzzing sound in her ears . . . She felt feverish . . . She hadn't taken her pills – she couldn't find them . . .

Eleanor admitted to herself that she had acted rashly, with little reason. She had no use for the Tricia Swindon ploy, not any more. How could she have forgotten? There would be no point in trying to persuade Corinne Coreille to agree to a meeting. Corinne Coreille would never agree to a meeting.

What could she have said to Corinne anyway, if Corinne *had* come to the phone? I am the mother of one of your victims – I am outside, in the greenhouse – come alone – you won't like what I've got to say to you, but we must talk nevertheless. I'd like to warn you that I won't really be responsible for my actions. The idea suddenly struck her as so hilarious that Eleanor started laughing. She couldn't help herself. *I won't really be responsible for my actions.* She shook with laughter. Sweet Jesus! She had to stuff her handkerchief into her mouth, that was the only way to stop herself. Then, of course, she started crying.

She was 'cyclothymic'. That was what her shrink had said. She went up – she went down. Pie in the sky – down in the dumps. Up, then down. Then up again. Like one of those yo-yos. She had been given medication for it. Those little pink pills – where *were* they? Like a pie in the sky! Eleanor's cheeks distended and she exploded once more into the rudest of noises. She clapped her hand over her

143

mouth. She felt so guilty for being amused, for laughing while Griff's ashes were trying to break out of that marble urn, that she became quite hysterical with grief. 'My boy, my child, please forgive me,' she sobbed, falling to her knees and bowing her head.

She didn't know how long she had remained kneeling but eventually she struggled up and stood silently by the glass panel once more.

The rain had stopped. It was very quiet. The night sky was clear and the moon had emerged – the enormous moon of antiquity – pale and mysterious and, oh so close! Eleanor held out her hands towards it yearningly. By its light she observed somebody leave the house on a bicycle and go down the drive. That boy with the sickly face, spiky hair and the single earring, which she now saw flashing in the moonlight. She had seen him earlier on. One of the servants, she guessed. *The boy who does the boots.* Where was that from? Belloc? For a couple of moments Eleanor toyed with the idea of running up to the drive, ambushing the boy and offering him money, a lot of money – *all her money* – in return for his assistance.

She needed a collaborator, somebody from the house. Somebody who could persuade Corinne to come out on some pretext – who would lure her into the garden. The boy could cosh Corinne when there was no one around, then drag her out and deliver her inside the greenhouse. Why, he could even kill Corinne for her, if she told him to! Some people would do anything for money. Teenage boys in particular. Boys were notoriously greedy, reckless, violent. Boys indulged in cruelty for cruelty's sake. They would smash a puppy's head with a piece of brick without thinking twice about it. Eleanor would gladly give every dollar she had in the bank for the joy of seeing Corinne Coreille lying prostrate among the dead plants, or on her knees begging for mercy . . . That boy would do the job. Get him, Eleanor told herself, and she might have carried out the idea but by the time she reached the door, the boy with the bike had disappeared into the night . . . She needed to think of something else . . . . Could she set some kind of trap?

*J'ai vu son visage tout au long de ma vie.* It was earlier on, as she opened the greenhouse door to get some fresh air, that she had heard Corinne sing in the house and now she couldn't get the song out of her head . . . Corinne had been giving a live performance . . . *J'ai vu son visage* –

Eleanor rubbed her temples. 'Go away,' she said and she made a pushing movement with her hands. *'Go away.'*

She remembered reading an article in which Corinne Coreille was mockingly referred to as *la grande anesthésiste.* Something about her sentimental songs having a softening effect on people – like meat that was being tenderized. Had she anaesthetized Griff as well? Perhaps Griff didn't feel anything at all?

The blood – that bath – Griff's face –

She needed to strike soon. Tonight. She glanced up at the full moon. Her solitary vigil had lasted long enough . . . She couldn't stay holed up in the greenhouse for ever . . . 'I think my days at Grey Gardens are limited,' she said, sounding exactly like 'Little' Edie Bouvier. 'I need to strike soon . . .' *Yes.* It had to be tonight. Tomorrow it would be too late . . . *Forget domani* . . . Perhaps she could set the house on fire? And strike as Corinne Coreille ran out in her nightdress, like a rabbit that had been smoked out of its warren? She had her knife in her bag . . . That white throat, so smooth and supple! She could hear Corinne's screams – her sobs – her pleas that she be spared. The thought excited her. There'd be no mercy . . . Blood called out for blood . . . There would be no point talking to her, really.

Eleanor consulted her watch: twenty to eleven . . . The moon grew larger and brighter . . . She saw Abraxas cross the lawn, his evil chanticleer's head once more turned towards her, his serpent's tail zigzagging behind him. He was coming from the direction of the house. She was not in the least surprised . . . When she looked at her watch next, it was five minutes *past* eleven.

She needed to set herself a deadline. Midnight? Yes. Corinne must die before midnight. Only that was easier said than done. How could she do it? The idea of setting the house on fire was fine, but she didn't have any matches . . . Break into the house when everybody was asleep – find her way to Corinne's bedroom? There might be a window left open somewhere on the ground floor, but which one *was* Corinne's bedroom?

Ten past eleven . . . Suddenly her mobile phone started ringing. Eleanor gasped and for a moment she stood very still. She then took her phone out of her bag with a trembling hand and stared down at it. Who could it be? No one knew her number. She flashed her torch at the display – *Unknown number.* She put the phone to her ear and pressed the button.

'Hello?' she said tentatively. She heard terrible crackling noises. 'Hello? Who is it?'

A voice spoke – extremely muffled – it sounded as though it was coming from some great distance. 'At last! I've been trying to – ' It was a young man's voice – breathless – speaking with an American accent.

'Who is this?' Eleanor's throat had gone extremely dry.

'Mother?'

No – *no.* It couldn't be. She felt the torch slip from her hand. She saw it go out as it hit the ground. 'Griff?'

I am not ready, she thought in a panic. I look terrible. I need a mirror. I need to put on my lipstick. Griff hates it when I am without my lipstick.

'Mother? I can see you now. Very clearly. I can see inside your head. Every thought. It is like looking into a crystal ball. All your thoughts are scarlet.'

Eleanor gasped again. *Her thoughts were scarlet.* Griff knew what she was planning to do! Of course he did. The dead had special powers. Though of course Griff was not dead – not any more. *He had come back.* She looked frantically around – peered outside at the lawn bathed in moonlight – glanced up towards the sky – she thought she might see him descending slowly, his hand raised in greeting, but there was no one. She thought she felt a draught, a sudden gust of cold air. She found she was shaking. She

146

realized she felt extremely frightened. 'Mother? Are you there?' she heard Griff say.

She was witnessing a miracle – and the miraculous was always frightening. Witnesses to the resurrection of Lazarus must have been terrified.

'Griff? Oh my God. Is that really you?' Her voice sounded very hoarse. '*Where are you?* Are you really at Chalfont?'

'I can see you,' he said again in a sing-song voice, a rising 'see', a falling 'you'. 'Can't you see me?'

'Oh my God. Are you – in the greenhouse? I can't find my torch – Where *are* you?' Eleanor screamed. 'Where? *Griff?*'

She heard a screeching sound, like a soul in great torment being sucked into hell, then the line went dead. 'Griff – Griff!' Eleanor cried, tears running down her cheeks. 'Oh Griff – please, speak to me.'

But the phone remained silent.

So shaken was she by the experience that it never occurred to her that Griff had always called her Eleanor – never Mother.

# 21

# The Man Who Knew Too Much

When they bumped into her on the landing, Maître Maginot had changed into a short black jacket trimmed with fur, jodhpurs, shining leather boots and a black beret, and she wore black gloves. The kind of outfit that might have been supplied by the French version of the Norfolk Hunt Club, Major Payne whispered, making Antonia giggle – if they had any such thing in France – or perhaps la Maginot was striving after the resistance fighter look *circa* 1940? What was it they called themselves? The *maquis*? All she was lacking was a fuming cheroot sticking out of the corner of her mouth. Her eyes were bloodshot, her face extremely flushed – it showed purple under the white powder. She bared her teeth at them in what might have been a smile, and she shook her fist above her head in some kind of revolutionary salute. Too much wine, Antonia thought.

Maître Maginot appeared to be in a state of considerable excitement and, despite the latish hour, bursting with energy. She looked determined – in a dangerous mood. In her right hand she held an ancient golf club, which Payne recognized as one belonging to his late uncle, though it was unlikely that she was on her way to practise shots on the lawn. Payne said later he wouldn't have been surprised if she'd come up with something on the lines of *'Vive la guerre!'*

It was twenty-five minutes past eleven.

* * *

There was a knock at the door. 'Who is it?' Antonia looked up. She was sitting at the desk in their bedroom, pen in hand. She had been writing her diary.

'Jonson . . . Andrew Jonson.'

'Oh, come in.'

As Jonson entered the room, the door to the en suite bathroom opened and Payne appeared in his pyjamas and dressing gown. 'Hello, old boy,' he said. 'How's tricks?'

Jonson had changed into a V-neck pullover, a striped scarf and slacks. Something of the boy prefect about him, Antonia thought. He looked worried. He said, 'Nothing much. Terribly sorry to bother you like this. Um. Checking the house once more –'

'Gosh, yes, the checks. We'd completely forgotten.'

'Is everything all right?' Jonson looked round the room.

'Yes, shipshape and Bristol fashion. Would you like to look under the beds? Inside the wardrobe?' Payne suggested in serio-comical tones.

'I know it's silly. No one could have got into the house. All the downstairs doors and windows are locked and bolted, but these are Maître Maginot's instructions. She's gone out to check the grounds.' Jonson looked slightly sheepish.

'Was that where she was heading? The grounds . . . It's a beautiful night. We bumped into her on the stairs. Made me think of those hurricanes to which women's names are given. Incidentally, what is Maître Maginot's first name?'

'I'm afraid I have no idea.'

'I assume she has one? Does she really believe she might come across the Merchant?'

'I don't know . . . Probably not . . . She just wants to make sure . . .'

Major Payne cleared his throat. 'We were rather intrigued by the birdie brooch she had pinned to her beret. Earlier on it was on her turban. I am sure you noticed?'

Jonson looked blank.

'She doesn't seem to want to be parted from it,' Payne went on. 'Is that another talisman? To protect her against the evil eye perhaps?'

Jonson gave a polite smile. 'I am sorry, sir, but I must go.'

'This is actually jolly important, old boy –'

'I'm afraid I can't stay long,' Jonson said uncertainly, looking back at the door, then at his watch. His hand went up to his chest where there was a slight bulge. His mobile phone, Antonia guessed, was in his inside pocket. Was he expecting a call?

'I am sure you can. *Festina lente* and all that. Didn't they teach it to you at school? Wouldn't you care for a snifter?' Payne gestured hospitably towards the whisky decanter and siphon on the side table. 'A nightcap? No? Sure? Not while carrying out your duties – same as the police, what? Golly. Had no idea you abided by the same rules. Antonia? No? I'll have one m'self, if you don't mind.' After he had poured himself a whisky into a cut-crystal glass, he took a sip and said, 'Look here, old boy. We are going to put our cards on the table. You are a decent sort of chap – we have no doubt about that, do we, my love?'

Antonia smiled and gave a nod of mock solemnity. She never failed to be amused when her husband struck one of his Blimpish poses. If he had had a moustache, he would have stroked it with the thumb and forefinger of his right hand. It was an act he put on. No one took the Blimp seriously. People's lips twitched into smiles, they relaxed their guard and then they could be tricked into blurting out things heedlessly, into giving themselves away through their disparaging attitude – and when they did, he pounced on them – figuratively, of course.

'We've been ferreting things out, you see, but there are a couple of loose ends we're a bit puzzled about . . . I had a talk with my sister earlier on,' Payne went on, 'and she happened to mention that my cousin Peverel had an affair with Corinne Coreille back in the early '70s. Is that what you told him yesterday? That you knew about it?'

There was a pause. 'I had no idea your cousin had had an affair with Mademoiselle Coreille. I told him that I had seen his photograph on her dressing table, that's all,' Jonson said. 'I realized that I hadn't met him in person, only seen his photograph. I could see he was startled. It was clear he didn't like to be reminded . . . I don't think that has anything to do with the death threats.'

'Hasn't it? Perhaps not. It's good to eliminate the irrelevant and the superfluous, clear away the tangle of extraneous bushes from the main path of inquiry, as they say – so that we can concentrate on what really matters, wouldn't you agree? What about that other business – the blood bond between la Maginot and Corinne? Isn't that relevant to your investigation?'

'Sorry?'

'The bond of blood, old boy. The tie that bindeth. The old DNA . . . Maître Maginot and Corinne Coreille are mother and daughter, aren't they?'

There was another pause, a longer one this time. Antonia was watching Jonson and she saw the blood drain slowly from his face. He remained standing by the door, stock-still, his arms hanging at his sides. Payne, whose eyes too had been fixed on Jonson, nodded in a satisfied manner. *They are*. Thank you. You may be an excellent detective and a first-rate mimic, but you aren't a terribly good actor. You wear your heart on your sleeve. A most endearing characteristic.'

Jonson ran his tongue over his lips. 'How did you find out?'

'Well, we noticed the resemblance. They have the same eyes. They make the same gestures – the way they tilt their heads to one side in particular. Then there is the brooch.'

'The brooch?'

'Maître Maginot's brooch, yes – or rather, the brooch the woman calling herself Maître Maginot is wearing at this very moment. I did mention it earlier. Two silver ostriches linked together by their tails. Rather whimsical and dashed memorable. You see, m'wife and I happen to be jolly observant. We rarely miss a trick. We had seen the brooch in a photograph – it's in one of my aunt's scrapbooks. Maître Maginot wore the brooch pinned to her turban at dinner first, then to her beret. She is clearly attached to it. That was jolly careless of her. She didn't seem to think that

151

Aunt Nellie would notice – or remember.' Payne paused. 'You see, the brooch was given to Corinne's mamma by my aunt when they were debs together in post-war London.'

Jonson stared back at him. 'Your aunt – gave Corinne's mother the brooch when they were debs together?'

'That's right.' Payne took another sip of whisky. 'In post-war London. You know the kind of thing. Glamour gels in off-the-shoulder gowns, exchanging wide-eyed glances with other glamour gels and flashing little smiles at the men, continually checking their cards to see if they've got their dances down right . . .'

There was a pause. Antonia was puzzled by the change that had come over Jonson. The tension, the anxious look, the guilty air – they had all left him. Disconcertingly, Jonson seemed to have relaxed. She saw a light spring into his eyes and a little smile, half amused, half scornful, appeared on his lips. It was as though Jonson had suddenly seen a large hole in his opponent's reasoning. She nearly expected him to say, 'Oh yes?' but he merely resumed his blank expression. She didn't quite know what to make of any of it.

Jonson said, 'I see . . . Well, what are you going to do about it?' His voice held a defiant note.

'Haven't decided yet . . . It would be interesting to know how you discovered that Maginot was Ruse.'

'Ruse?'

'Sorry. That's her nickname. Ruse – short for Rosamund. Corinne's mamma.'

'Yes. Rosamund. That's right,' Jonson said. The flat voice again. Antonia frowned. He's going to tell a lie, she thought. 'Well, I found out who she was entirely by accident. It happened while I was in Paris – at their house – looking for the person who had been leaking stories about Corinne. I saw something – some papers.'

'Is Ruse aware that you know her true identity?'

'Yes.'

Payne looked at him. 'You realize of course that Ruse has perpetrated several deeds that are punishable by law? She's been accomplice to embezzlement and theft. She has assumed false identity, perpetrated impersonation and, very possibly, condoned double murder.'

'What double murder?'

'That of a Dutch couple in Africa – it was their bodies that were passed off as the bodies of Ruse and François-Enrique.' There was a pause. Payne pushed his hands deep into his dressing-gown pockets. 'You aren't by any chance blackmailing her, are you? Or should I say "them", since Corinne too is involved. I believe she'd do what her *chère maman* tells her . . . Corinne's got oceans of dosh –'

Suddenly Jonson laughed. 'No, I am not blackmailing them.' He sounded genuinely amused and perfectly truthful. Antonia's bewilderment deepened. '*No*,' Jonson said again. 'I'm afraid you've got the wrong end of the stick altogether. Goodnight.'

He turned round and, without another word, left the room. Antonia and Payne looked at each other. 'I don't know exactly how,' Antonia said slowly, 'but I think he is right – I do believe we've got the wrong end of the stick. Not only about the blackmail, but altogether.'

'But he admitted they were mother and daughter!'

'He did – and I don't think he was bluffing. The whole thing is very confusing, I know.' Antonia frowned. 'I seem to have a glimmer of the truth . . . That photograph – the photograph I found in Jonson's case. There was something in it – that shouldn't have been there at all – I am sorry, I am too tired . . . Does that make sense?'

'Not in the least.' Major Payne yawned prodigiously. 'I am terribly tired myself. Can hardly stand on my feet. Time for Bedfordshire, wouldn't you say?'

# 22

# The Rising of the Moon

Lady Grylls peered at her god-daughter through her thick bifocal glasses. 'I just came to check if you have everything you need, Corinne. Are you comfortable? I've brought you a bottle of mineral water. Hope you don't mind it's Hildon and not Evian or Volvic. I always buy British.'

She had given her god-daughter the best room – the Cynthia Drake. Who Cynthia Drake was, or whether she had existed at all, Lady Grylls had no idea. The association was lost in the mists of time. She wondered whether it had been some old flame of Rory's, but she doubted it. She looked round. Pale pink walls, thick cream carpet, silk lampshades, two little gilt chairs covered in ivory watered satin, a painted escritoire.

Her god-daughter was sitting on the bed. She had changed into a dark blue peignoir with white trimmings around the neck and cuffs. She held her hands clasped in her lap. Her fringe reached down to her eyes. She looked absurdly young and somewhat forlorn. Poor Corinne. She brought to mind a novice nun. Lady Grylls was filled with sudden pity.

'Oh, thank you very much, Aunt Nellie. Everything's perfect. Thank you for the snowdrops and the crocuses.' Corinne pointed to the two tiny vases on the mantelpiece. 'That was sweet of you . . . There is an owl somewhere outside. Can you hear it? It keeps hooting.'

'Perhaps that's his way of keeping himself warm. Don't

worry, my dear.' I should stop talking to her as though she were a child, really, Lady Grylls thought. 'So cold, isn't it? Or is it just me? Would you like a hot-water bottle in your bed?'

'No, thank you. It's not too cold. I think when the owl hoots, it means he's trying to mesmerize little birds and mice, so that he can find easy prey . . . There it is again . . . It sounds almost human.'

'It does, doesn't it? Easy prey, that must be the reason, yes.'

'The door, it does not lock. Is there a key?'

Lady Grylls squinted down at the lock. 'Goodness, you are right. The key's gone. The way things disappear in this house! We had a problem with keys disappearing some time ago. Nicholas thinks it's a poltergeist, but don't worry – it isn't. You aren't nervous, are you?'

She received a pale smile. 'A little . . . Is Chalfont haunted?'

'No. Of course not. That stupid boy claims there is a chilly patch on one of the landings, but he doesn't know what he is talking about. I've never felt anything myself. A poltergeist indeed. Ridiculous. He says all sorts of things – he even claimed he'd seen Cynthia Drake!' Lady Grylls guffawed.

'The *fantome* of Cynthia Drake?'

'All bosh. Forget I said it. Don't worry. Nicholas is interested in magic and things like that. He takes dope. I should report him to Social Services, really, but I understand they are absolute pests, so I won't. Besides, it would mean getting Provost in the soup. That's Nicholas's papa. I am sure Nicholas will grow out of it.'

'I keep thinking about those letters,' Corinne said with a sigh. 'The American woman who wrote to me . . . I do feel sorry for her and her son.'

'Yes, yes. All terribly morbid. Better not brood on it. Mad as a hatter. Not your fault,' Lady Grylls delivered in brisk tones. 'I can have you moved to another room, if you like? Where the door locks properly.'

'No, thank you. It's very late. I can always put that chest of drawers against the door, if that's all right?'

'Goodness. Yes – by all means. I am a terrible hostess, I know. The trouble is I don't get visitors often these days – apart from my nephews. They don't seem to mind when things go wrong, but the truth is the house is going to the dogs . . . The last time we had proper visitors was more than twenty-five years ago – the Alec Douglas-Homes. Such sweet, unassuming people. So terribly unworldly. No trouble at all. Not a word of complaint . . . The curtains – you want them drawn, don't you?'

Lady Grylls started walking across to the window. Passing the dressing table she stole a glance at the array of bottles and pots and tubes and a little box or two that constituted Corinne's 'clamjampherie' – that was the word Lady Grylls's Scottish nanny had been wont to use. Amidst it all Lady Grylls was startled to see a pair of human hands lying side by side. It was gloves, of course, flesh-coloured, made of some delicate material, the nails painted in. Like discarded snakeskin, she thought, and she squirmed internally at the idea. For some reason she remembered that Eleanor Merchant had called Corinne a witch in her letter.

'Full moon,' she heard Corinne say. 'I can see it from here.'

'Full moon, yes.' Lady Grylls stood gazing out of the window. 'Your mamma hated full moons. Said they made her feel tense and fearful and heavy – as though somebody was sitting on her chest – like in that nightmare picture – you know the one with the squatting succubus and the mare's head? No, I don't think "succubus" is right – succubi are female, aren't they? Ruse said she couldn't sleep properly when there was a full moon. Full moons gave her nightmares. She always had the feeling of impending disaster. *Isn't* that when people are supposed to go berserk?'

Enough nonsense – but what *did* one talk to Corinne about? She couldn't possibly ask her how she had kept herself so young-looking – or why she had given Ruse's brooch to Maginot. Or, for that matter, what Maginot's first

name was. For some reason Lady Grylls felt curious . . .
One couldn't imagine Maginot being called Bernadette or
Françoise or Cécile or Mireille. Women like Maginot didn't
seem to have a first name. One couldn't imagine them ever
having been young – or ever having been in love. The idea
of Maginot in love seemed grotesque. Had Maginot any
family? She was too much of a *type* somehow. The megalo-
maniac monster. One-dimensional – like the humours in
Ben Jonson or in the *commedia dell'arte*. One couldn't
imagine Maginot separate from Corinne – leading an existence which was independent of the life and career of
her charge.

Lady Grylls experienced an odd sensation – she couldn't
quite explain it – as though she were standing on the brink
of some momentous discovery, but the feeling passed. I am
exhausted, she thought. It's been a long day. I am becoming fanciful. She pulled the curtains together. Turning
round, she asked, 'Do you remember your mamma at all?
Hope you don't mind me asking, my dear?'

'I don't mind.' The pale smile again, the right hand
going up to the fringe, then down to the lap to join the
other. Lady Grylls's short-sighted eyes fixed on Corinne's
hands. Well, there was nothing wrong with either of them;
they struck her as smooth and supple, certainly not the
hands of a fifty-five-year-old. Why did she wear gloves
then? Not a single wrinkle or brown speck, not the merest
hint of a liver spot either, as far as she could see, but then
she couldn't see properly. Lady Grylls pushed her glasses
up her nose. She must have that cataract operation sometime soon. She was annoyed with old Morgan nagging at
her, but it was rather unwise of her, she had to admit, to
keep calling off the operation the way she did.

'I do remember my mother, yes . . . *vaguely*. I was very
young when she died.'

'Yes, yes. Terrible business, ' Lady Grylls said quickly.
'Your mamma was a most colourful character. We were
great chums. I do miss her sometimes,' she added untruth-
fully. She meant to be kind. She was filled with compassion: the poor thing needed encouragement, bolstering –

she had such a 'lost' look about her! 'What is it you remember? What would you say was the most remarkable thing about your mamma?'

'Her voice . . .'

'Her voice? Well, it was low and husky and rather attractive, men liked it and all that, but of course Ruse couldn't sing for toffee.' Lady Grylls laughed. 'I was a better singer than she ever was. Your papa had sung in a church choir as a boy, but it was his parents who made him do it. Now I adore the way Frenchmen talk, but his voice wasn't in any way remarkable either. That's why everybody was so stunned when you turned out such a miracle.'

'I remember a song. I was very young, but I remember listening to it – it was probably the first song I actually liked . . . "Love Story" . . . Of course it was my mother who –' Corinne broke off and looked down. She suddenly looked confused – frightened – as though she'd said something she shouldn't . . . I am imagining things, Lady Grylls thought.

'I mean, of all the songs I sang, "Love Story" was my favourite,' Corinne went on. 'My mother would have loved it, I always felt. I sang its French version. "Histoire d'Amour".'

Lady Grylls frowned. Everything seemed to be out of focus somehow . . . What was the girl on about? She didn't make sense. She was rambling – must be frightfully tired. She must be suffering from a *crise de nerfs*. Lady Grylls felt sure Corinne had been about to say something different. *Of course it was my mother who* – What? What had she meant to say? Ruse wouldn't have loved 'Love Story'. Ruse had been the most unsentimental person who ever lived, cynical, pragmatic and as tough as old boots.

'Oh yes? That's from the film, isn't it?' Lady Grylls said. '*Love Story*. Rather sad, I remember. The gel dies at the end –' She broke off. Mustn't talk about death and gels dying, she thought.

She heard the grandfather clock in the hall downstairs chime the half-hour.

Half past eleven.

That was the last time Lady Grylls saw her.

The following morning, 4th April, at eight o'clock sharp, when Provost went to Corinne Coreille's room to deliver her cup of early morning tea – very pale Earl Grey, flavoured with a slice of lime, as she had requested – he found the door ajar. He knocked, then called out 'Miss Coreille?', but receiving no answer, pushed the door open and entered.

The room was empty. So was the bathroom. The bed, he observed, was made. He didn't immediately assume that it hadn't been slept in. There were no signs of any disturbance. He then went into the room next door, which was Maître Maginot's. The night before the 'old Frenchwoman', as he called her, had asked for a cup of camomile tea sweetened with honey for the morning. This room too was empty. He looked around: at the kimono with an elaborate floral pattern on the bed, the cellophane bag of sugared almonds and the tatty book – *La Langue des Fleurs* – on the bedside table. Next to the book lay two folded newspapers: the *International Herald Tribune* and *Le Monde*.

'Where could they have gone, Provost?' Lady Grylls wheezed as she sat in her bed, propped up between several large pillows, looking very pink. Her hair was in a hairnet and, as usual, she was wearing a pair of Rory's old striped pyjamas – so much more comfortable than any of her nightdresses. She sipped the strong Assam tea, bit into a slice of buttered toast, drew on her cigarette, her first for the morning, and cast an eye over *The Times*, which Provost had placed on her tea-tray. She was smoking a Balkan Sobranie – they had been a present from Corinne. As she sat lost in thought, it looked as though she had a decadent mauve lipstick hanging from the corner of her mouth. Her glasses had slid down her nose but she didn't push them up.

'Perhaps they've gone for a walk – in the garden,' Provost suggested. 'It's a lovely morning.'

Lady Grylls glanced across at the window, blinking at the bright sunlight that turned her white lace curtains golden. 'So it is,' she agreed. 'Looks like spring's come at last . . . About forty-five years ago there was quite a craze for something called "rhymes of impending disasters" – remember them, Provost?'

'I am afraid not, m'lady. Before my time.' Provost cleared his throat. 'I am forty-four.'

'Goodness, I thought you were thirty-six.'

'That's Shirley's age, m'lady.'

'Of course – she was younger than you. I keep forgetting. You don't think that was the reason why she –' Lady Grylls broke off. 'I remember I was supervising the children – it was somebody's birthday party, John's or Patricia's, I think – and I encouraged them to write as many rhymes of impending disasters as they could think of. Peverel – my nephew, you know – wrote something on the lines of "Aunt Nellie's mislaid her glasses and thinks the burglar's making passes". He accompanied it with a silly drawing of a simpering fat woman being manhandled by a masked marauder. He must have been eight or nine . . . A puerile squib, you'd no doubt say, but, as it happened, I *had* mislaid my glasses, just before the party started, actually, so I was disproportionately upset by the whole thing . . . I don't suppose I ever forgave Peverel.'

'No, m'lady.'

'Have you forgiven Shirley? I mean for leaving you and all that?'

'I don't know, m'lady . . . I don't think so.'

'You must forgive her. I must try to forgive Peverel too. But we must forgive ourselves first . . . Have you ever taken dope, Provost?'

'Once or twice, m'lady. In my younger days.'

'I too snorted cocaine once or twice – at a London night-club called Ludovigo's. Many years ago. I never became a dope fiend, mind – nothing like that boy of yours.'

'No, m'lady.'

'I was with a Frenchman. He made me do it. I didn't really like it, but I was potty about him –' Lady Grylls broke off. 'I don't know what the matter with me is this morning. I am in a bloody peculiar mood. Impending disasters – whatever gave me the idea of impending disasters? I suppose it's age . . . Age, with his stealing steps – it claws you closely in his clutch.'

'I don't think Age has "clawed you in his clutch", m'lady – not yet. If I may say so.'

'You may say so. Sweet of you . . . Bobo Markham says I don't look a day older than fifty-eight, which of course is complete nonsense . . . See where they are, will you, Provost? I mean Corinne and that terrible woman. Scour the garden. When you find them, check if they need anything, apart from croissants and coffee, that is. You've got the kippers for Corinne, haven't you? She seems to like kippers. Tell them I'll see them at brekkers.'

For some reason Lady Grylls's vague stirrings of anxiety intensified. It would be most peculiar if her two visitors had really gone out so early in the morning, she thought, all by themselves, considering the preposterous safety checks Maginot had insisted on the night before! Unless Andrew was with them? It would make more sense if Andrew was accompanying them. She called Provost back and asked him, but his answer failed to reassure her: Mr Jonson was in his room, shaving. Mr Jonson had no idea where Miss Coreille and the old Frenchwoman were.

'No idea, eh?' Something isn't right, Lady Grylls thought.

That was an understatement. Things were very wrong indeed. When Provost, after a fruitless search of the garden, eventually noticed that the door of the greenhouse was gaping open and went in, he found a dead body lying there.

She had been bleeding profusely from a wound in the throat. There was so much blood, it made him sick.

That and the shock.

# 23

# Bodies

At several minutes after eight o'clock Antonia came down to breakfast, alone. (Hugh wanted to sleep in.) Apart from Nicholas, the dining room was empty. The boy was placing covered dishes on the sideboard. She wished him a good morning and received the usual indistinct reply. Nicholas looked as though he had had very little sleep the night before, though his hair was as spiky as ever. A long way from the powdered be-wigged footmen of yesteryear, Antonia reflected, amused.

She helped herself to scrambled eggs. She thought she could smell kippers. She frowned. Kippers were in some way important, though at the moment she couldn't think how . . . The coffee was excellent. It was a wonderful morning: beautifully still, crisp and cold, the slanting sunbeams shining in streaks like the haloes of saints. An hour earlier she had stood at her bedroom window, watching the mist rise from the valley beyond the garden. The mist had gathered, rolled, crept up the field and within several minutes had gently lapped the house. Nothing had stirred. There had been a stillness. An absolute silence, in fact.

Later Antonia was to reflect that the weather had been like the dresses of Hitchcock's heroines: dramatic and tempestuous in the neutral scenes, quiet and understated in the action sequences.

Suddenly she heard the front door bang, then the sound of running feet and Provost staggered in. He looked dreadfully pale and wild-eyed. He gestured towards the window, his mouth opening and closing.

Eventually he managed to speak. 'She's there – something terrible – in the greenhouse. Please, come with me – she is dead –'

'Oh my God – Corinne?' Antonia rose at once. No, that's impossible, she thought.

As they crossed the hall, Provost muttered, 'Police – ambulance – we must – she is dead – so much blood!' He led the way out. Antonia and Nicholas followed. Unless she had imagined it, Nicholas had perked up as soon as the word 'blood' had been uttered. They moved rapidly across the broad swathe of lawn, through the wet grass that badly needed mowing, in the direction of the greenhouse.

They walked past a tiny ornamental pond with goldfish and rushes. The hedgerows had all burst into green. Her nostrils twitched at the strong earth smell, a smell of freshness of spring and flowers. A time of hope and reawakening . . . Pigeons were cooing somewhere. A couple of blackbirds flew up, flapping their wings, startled by a branch snapping. She didn't quite know whether she was treading on air or land. Her hands were clenched in fists . . . Her thoughts were chaotic and inconsequential . . . There had been a grim and rather surreal inevitability about it all . . . Jonson had failed in his duty of protecting Corinne Coreille's life . . . This kind of thing simply didn't happen . . . It was a scene from her next novel . . . For some reason Provost had made it all up . . . Provost was the killer . . . No, the butler was never the killer . . . Why was she wearing such a smart twin-set and pearls? . . . Any moment now she would hear the director shout, 'Cut!' . . . That photograph . . . The photograph she had found in Jonson's case . . . It showed Corinne sitting in front of her dressing table, making her face up . . . Well, there was something about that scene that was wrong . . .

No *kipper*, she thought. That was it. Jonson had said there was a kipper on a plate on the dressing table – but there wasn't. He had made that up. He had blushed. He had been about to say something different – and she knew very well what, since she had spotted it.

The greenhouse was Gothic in structure and it had clearly seen better days. Once no doubt it had been the kind of place where Cecily and Gwendolen might have reclined among the greenery, sipped pale China tea and bantered, but no more. It had a bleak and disused air about it . . . Now it had become a house of death . . . The windows were blood-red with the rays of the early morning sun . . .

They went in.


The body lay very close by the greenhouse door and they nearly fell over it. Provost gave a warning cry. Nicholas whistled. Though Antonia had been prepared for it – though she had seen a dead body before – she started shaking as soon as her eyes fell on it.

'But that's Maître Maginot,' she whispered. She felt rather nauseous but she also experienced sudden relief.

'Yes, yes,' Provost said. 'The old Frenchwoman. That's her. Oh my God.'

'She's been shot,' Nicholas said, pointing a forefinger at Maître Maginot's neck. He sounded gleeful, excited. 'At close range. At *very* close range. I can tell. I've seen pictures of dead bodies on the internet. There's a website. Violentdeath.com,' he rambled.

'You shouldn't be looking at such pictures, Nicholas,' Antonia reprimanded him. Her voice sounded high, absurdly schoolmistressy. Displacement activity, she thought. We are in a state of shock.

'Why not?' Nicholas challenged her. Then he sneezed. 'I am allergic to plants,' he mumbled.

'What plants?' Antonia felt the urge to laugh. I mustn't get hysterical, she thought.

'Don't know which ones – it always happens when I come in here.'

Maître Maginot lay sprawled on her back, the black beret still incongruously on her head. The terrible deformed face under the beret was the colour of tallow, which, Antonia reflected, was also the colour of tripe. It might have been one of Madame Tussaud's Chamber of Horrors wax effigies lying there . . . They drank tripe soup in France, didn't they? The moment she thought that, Antonia feared she might disgrace herself and be sick. Maître Maginot's face was frozen in a ferocious grimace: her eyes were bulging. Her lips were parted – her teeth bared –

The wound was a terrible gaping black hole in the side of Maître Maginot's throat. It was evident she had bled profusely from it. Her clothes were saturated with blood and there was more blood on the ground around her. The blood was dry and was of a dark brownish hue. It was clear she had been dead for some time, several hours probably. Her mobile phone stuck out of a pocket in her breeches. A torch lay beside her right hand, which was gloved. Maître Maginot's left hand was bare and Antonia found herself staring at it, at the scarlet nails.

She noticed something very curious – a freakish detail, one might call it. She knew that was important – she couldn't say how – in the same way as the absence of the kipper from Corinne's dressing table was important . . . Was she thinking straight? She hoped she wasn't losing her mind!

'We must call the police,' she said.

'Dad's gone back to the house,' Nicholas said. 'He's gonna do it.'

Antonia looked round the greenhouse. She saw lots of potted plants, empty pots and blue-and-white Chinese containers and censers. Garden tools. A garden bench, a bamboo table and a chair. A mobile phone lay on the floor beside the chair. A *second* mobile?

The next moment she felt Nicholas tugging at her arm. 'Miss – look! There's a leg over there. *Look.* Over there. It's another body!'

Antonia started up, though not too violently. She was getting anaesthetized, she supposed. Her first thought was that the boy had imagined it, but when she followed his pointing finger, she saw he hadn't. There was a leg there all right, exactly as he had said – a woman's leg in a torn stocking – the foot in a flat shoe. The leg was sticking from behind two large potted palms. There was a woman's body lying there all right. Nicholas started walking towards it, but sneezed twice in quick succession and went back. *'Fuck,'* he said.

Antonia moved like one in a trance. Inside the green-house it was freezing cold, colder than outside. For obvious reasons, it made her think of a mortuary. *Morgue,* in French. *Les cadavres sont dans la morgue.* No French grammar book would include a sentence like that. She imagined that there was a metallic smell of blood in the air . . . She stumbled on something – the niblick. Maître Maginot had been brandishing the niblick the night before – when Antonia and Hugh had met her on the stairs. Maître Maginot had been on her way out – she had intended to check the grounds. She had been on her own – unwisely, as it turned out – it had cost her her life –

Antonia's eyes were fixed on the leg in the flat shoe. Her next thoughts ran as follows: Corinne – so they got her after all – poor Corinne – Corinne and Ruse – mother and daughter – both dead – is there a new pattern emerging?

But it wasn't Corinne Coreille's body that lay behind the palms.

It was the body of a stranger: a middle-aged woman in an extremely dirty mink stole, wearing yellow gloves. She too lay on her back, in a pool of frozen blood, and, like Maître Maginot, she had been shot. Antonia gasped. This was much worse than the wound inflicted on Maginot! Part of the woman's head, just above the right temple, was missing – it had been blasted off. The woman's mouth was covered in bright red lipstick and it was gaping open. Her eyes were open too; they were round and glassy and staring. Rather foolish, Antonia thought. No, not foolish – demented.

The next moment Antonia noticed the gun. The gun was clutched in the woman's right hand. She bent over and looked at it without touching. A Colt .357 Magnum. The gun's muzzle was pointing upwards. It nearly touched the woman's chin. It looked as though she had done it herself – as though she had blown her brains out on purpose, of her own free will, in one final act of desperation.

An expensive-looking handbag made of crocodile skin lay beside the body. It had burst open and most of its contents were scattered around. It seemed the woman had been searching for something in a frantic manner. (The gun?) Antonia saw banknotes and tissues, a handkerchief, a powder compact, a carving knife, a purse, some news-paper cuttings, a passport –

She heard Nicholas call out, 'Is the gun there?'

'Yes.' The gun had a silencer, she noticed.

Antonia picked up the passport gingerly, holding it at the corner between her thumb and index finger. She knew she shouldn't have done it, yet had been unable to help herself.

It was an American passport, as Antonia had known it would be. Opening it, she saw a folded plane ticket . . . Boston–Paris . . . One way . . . Hadn't she intended to go back? The face that stared back at her from the photograph was interesting; it could even be called pretty, in a freakish kind of way – blonde hair swept back – light blue eyes open wide in a parody of earnestness – lips curved up in a knowing smile.

Antonia read the name without any particular surprise: *Eleanor Merchant.*

## 24

## *Vous Qui Passez Sans Me Voir*

Jonson and Major Payne appeared at the door. Neither of them spoke. Jonson was fully dressed. Payne was wearing his trousers, pyjama top and dressing gown.

Antonia's eyes fixed on Jonson. He looked unwell – troubled. His face was extremely pale and a little puffy, with dark circles round his eyes. His hair was uncombed. He seemed to have aged overnight. She saw him shut and open his eyes several times, then shake his head, the way people did when they imagined they might be dreaming. He then spoke and made it clear to the boy Nicholas that he wanted him out of the greenhouse that very minute. At first Nicholas pretended he hadn't understood, but eventually he obeyed, though with sulky ill grace.

For several moments Hugh and Jonson stood silently, looking down at the bodies of the two women. The scene could be described as terrifying, yet with every second that elapsed, it seemed more and more unreal . . . Antonia was put in mind of the time they had done *The Duchess of Malfi* back at school and the fun they had had, splashing red paint about and over each other.

She showed them the passport.

It was Payne who broke the silence. 'The Merchant. Incredible. So she did manage to get here after all!'

Jonson passed his hand over his face and Antonia heard him take a deep breath. 'Yes . . . It is – incredible . . .'

'It looks as though Maginot found the Merchant lurking

168

here and the Merchant shot her,' Payne said. 'After which she proceeded to blow her own brains out . . . Maginot intended to check all the outbuildings last night, didn't she?' He turned towards Jonson. 'Did you know Maginot was coming to the greenhouse?'

'Not to the greenhouse, specifically. I knew she was checking the grounds. I did insist I do the outside and she the inside, but she said no.' Jonson spoke haltingly. 'She asked me to go around the house – check all the rooms . . . The lofts and the cellars . . . It – it should have been the other way round, but she wouldn't be swayed – she got angry when I suggested it.'

'She looked exalted,' Payne murmured. 'Unstoppable. Bursting with confidence. Dangerously bellicose –'

'*Vive la guerre*,' Antonia said.

'Quite – the way she brandished Uncle Rory's niblick. Not that it helped her –'

Antonia reflected that no one was pretending to be in any way saddened by the deaths. Shocked and unsettled and sickened, yes, but no more than that. They had never known Eleanor Merchant, but the picture that had emerged from her letters gave one a strong dose of the shudders. Maître Maginot, while alive, hadn't invited any warm feelings either. Contrary to what John Donne wrote, not every death diminishes us – there are deaths that simply don't, Antonia thought.

She saw her husband's eyes travel from the gun clutched in Eleanor Merchant's hand to the torch that lay beside Eleanor's body. He then looked at Maître Maginot's body and back at Eleanor's. He seemed to be trying to estimate the distance between the two bodies. He cleared his throat. 'Yes, it does look as though Maginot discovered the skulking Merchant, who panicked, whipped out her gun and shot her. I don't suppose the Merchant had any idea as to who it was she had shot –'

'Stop calling her the Merchant,' Antonia said. She was annoyed by his flippancy. They didn't have to stand around with bowed heads and whisper and put on a show of respect they did not feel, but it was poor taste, making someone who had died a horribly violent death appear ridiculous.

'I stand corrected . . . We can assume that Mrs Eleanor Merchant went to the body and flashed her torch on it. I don't suppose Maginot's face meant much to her, but one thing Mrs Eleanor Merchant must have become aware of at once – namely, that she'd never be able to get Corinne now, not after what she'd done. She must have realized she'd lost the game. So – she turns the gun on herself and pulls the trigger. She probably meant to kill herself all along, wouldn't you say?'

'Well, she bought only a one-way ticket . . . Her son had killed himself . . . A suicidal streak might have been in her blood,' Antonia said thoughtfully. She found she was standing by the bamboo table. There was a book on it: *Who's Who in EastEnders*, also a magazine: *Vogue*.

'What did you do last night?' Payne asked Jonson. 'I mean, after you checked the bedrooms?'

Jonson said that he had gone to bed. He had fallen asleep almost at once. He had been dog-tired. Jonson spoke haltingly. 'It was about midnight. Maître Maginot said she'd call me on her mobile if she noticed anything suspicious, only she didn't, so – so I assumed everything was fine and that she'd come back to the house and gone to bed herself. I heard no noise. Nothing. No shots.'

'No one would have heard any shots. The gun's got a silencer,' Payne said.

'I never thought Eleanor Merchant could be anywhere near the house.' Jonson shook his head. 'I didn't think she could be in England . . . I didn't think it possible . . .'

There was a pause. 'That phone call last night,' Payne said. 'The American woman who rang while we were having coffee. She introduced herself as a – chat-show hostess? She wanted to talk to Corinne. What did Provost say her name was?'

'Thora – no, Tricia – Tricia Swindon,' Jonson said. 'Some such name.'

'And she rang off as soon as she heard Maginot's voice? That must have been Eleanor Merchant.'

A muffled noise was heard from the doorway. Nicholas was standing there furtively, looking in, his hand cupped over his nose.

'I told you to go away,' Jonson called out to him. The boy disappeared, this time for good. They saw him through the window, walking across the lawn towards the house. Jonson said, 'It must have been Eleanor Merchant who phoned, yes. On her mobile. Heaven knows what she'd been hoping to achieve.'

'She probably didn't know herself,' Payne said astutely.

Antonia was looking down at the cover of the magazine, at the picture of the super-thin model and the Siamese cat. For some reason she found herself thinking of the photo she had found in Jonson's case once more . . . Corinne Coreille had been snapped sitting at her dressing table – she had taken time off from applying her make-up to stroke a kitten . . . A kitten, yes. A live kitten. The kitten seemed to have jumped on the table . . . There was no kipper on the table – Jonson had made that up. He had been about to say 'kitten' but had changed his mind . . . Nicholas on the other hand kept sneezing because he was allergic to plants . . . Now, why did she think there was a connection between the two? An association of ideas . . .

Antonia frowned. Something was stirring at the back of her mind. A memory was about to surface – it was something both Lady Grylls and Peverel had mentioned . . . Hope I am not getting unhinged, she thought, casting a glance at Eleanor Merchant's body and immediately looking away.

'That kitten in the photograph,' she said aloud. 'Where did it come from?'

Jonson stared at her. He looked like a man who was waking up from a dream. 'It was a stray – one of the gardeners had found it and brought it into the house. Mademoiselle Coreille apparently took a fancy to it.' He spoke mechanically. 'I understand Maître Maginot and Mademoiselle Coreille had an argument about it. Maître Maginot objected strongly –' He broke off. 'How do you know there's a kitten in the photograph?'

171

'You told us,' Antonia said.

'I didn't –' Suddenly Jonson looked terrified.

'Oh, but you did.' I can bluff too, Antonia thought, though she felt rather sorry for him. 'Kipper', he had said to avoid saying 'kitten'. A silly lie – he'd been unable to think of another word. He was a poor liar.

'We must be getting back to the house,' Payne said, looking at his watch. 'I expect the police will be here any moment now and they will be cross if they find the three of us cooped up with the bodies.'

'Yes,' Jonson said. 'Yes.' Without another word, he turned round and left the greenhouse.

'I touched Eleanor's passport,' Antonia said.

'You shouldn't have,' Payne said.

'I held it very lightly – by the corners.'

'It doesn't matter. You've as good as signed it with your full name. There's no escape from the old DNA. If the police decided the Merchant didn't do it after all, you'd be their next prime suspect, d'you realize?'

Antonia cast one last glance at the bodies. The good ended happily and the bad ended unhappily, she thought absurdly.

'What was Corinne's reaction to the news?' Antonia asked a few moments later as they were walking across the lawn towards the house.

'I don't know if she's been told anything yet. Somehow, I don't expect her to have hysterics – do you?'

'No . . .'

'You'd never believe this, but it's like in that damned French song Antonia was talking about yesterday morning. The one she heard in a dream,' Lady Grylls said as soon as she saw them. 'What was it called? "Vous Qui Passez Sans Me Voir".'

'What do you mean, darling?' Payne frowned.

'Corinne's disappeared – and no one's seen her go. She is nowhere to be found. Her bags have gone too.'

# 25

# The Unexpected Guest

They had come upon her in the hall, tending to Provost who gave every impression of being in a very bad way indeed. He was sitting on a spindle-legged gilt chair, staring before him. Lady Grylls had made him a cup of tea. She seemed to have emptied almost the whole contents of the silver sugar bowl into the tea; she kept urging him to drink it. The air was filled with the old-fashioned smell of valerian. There was a bottle of brandy on a salver on a small round table, also, inexplicably, a thermometer.

Provost was clad in the black-and-yellow striped waist-coat à la Maxim's but his stiff gleaming-white collar had been removed and it too could be seen on the salver. Lady Grylls was wearing a dressing gown and she had also put an elaborate choker with a large ruby clasp around her neck. She was smoking another purple-filtered Balkan Sobranie cigarette. The morning light, filtered through the fanlight, filled the hall with the murky yellow tones of a sepia print and, Payne thought, it made it look rather like a scene out of some quaint Edwardian farce on the twin subjects of *noblesse oblige* and the feudal spirit. (*Lady Grylls Pulls It Off? Baroness to the Rescue?*) The mundane conclusion of course was that murder made people act irrationally.

'His legs buckled under him like one of those collapsible card tables. Good thing I was here to catch him as he fell . . . He can't cope with things like that. He's a weak man . . . Peverel's here,' Lady Grylls went on with evident distaste. 'As though we haven't got enough to think about.'

Payne's brows went up. 'Peverel? I thought he wasn't coming back?'

'Well, he has. He drove all the way down from London. Must have started at some unearthly hour. He's in the dining room, drinking coffee. He looks like a funeral director, quite unlike himself. He seems to know about it already –' Lady Grylls broke off. 'Provost says Maginot has been shot – is that correct?'

'Yes.' Payne then told her to prepare for another shock. 'Maître Maginot's body isn't the only one in the greenhouse, darling. Eleanor Merchant is there too – shot as well . . . It looks as though she killed Maginot and then committed suicide.'

'You don't mean that, do you, Hughie?'

He said he did. He swore he wasn't making it up.

'That's a pretty kettle of fish,' Lady Grylls said after a pause. 'So *that's* what Peverel meant when he said there were two of them. I thought I'd misheard. Goodness. That woman came all this way from America to shoot herself in my greenhouse. Incidentally, do you remember that awful weepy, *Love Story*? When was it made, can you tell me?'

Major Payne blinked. 'Sorry, darling? What love story?'

'*Love Story*. The film. When was it made?'

'When was it –? Early seventies . . . 1970, at a guess. '

'1970. I thought as much.' Lady Grylls nodded. 'In 1970 Corinne was twenty-two. I knew she was talking bosh. You see . . .' She then told them about the extraordinary conversation she had had with Corinne the night before. 'And she said that she remembered her mother's voice! That was the other rum thing. It didn't make sense. There was nothing memorable about Ruse's voice, but Corinne spoke as though it had been something quite exceptional.'

Antonia and Payne found Peverel in the dining room, standing by the fireplace, a large white coffee cup in hand. He was wearing a black coat with a velvet collar and a long white silk scarf. He did look solemn and – not sad, exactly, Antonia thought, but preoccupied, in a pensive mood. 'I thought you were the police,' he said, glancing at the clock. 'They are always late, aren't they?'

It was then that the possible importance of something Lady Grylls had said dawned on Antonia. She asked, 'How do you know what happened?'

He shrugged – took another sip of coffee. He was drinking it black. There was a faraway look in his eyes. For some reason Antonia had the idea that he was reflecting on the past.

'How did you know there was a second body there?' she persisted.

He gave a little smile. 'That boy told me. Nicholas.'

There had been a brief pause and a scowl, as though he had had to think about it – or was Antonia imagining it?

'I thought you had no intention of coming back,' Payne said.

'I discovered I'd left something behind. I came to collect it.'

'What a bore for you. Must have been something very important. '

'Oh, it is. It is.' Peverel took another sip of coffee. 'Terribly important.' He gave no more details. 'In your kind of detective story, Antonia,' he went on, 'the police always blunder in the dark, don't they, and it is invariably the gifted amateur detective who gets to the truth?'

'It's a convention . . . Part of the game . . . One of the genre's requirements.' Antonia frowned: there had been an odd intensity about Peverel's voice. 'Readers still seem to like it, though of course everybody knows it's got nothing to do with real life.'

'Real life . . . Oh, how I wish –' Peverel broke off. He put down the coffee cup and looked towards the window.

There was a pause. Antonia's eyes remained fixed on him. How he wished – what? That the police did blunder in the dark not only in detective stories, but in real life as well – that the police never got to the truth?

Now that was interesting – extremely interesting.

(What *was* the truth?)

The next moment they heard a siren.

# 26

# An Inspector Calls

The police took control of the situation briskly and efficiently. They told everybody to stay inside the house, they then cordoned off the greenhouse. Antonia watched them do it from the drawing-room window. She wondered how long it would be before the bodies were taken away in body bags. Some half an hour later a police inspector called Lyttleton came to the house and said he would like to take a statement from each one of them. Lady Grylls suggested he use her late husband's study on the first floor.

The study was panelled in dark oak and across the windows there were crimson plush curtains. The small fireplace was suitable for burning coal and it was surrounded by painted tiles depicting a hunt: a lot of horsemen in scarlet coats frantically chasing after bushy-tailed foxes which appeared oddly nonchalant. An ancient leopard skin lay on the floor in front of the fireplace. The mahogany bookcase contained mainly game books bound in red morocco leather, garden catalogues and a number of stamp albums: as a young man the late Lord Grylls had been an ardent stamp collector.

The walls were adorned with several indifferent pastoral landscapes and two huge Wootton pieces. An oil portrait of Lord Grylls in the Robes and Star of the Order of the Garter hung above the fireplace. Lord Grylls's pale puffy face, placid expression and blond hair put Antonia in mind of portraits of George IV's brothers by Liotard. The desk was well worn and massive and it rather dwarfed Inspector Lyttleton who seemed to live up (or should it be 'down'?) to his name.

Antonia was the last to be questioned. What was Miss Darcy's occupation? She was a detective story writer! Really? Well, well. The inspector leant back in his chair and gazed at her with interest. He was in his late forties or early fifties and looked benevolent, though Antonia was convinced that was just an act. Had he read any of her books? he wondered. She had written only two, Antonia said. She was sitting beside a small table and she put her hands under it and held them on her lap – like a well-behaved child at a party, she thought nervously . . . What were her books called? She told him. No, he didn't think he had read them. 'I must make a note of your name,' he said. 'Crime writers usually get almost everything wrong, mind. Even those who do "research" . . . ' He gave a superior little smile and went on to say that in his experience those crime writers who did 'research' were the worst.

'I never do any extensive research,' Antonia said and was at once annoyed at herself for sounding defensive. She didn't write police procedurals, forensic crime or historical crime, she started explaining. He cleared his throat. He did read the odd detective story every now and then, he said, when he was on holiday. Some detective stories were 'clever' – nothing like the way crime happened in real life of course. His wife now was a great fan of detective stories – she was always comparing him to fictional detectives. Wasn't that silly? He shook his head.

Miss Darcy must find it very odd, being involved in a real-life murder case? Antonia agreed that it was very odd. She didn't say it had happened to her once before. (He was bound to think that extremely odd and might become suspicious of her.) She then told Lyttleton what she knew about Corinne Coreille and the anonymous death threats constructed with letters cut out of the *International Herald Tribune*. He knew all about them – Jonson had already shown him the death threats – as well as Eleanor

Merchant's letters. Antonia mentioned the phone calls that had been received at Chalfont. The last time she had seen Maître Maginot? The night before – on the stairs – Maître Maginot had been on her way down. The time? Some minutes after eleven o'clock.

The inspector was taking laborious notes in a little black notebook. No sergeant, Antonia suddenly thought. How odd. That was what happened in her previous detective novel. She had omitted the sergeant and had been criticized for it by one reviewer . . . Antonia detested police procedurals, thought them tedious in the extreme; in her novels she delayed the appearance of the police for as long as she could, till chapter twenty-five, say, or thereabouts, and then gave them the shortest of shrifts . . . Surely it was irregular for the inspector not to have a sergeant? She meant to ask him, but decided against it . . . She experienced a sense of unreality . . . It was almost as though they were characters in one of her novels . . . He reminded her of her late father a little . . . *Was* he real – or had he emerged from the depths of her mind?

She was feeling light-headed . . . She shut her eyes and rubbed at them. Delayed shock . . . Curb your imagination, she told herself.

She heard him clear his throat.

'I am sorry!'

'Aimless reverie or profitable reflection?' Inspector Lyttleton smiled. He then asked her a question. When was the last time she had seen Corinne Coreille? The night before, at dinner. How had Corinne struck her? Antonia described Corinne's manner as 'quiet, subdued, neutral'. 'The most remarkable thing about her was her passivity,' she said. No, Corinne hadn't looked particularly anxious. It was Maître Maginot who had shown signs of considerable agitation – especially after the phone call from the woman who had introduced herself as Tricia Swindon.

Inspector Lyttleton nodded. That call had been made by Eleanor Merchant, he ventured – they had examined her mobile phone; as a matter of fact Eleanor Merchant had made several calls to Chalfont Park. And there was a little mystery – Eleanor Merchant had received a phone call at ten minutes past eleven. 'Who from?' Antonia asked, greatly interested.

'The caller's number was unknown,' Lyttleton answered. 'We don't think it has any bearing on what happened, but of course we are keeping an open mind.'

Had Antonia heard any suspicious noises during the night? She said no, pointing out that the gun had a silencer, at once regretting it for the inspector looked displeased. He said he wished they hadn't gone inside the greenhouse at all! The shot that killed Maître Maginot had been fired at a very close range, Inspector Lyttleton said thoughtfully – Eleanor Merchant must have been standing beside the door as Corinne Coreille's legal adviser entered the greenhouse. Eleanor might have been aware of Maître Maginot's approach – it looked as though she had been waiting for her . . . Was it possible that Eleanor Merchant had taken Maître Maginot for Corinne? Physically the two women couldn't have been more different – unless Eleanor was completely unfamiliar with Corinne's appearance? No, that was not very likely, was it?

'Well, Mrs Merchant seems to have had very serious health issues – judging by the pills we found in her bag. I mean her mental state –' He cleared his throat. He implied Mrs Merchant's mental state provided the only explanation necessary for what she had done.

Had Miss Darcy heard any other noises? Footsteps – raised voices – commotion of any kind – the roar of a car engine perhaps? No?

'I didn't hear a thing,' Antonia said. How interesting that Maginot should have been shot at a close range, she thought. A picture rose before her eyes, of the two women locked in a mortal combat, lurching about against the backdrop of all those decaying plants, the gun between them . . . No, no – of course not – that wasn't how it had happened . . . The gun – where *did* the gun come from?

'I don't suppose you can help having ideas?' Inspector Lyttleton said with a smile.

Antonia admitted she couldn't. There was a pause, then

he changed tack. Why hadn't they called the police earlier? Why a private detective and not the police? Antonia explained that that had been Maître Maginot's idea. Maître Maginot had done it out of consideration for Corinne Coreille and her career – she had been afraid of adverse publicity. Adverse publicity, he muttered. So, in a way, Maître Maginot had brought it upon herself. He shook his head.

No one, Antonia emphasized, had imagined that Eleanor Merchant would be able to find Corinne's whereabouts. He agreed – that was one of the most amazing aspects of the whole affair. He scrunched up his face.

However had Eleanor Merchant managed to get hold of Lady Grylls's address?

# 27

# The Killing Doll

How indeed?

That was a question – one of the questions – that had been bothering Antonia. How could Eleanor Merchant have known where to find Corinne Coreille, given Maître Maginot's obsession with secrecy and security – considering how carefully she had orchestrated operation 'Safe Haven'? Maître Maginot had explained that the reason for not taking any 'entourage' with them was to avoid attracting any attention at any stage of their journey.

No, Antonia had no idea where Corinne Coreille had disappeared or when she could have left the house. The oddity and reclusiveness of the French singer were touched upon, together with her memorable haunting voice. Surprisingly, it turned out Inspector Lyttleton was familiar with Corinne Coreille. He remembered the occasion well. He had seen her on TV in the early '70s – the Ed Sullivan show – Corinne Coreille had sung in duet with Eartha Kitt – the two of them had been kitted out as comic vamps – feather boas and fishnet stockings – they had sat on top of a grand piano. 'All white. The piano, the roses, the snow . . . It was a Christmas special. The pianist smoked a cigarette. They let people smoke on the box in those days. *C'est si bon*,' Lyttleton hummed and wriggled his shoulders lightly. 'Variety. I've always been fond of variety,' he said.

Had Corinne Coreille perhaps panicked and run off in

the early hours of the morning? That at once suggested that somehow she knew what had taken place in the greenhouse. What was Miss Darcy's view? Antonia shrugged. It was possible. She felt reluctant to swap theories with him. Could Corinne have heard a noise from outside, gone to investigate and found the bodies? Possible again, Antonia said, though she thought it highly unlikely. Corinne would never have left the house in the dark, all by herself. If she had heard a suspicious noise, a cry, say, she would have sought Jonson out, the man they had hired to protect her. But Jonson had been asleep in his room, or so he claimed. He had heard nothing . . . Had Jonson told the truth? Such a likeable young man, but – Antonia reminded herself – one thing one should never do in a case of murder was to warm to likeable young men.

There was also the question of transport. It had been a cold and wet night. Corinne couldn't simply have walked out of the house, carrying her bags. The house was on the outskirts of the village. There was a cab service in the village, but the police had already ascertained that no cab had been called from Chalfont Park at any point in the night or in the early hours of the morning. A search, Antonia understood, was under way.

Where *was* Corinne? She seemed to have vanished into thin air. Without a trace. The way the inspector said it, the way he paused and frowned and shook his head, suggested that he thought Corinne Coreille too might be dead. Suddenly, he asked Antonia if she knew anything about the doll that had been found on the stairs. Where had it come from? She stared at him. She knew nothing about a doll – what doll?

He produced a see-through plastic bag from his brief-case and handed it to her across the desk. The doll was inside the bag. 'Don't take it out,' he warned her.

'I wouldn't dream of it,' Antonia said.

There were two large hatpins sticking out of the top of the doll's head, two more had been run through its eyes, another two through its ears. A pin that was larger than the others stuck out of the doll's mouth. Antonia shuddered. A voodoo doll? The next moment she realized with a start that it was a Corinne doll. Peverel had told them about it – and of course Eleanor Merchant had written about it in her first letter. The doll was about five inches long and it was instantly recognizable as Corinne. There was the fringe, the demure expression, the blue dress, the red bow. The eyes looked somewhat 'Japanese'. Well, the doll had been made in Japan, to coincide with Corinne's Osaka comeback concert.

The inspector had read Eleanor Merchant's description of how she had set about sticking pins into a Corinne doll, turning it into a 'pincushion' and feeling 'better' as a result. Eleanor had asked Corinne whether 'it hurt'.

It looked as though Eleanor Merchant had brought the doll with her, all the way from America. But Eleanor had died in the greenhouse. How had the Corinne doll landed on the main staircase at Chalfont? That was where Provost had stumbled on it in the morning . . . Could Eleanor Merchant have sneaked into the house at some point? It was Antonia who asked the question. Well, no door or window had been forced . . . Eleanor could have been let into the house by somebody, Antonia imagined. She might have had an accomplice.

The inspector said guardedly that they were not looking for anyone else. Of course the search for Corinne Coreille would continue.

Soon after the interview was over and Inspector Lyttleton left. Antonia had kept to the known, plain facts. She had made no mention of any of the fancy trimmings. Peverel's involvement with Corinne over thirty years previously, the fact that Corinne Coreille had given birth to his child, the idea that Maginot was in fact Ruse, Corinne's mother, the strong suspicion that had now become a certainty that Jonson knew more than he had told . . . Did any of these have any bearing on the two deaths? Antonia was set on continuing with her own inquiry . . . She hadn't mentioned the kitten either, though the kitten was very much on her mind.

The kitten in the photograph . . .

She didn't leave the study at once. She sat at Lord Grylls's desk, in the revolving leather chair the inspector had occupied. She ran her hand across the desk surface . . . She liked the feel of the desk. It was the kind of desk she could write a novel on. She always wrote by hand first. She was funny about desks. Some desks simply didn't feel right. There were desks that repelled her – stalled her creativity. Hadn't Muriel Spark had a similar thing about pencils? Lady Grylls had asked her what she wanted for a wedding present – Antonia wondered whether she could ask for the desk?

Idly she reached out for one of Lord Grylls's stamp albums and started leafing through it. A series of French stamps showing the face of Marianne in red, in white and in blue, drew her attention. Corinne's face had been used as a model for Marianne in the '70s. Once more she saw Corinne's face, the way it had been in the photograph she had taken out of Jonson's case – youthfully smooth –

But it wouldn't have remained smooth if she had been stroking a kitten . . . Antonia nodded slowly . . . She had known all along there was something wrong about the photograph Jonson had brought with him to Chalfont Park. The kitten shouldn't have been there. Her sub-conscious had registered the fact – but she had been distracted by the photograph of Peverel on Corinne's dressing table.

Jonson of course knew. He hadn't wanted them to see the photograph because he feared they might be able to deduce the truth.

# 28

# A Case of Identity

It was two o'clock in the afternoon.

Major Payne and Antonia were in the library. They were standing by the window, watching as the police cars started leaving. The day had clouded over and once more it promised rain – but it had got milder. Payne opened the window a crack, to let in some fresh air. They heard what they believed to be a nightingale, but there was no final chug-chug-chug, so they decided it was a blackbird.

'The Victorians maintained that a death without a death-bed was a horrid thing,' Payne murmured.

'Unless it took place on the field of battle – or in the missionary field.'

'How does one die in the missionary field?'

'Man-eating tigers – mosquito bites – snake bites.'

'Cannibals?'

'The police have gone,' Antonia observed.

There was a pause. 'Well, that's that, my love,' Payne said. 'An open-and-shut case if ever there was one. Eleanor Merchant's fingerprints on the gun. Cuttings from the *International Herald Tribune* in Eleanor's bag. Aunt Nellie's address and telephone number in Eleanor's address book . . . She made a hash of it at the end when she lost her nerve and killed the wrong person. She must have been getting frustrated and desperate. She must have reached the state known as panic depression . . . What Arthur Machen, I believe, called "horror of the soul" . . . The police thought she must have spent at least one whole day in a confined space. She had had very little food and drink. She was cold. All that would have made her highly strung, jittery and trigger-happy. The police are perfectly satisfied.'

'They are, aren't they?' Antonia said.

He cocked an eyebrow. 'You are not?'

'The address and the phone number. How did she manage to get them so easily? Then there's the gun. How did Eleanor manage to obtain a gun? There was a knife in her bag. She might have been preparing to *stab* Corinne. She couldn't have brought a gun with her on the plane from the United States. She couldn't have got the gun in France and then boarded the Eurostar either. Not with the kind of security there is at the moment . . . OK. She might have bought the gun on the black market, after her arrival in London, but I am far from convinced.'

'What other solution is there?' Payne started filling his pipe. '*Could* Corinne have done the double shooting? It might have been her way of overthrowing the Maginot regime . . . Corinne's plan might have been to make the Merchant look like the guilty party – but she lost her nerve and fled . . . Corinne might be much more devious and cunning than she appeared. Perhaps it was she who led the Merchant on, making sure she got Aunt Nellie's address and phone number and so on?'

'Well, somebody did lead Eleanor Merchant on,' Antonia said.

'Who? You don't think it's Jonson, do you? Maginot? No, can't be Maginot – doesn't make sense. Incidentally, what about our theory that Maginot is in fact Ruse? Where does it fit in precisely?'

'It doesn't fit anywhere.'

Payne had struck a match and was about to put it to his pipe. He looked at his wife across the tiny flame. 'It doesn't?'

'It doesn't. We were wrong. Maître Maginot isn't Ruse.'

'What do you mean? We noticed the resemblance!

Maginot *is* Corinne's mother – it was confirmed by Jonson – remember the way he stood and stared?'

'Only for a minute – his expression changed as soon as you said your aunt and Ruse had been debs together in pre-war London. He was right when he told us that we'd got the wrong end of the stick altogether.'

'Maginot can't be Ruse because . . . Corinne isn't Corinne? No, that's not it.' Payne rubbed his forehead. 'Impossible. I don't know why I said it –'

'It isn't impossible. Far from it.'

There was a pause. 'Corinne isn't . . . Corinne?' Payne repeated.

'No. In that photograph – the photograph I found in Jonson's case – Corinne is seen stroking a kitten – but she couldn't have – it would have made her feel very ill – might even have killed her. *Corinne suffered from an acute allergy to cats.*'

Payne stared at her. 'She came out in red blotches after sniffing a cat, Aunt Nellie said. Golly . . . *Yes.* The woman in the photo clearly had no problems with cats. Clever of you to notice. How did you –'

'There was a magazine on the table in the greenhouse – *Vogue* – it had the picture of a model holding a cat on the cover,' Antonia explained. 'Nicholas is allergic to plants – he kept sneezing. The two things suddenly clicked in my mind.'

'Jonson said nothing about a kitten. He mentioned a *kipper* – I did think it damned odd . . . Jonson knows the truth, doesn't he?' Major Payne said quietly.

'He does. For some reason he is protecting that woman . . . He is either being paid hush money – or else he is in love with her.'

'In love with *la fausse* Corinne . . . How jolly complicated. An impostor, eh? A woman who bears an uncanny resemblance to Corinne in her prime . . . Last night she wore lashings of slap, did you notice?'

'Yes – for the wrong reason. It was the thick pancake variety – what ageing actresses put on to conceal deep wrinkles and other ravages of time, so that they can play the ingénue without provoking screams of derisive laughter. But her jaw-line is that of a young woman,' Antonia pointed out. 'She is youthfully slim. Her whole bearing is that of a young woman. Well, she *is* a young woman. I do believe that.'

'What you mean, my love, is that we've been witnessing the oddest of double bluffs.' Payne stroked his jaw with a thoughtful forefinger. 'Or is it triple? A young woman . . . pretending to be an ageing diva . . . who is doing her utmost to look young . . . Those creepy flesh-coloured gloves . . . The true reason again is not to conceal the fact that she has wrinkles but that she *hasn't got any*. The same purpose, one imagines, is served by her high-necked dresses and those enormous bows?'

'Correct. She doesn't want it to be seen that her throat is in fact smooth and unlined . . . As for the wig, I think she wears it not because she is bald or in any way deformed, but because her hair's a different colour and too short, and it would have been too much trouble if she'd had to grow it long, style it, keep colouring it and so on.'

'But – I say – look here, old thing. This young woman's features are very similar if not the same as Corinne Coreille's. More importantly, her *voice* is the same as Corinne Coreille's. You heard her sing last night. It would be madness to assume that there's a young woman who is Corinne Coreille's absolute double, or rather, younger version. Unless – ' Major Payne broke off, the idea at last dawning on him, as Antonia had hoped it would. 'Good lord. She isn't Corinne's *daughter*, is she?'

'She is. What you called the old DNA provides the only feasible explanation. Remember that Corinne *did* have a child,' Antonia said. 'By Peverel.'

'But she lost the baby! That's what my sister told me.'

'A story to that effect was put around, no doubt. That was the version of events they presented to poor Peverel. For good measure, it was even suggested that Corinne couldn't have any more children. I see Mr Lark's hand in it, don't you? It was done with the sole purpose of putting Peverel off, of severing all links between him and Corinne.

Peverel must have been seen as a threat to Corinne's career. Corinne could never be allowed the distraction of a boyfriend or a husband. Corinne's daughter was given away for adoption – or placed in the care of somebody they trusted . . . Some relative? Wasn't there an aunt, on her father's side, who was a Mother Superior at a convent outside Lourdes?'

'There was.' Major Payne puffed thoughtfully at his pipe, his eyes following the swirls of smoke as they rose towards the ceiling. 'The girl grows up looking the spitting image of her famous mother . . . She has also inherited her mother's amazing voice. She can sing like her. *Exactly* like her . . . Corinne's daughter is now – what – thirty-two – thirty-three years old?'

'Yes. She gave herself away last night – remember what your aunt told us?'

'I do remember. It all makes perfect sense now. Aunt Nellie asked her if she remembered her mamma, by which she meant Ruse, and she received an extremely curious reply. Corinne's daughter knows nothing about Ruse, who is her *grandmother* and who died in Kenya well before she was born. (We made fools of ourselves over that one, didn't we?) She said she remembered her mother's voice – then she referred to "Love Story". Her earliest memory of a song, she called it. The first song she really liked. That made no sense at all. It had nothing to do with Ruse, who couldn't sing for toffee, so Aunt Nellie was taken aback. Corinne's daughter was talking about her mother, the real Corinne. Then she realized she had blundered and said that of course that was the song *she* sang in French. "Histoire d'Amour".'

'Whereas it was the *real* Corinne Coreille who sang it . . . Yes. Corinne's daughter must have heard the song on the radio, or on television. Somebody – her great aunt – perhaps drew her attention to the fact. *Listen – that's your mamma singing.*' Antonia paused. '"Love Story". The song – as well as the film – was extremely popular throughout the '70s . . . Corinne's daughter was born in 1970 or 1971.

189

She must have been three or four when she heard the song for the first time. Her earliest memory, she said.'

Payne had been gazing thoughtfully into the bowl of his pipe. 'A daughter passing herself off as her famous mother . . . She even goes and gives a concert in Japan, to great acclaim and not a whiff of suspicion . . . Well, my love, as Sherlock Holmes puts it, life is infinitely stranger than anything which the mind of man could invent.' He looked up. 'Wait – the resemblance between Maginot and Corinne! It was there all right. Their eyes. The way they tilted their heads. I know we didn't imagine it.'

'We didn't,' Antonia said. 'They are mother and daughter all right.'

'But – but then that means –'

'Yes.'

'It can't be. No, no, no. Out of the question –' Payne broke off. 'Well, it must be. Maginot – is Corinne? Or rather – was?'

# 29

# Beauty and the Beast

'Correct. That's why Jonson suddenly relaxed. Jonson knows their secret and for some reason he is extremely protective of it. At first he thought the cat was out of the bag, but then realized that we'd been thinking of the *wrong* mother and daughter. Not of Corinne and her daughter, but of Ruse and Corinne.'

Payne said, 'We skipped a generation.'

'Corinne's little finger is as long as her index finger. Peverel told us about it – that bizarre detail has been mentioned on one of the websites devoted to her. I noticed it in the greenhouse this morning, when I stood looking at Maginot's body. Then there's Corinne's odd penchant for authoritarian figures. Napoleon – Miss Mountjoy. Corinne *did* enjoy playing the nagging dragon.'

'Yes . . . It might be said that from the very start there was a Maître Maginot lodged somewhere deep inside her consciousness – screaming to be let out.'

'Both Miss Mountjoy and Maître Maginot wore turbans and they liked to boss people round.' Antonia smiled.

There was a pause. 'Maginot looked nothing like Corinne. Too tall – too heavy. Could she have changed so much over such a short period of time? Her voice was rasping and crow-like – her face the face of a gargoyle – and she looked much older than fifty-five . . . On second thoughts,' Major Payne continued musing aloud, 'platform shoes would take care of the height – and people can age prematurely, through illness or stress or the wrong diet. Maginot did like her drink. Besides, she'd had a stroke. That too would have altered her appearance . . . Would it change it beyond all recognition, though?'

'Maybe not – but something else certainly would. Do you remember where Corinne was believed to have gone – at the time she disappeared from view?'

Payne held the bridge of his nose between his thumb and index finger. 'To Switzerland? One of Peverel's scouts was of the opinion that she'd had something major done . . . Good lord! You don't mean –'

'I remember reading a hair-raising article once, about what happens if your body proves intolerant to surgical intrusions. The silicone that has been implanted in your face starts moving, your eyes swell shut, your head balloons to the size of the Taj Mahal, then you get gangrene, which in turn may lead to "skin death" or necrosis . . . If you don't die, you never look the same.'

'Plastic surgery that goes wrong . . .'

'Here's a theory,' Antonia said. 'For some thirty years Corinne Coreille has been able to have a most successful singing career. Through regular diet, exercise and the latest in beauty care, she has managed to remain "young" – unchanged. She has contrived to preserve a certain memorable image. She has had at least one face-lift, various nips and tucks. However, age does catch up with her, eventually. She is forty-nine now and one day she discovers she doesn't look right any more – or perhaps the realization has slowly been creeping up on her?'

'Yes. She can't imagine going on stage, stepping out under the spotlight, looking haggard, her face collapsed.' Payne pulled a demented grimace. 'She cancels one concert, then another. None of the intensive beauty treatments seems able to erase time's satanic footprints. She grows desperate – decides on a radical solution. She'd have something major. A total image reconstruction. Nothing less would do. She disappears from view. She books herself into a superior Swiss clinic, from which she is confident she will emerge spectacularly rejuvenated from under the knife, thirty years younger – a girl once more!'

'Only she doesn't.'

'She doesn't . . . The surgery goes spectacularly wrong – some dreadful infection sets in – she nearly dies. Well, the doctors save her – she recovers – but she loses her face. It is patched up – however, she can no longer be recognized as Corinne Coreille. She looks like Godzilla. Something has gone terribly wrong with her vocal chords too, maybe as a result of the shock. The famous voice – the beautiful voice that had once charmed General de Gaulle – is no more – gone! Corinne Coreille has suffered a permanent *extinction de voix*.' Payne started relighting his pipe and he waved his hand as though to say, 'Over to you.'

He's enjoying this as much as I am, Antonia thought. She took up the tale. 'Corinne spends the next five years in the wilderness. She suffers severe depression, has a nervous breakdown, starts hitting the bottle, puts on weight. She becomes a hermit, leads a twilight existence, which for her, after so many years in the spotlight, is a living death. She ages – now she looks ten years older. Maybe she assumes a different name. She realizes that she is finished. She is haunted by the thought – tormented – crazed by it. Her mind becomes somewhat unhinged. Then – then something unexpected happens –'

Payne put up his finger. '*Corinne meets her daughter*. She hasn't seen her for quite a while, maybe she's never seen her as a grown-up woman at all, so when they stand face to face, she is struck by the remarkable resemblance her daughter bears to her young self. Then she hears her daughter sing. She is stunned – she can't believe her ears – that unique voice, the Corinne Coreille voice – *her* voice, as it was in her prime! She has the uncanny feeling that she is hearing one of her own early recordings –'

'Actually Corinne saw her daughter on video. It was the nuns who recorded the tape,' they heard someone say. 'Two flighty *soeurs* who had got tipsy on absinthe. It showed Monique dressed up as Corinne, singing one of Corinne's songs. The title of the song, prophetically enough, was "Je Reviens".'

Peverel had entered the library without either of them hearing him.

# 30

# A Star is Born

They looked at him in silence. They had no idea how long he had stood there.

'You might as well know the exact details. Corinne hadn't been in touch with her daughter for sixteen years,' Peverel went on. 'She was a terrible mother. She should never have had children. She was monstrously egocentric – dangerously self-obsessed.'

He spoke with great bitterness and ferocious passion. Antonia had never imagined Peverel capable of any strong emotions. He looked even paler than when they had seen him last.

'She wasn't like that to start with, when I first knew her. Of course not,' Peverel continued. 'She was a very confused child, true, but she had sweetness and gentleness as well as the capacity of giving and receiving love. Well, all that evaporated over the years, thanks mainly to her Svengali – the great Mr Lark. It was he who turned Corinne into this stylized, exquisite, equivocal creature. He stunted her emotional development quite on purpose – like those bonsai trees that forever remain the wrong size – like the feet of Chinese women of noble birth that were kept bound so that they could remain small and dainty! That was what the audience seemed to want, that's what he gave them. More and more of the *same*.'

'*La petite fille* with the upturned nose and the big bows and ruffles?' Payne murmured.

'Yes. Papa Lark made sure Corinne didn't grow up. He stopped her from seeing me. I believe that made her unhappy – I am sure she loved me – but she did give me up and accepted her lot, eventually. She did as Papa Lark decreed. I am sure it was under his dictation that she wrote the letter informing me that our daughter had died.'

'How did you know that it wasn't true?'

'One of the nuns told me. Sister Felicia.'

'So I was right,' Antonia said. 'Corinne's daughter *was* brought up by nuns.'

'Yes . . . She was sent to the convent outside Lourdes, where Corinne's aunt was Mother Superior at the time.'

Sister Felicia had discovered some papers in her Mother Superior's desk after her death, Peverel explained. There was a birth certificate – also letters sent to Corinne's aunt by Mr Lark. Mr Lark had written that on no account should Peverel be contacted and told that his daughter was alive. Mr Lark had made the convent a number of generous donations . . . The Mother Superior had complied with his wishes and she had preserved Corinne's guilty secret for more than quarter of a century, but now that she was dead, Sister Felicia saw no reason why the truth shouldn't be told. Sister Felicia had managed to find Peverel's address and written to him. 'She was a good and decent soul,' Peverel said.

'Was Monique a nun?'

'No. She had never taken a vow or anything of that sort, but she lived and worked at the convent. She worked on the administration side – a secretarial job. She seemed to be content. Sister Felicia wrote to me two years ago, on the day after Monique's thirtieth birthday. She also told Monique about me. She believed a great wrong had been perpetrated and she had made it her mission to set it right.' Peverel paused. 'I went to France to see Monique. Sister Felicia met me at the station and she took me to the convent – in an incredibly battered Citroën . . . Monique and I got on extremely well. She was very shy and reserved to start with, but she relaxed eventually. She clearly loved the idea of having a father.' Peverel smiled. 'She even asked me for a photograph!'

'The photograph on her dressing table?' Antonia said.

'Yes . . . You do seem to know an awful lot . . . I didn't let my bitterness about Corinne spill out. Monique hardly knew her famous mother. She bore a striking resemblance to Corinne, only she was blonde. She could also sing like her. *She had the same voice.* You were right about that too . . . As it happens, Sister Felicia and Sister Fortunata had just recorded the video – Monique made up as Corinne. The resemblance was uncanny. The nuns were in their early sixties and they were both great fans of Corinne Coreille. No one else knew what they had done . . . I understand they have died since. Pity. I liked them enormously. They played the tape for me – danced to it. They were totally eccentric. Terribly sweet.'

'You said they sent a copy of the tape to Corinne too?'

'Yes – care of her record company. In fact they asked me to post it. We wondered about the effect the tape would have on Corinne. It was sixteen years since Corinne had last seen Monique. Monique had been fourteen then – a gawky, awkward teenager. I learnt that Corinne had been sending money to Monique regularly, so she couldn't be faulted on that count.'

'So you have known about the impersonation all along?'

'No – not all along. Monique only told me this morning. Corinne had sworn her to absolute secrecy. Corinne, you see, went to the convent as soon as she saw the video. Under an assumed name, though no one would have recognized her anyhow. She passed herself off as an aunt of Monique's. She asked Monique to do a repeat act. Make herself up as Corinne, put on the wig and so on, and perform once more. She was stunned by the result and, I expect, she had her brainwave there and then. That same day she took Monique to Paris with her.'

'Corinne saw in Monique her chance for revival?'

'Yes, Antonia. The chance to re-create herself – to make a spectacular comeback – to resume her singing career afresh. Corinne had been getting invitations for concerts from all over the world but had been turning them down. Her secret had been well kept – miraculously, there hadn't been a single rumour about her failed plastic surgery, so no one knew. Corinne wasted no time and started coaching Monique – she taught her her gestures, mannerisms, tastes, everything! Before the trip to England she told her all Monique needed to know about Aunt Nellie – about Hugh as well – where and when they had met, about his sister Amanda and so on . . . As it happened, Monique proved an excellent student – *she became her mother.'*

'It's a most fantastic thing – relinquishing one's identity and living somebody else's life. Becoming one's mother!' Payne exclaimed. 'Not many people would agree to it.'

'No. Well, Monique was tempted. That's what she said. She had always wanted to perform. She had dreamt of singing in public, on a stage, in front of an audience, but had been pathologically shy, too shy to do anything about it. She had led an extremely sheltered life, a most secluded provincial existence. She lacked the confidence. She was gauche. What her mother offered her was not merely a chance to sing on stage, but a shortcut to fame – something Monique had never thought possible, never contemplated, not in her wildest dreams! So she jumped at the opportunity. She knew she had a very good voice but she had always thought of it as old-fashioned –'

'*Le goût de papa?'* suggested Payne.

'You may put it that way. That she sounded exactly like her mother, Monique regarded as something of a disadvantage. She had never imagined she would be able to make a career as herself – not a major one at any rate. It was one thing to have your voice noticed at matins, another to be an international star. But as the celebrated Corinne Coreille she would be able to do it – start as world famous – as legendary! There would be no need for her to establish herself – she would emerge fully formed.'

'Like a butterfly out of a chrysalis.'

'She'd sing to audiences that knew her – that were there to adore her – audiences that had been waiting for her – wondering what had happened to her – *longing* for her voice. She said it was a very peculiar feeling she had in Japan – standing under what amounted to a floral shower, being applauded for her voice, which was also *not* her voice. The only real problem had been her youth, the fact that she was twenty-two years younger than Corinne, but there were such things as wigs and make-up.'

There was a pause. 'When did she tell you all this?' Antonia asked.

'Last night, or rather in the small hours of this morning. She phoned me on her mobile. We talked for at least an hour. She needed to talk desperately. She was frightened, terrified. The death threats, the anxiety that she might get something wrong at dinner, then her mother getting killed. She couldn't face being interrogated by the police. Besides, there was something wrong with her make-up. Either that, or it was because her hands were shaking too much. She was in a state of panic. She couldn't go through with it.' Peverel paused. 'That's why I came. I had to. In case any suspicion fell on her. In case the police attributed her disappearance to guilty conscience. I wanted to see what line the police would take. I suppose I'd have told them the whole story if they got it into their heads that Monique had anything to do with the two deaths –'

'And hasn't she?' Major Payne said quietly.

Peverel ignored this. 'I also wanted to see how serious Andrew Jonson's intentions were. They are thinking of getting married. Oh, you didn't know that, did you? You seem surprised. I thought you knew everything,' Peverel said with a return of his sardonic manner.

# 31

# A Family Plot?

'Ah, there you are,' Lady Grylls said, entering the library. She was holding a glass of brandy in her hand. 'I've been looking for you. We are going to have hot onion soup and ham sandwiches in the dining room. I've scrapped the original menu, for obvious reasons. All will be ready in about half an hour, I am told. Hortense is coping extremely well, all things considered. But there's something else I meant to tell you – now what *was* it?' She raised the brandy to her lips and took a swig.

Peverel said, 'Really, darling, at your age, the consequences of a midday binge could be catastrophic.'

'Oh yes.' Lady Grylls turned to Antonia. 'There's been a rather sensational development, though I suppose you'll disagree. I mean, it's *never* the person who's seen leaving the scene of the crime at the crucial time, is it?'

Antonia decided to humour her. 'You don't mean somebody's been seen leaving the scene of the crime at the crucial time?'

'Yes, my dear. *A stranger.* That makes the possibility of him being the murderer even more remote, doesn't it? I can tell from your expressions that you've been juggling with conjectures, so you might as well consider this one as well.' Lady Grylls paused. 'The boy Nicholas – Provost's son – is certain he's seen the killer. Of course he didn't know at the time it was the killer . . . He doesn't want to talk to the police about it because, you see, he doesn't *trust* the police.'

'Nicholas believes he has seen the killer?'

'That's exactly what I said. Yes.' Lady Grylls raised the brandy glass to her lips once more. 'Man in a car. Looking bleached.'

Peverel said pointedly, 'Conspicuous consumption.' It wasn't clear whether he meant Nicholas and drugs or his aunt and alcohol. Antonia suspected it was the latter.

'Darling, shouldn't you start at the beginning?' Major Payne said gently.

'Last night Nicholas left early. We hadn't finished dinner yet. I didn't mind. I thought Provost was perfectly capable of coping on his own. Anyhow, last night Nicholas said he was going to this disco in the village. It's organized by the youth club, apparently. He went on his bike. As he was coming back, at about half past two, he saw a car coming out of the gates and he nearly crashed into it. He fell off his bike and the car slowed down but didn't stop. There was a full moon. Nicholas saw the driver very clearly. The driver turned his head and gave him a look. It was a young man.'

'A young man?'

'That's right. A pale thin young man, with short cropped hair that was very fair, almost bleached white. Ghostly pale. Liquid eyes that gleamed in the moonlight like a cat's. Somewhat effeminate – "girlie" was the way Nicholas put it –' Lady Grylls broke off. 'I'm afraid I don't feel frightfully well. It's been a ghastly morning. Absolutely dreadful. Just a minute ago Bobo Markham phoned and said he's got two new pigs and would we all like to go and see them!'

Payne suggested that she sit down. He led his aunt to one of the grandfather armchairs. '*Her glass – take it away,*' Peverel whispered.

'Thank you, Hughie . . . Well, it's an extraordinary story, you've got to agree . . . No, leave the glass. I haven't finished . . . Leave it, I said . . . At first I thought that Nicholas must have had a drug-induced mirage of some

sort,' Lady Grylls went on. 'Heaven knows what sub-
stances he took last night. Now you wouldn't believe this,
but my second thought was that the young man was that
American woman's son. Eleanor's son. She expected him
to appear, didn't she? That's what she wrote in one of
her letters.'

'You thought the young man with the car was Griff?'

'I imagined his ghost might have come back from the
dead, yes.' Lady Grylls shook her head. 'This is all terribly
embarrassing. Totally unlike me . . . Nicholas said he saw
the car moving but he *didn't hear a sound* . . . You see,
Corinne and I talked about ghosts last night – Cynthia
Drake and so on – *that's* what must have put ghosts into
my head . . . Incidentally, who *was* Cynthia Drake?'

'The Hon. Cynthia Drake? The social editor of *Weekend
Whirlwind* – a magazine now defunct,' Payne said. 'Back in
the '50s, I think.'

'All those satin chairs . . . How peculiar. I wonder
whether Rory – Anyhow. There are no ghosts. It's obvious
what happened. He – that young man, whoever he is –
must have turned off the engine. The drive slopes – from
the house to the gates, what's left of them, it's all downhill.
He clearly didn't want anyone in the house to hear him, so
he pushed the car and jumped in.'

'That makes perfect sense,' Antonia agreed. ' Who could
this young man be?'

Payne had gone to the window and was standing beside
it, looking out. 'Jonson's car is gone. Do you know where
it is? He's still here, isn't he?'

'Andrew? He is here, yes,' Lady Grylls said. 'Saw him a
minute ago, in the hall, talking to someone on his mobile.
He was looking terribly worried, poor boy.'

Payne turned round slowly. 'Terribly worried, eh?'

Peverel cleared his throat. 'The "girlie" young man
Nicholas saw last night was in fact a girl. It was Monique.
She was in Andrew's car. Andrew let her use it. Monique's
hair is very fair and she's had it closely cropped, she told
me. It makes it easier to put on the wig. Without her make-
up and wig she'd be unrecognizable. She looks bleached,

almost. Not unlike Jean Seberg in *Bout de Souffle*. Remember her?' He smiled. 'I imagine she'd look like a delicate boy in the moonlight. And I believe she was crying – that's why her eyes "gleamed".'

'What are you talking about?' Lady Grylls asked. 'Who is Monique? I believe that was the name of the person Andrew was talking to on the phone. He walked into the drawing room as soon as he saw me. Didn't want me to overhear, clearly.'

Payne was looking at his cousin. 'Where did she go?'

'To London. To Andrew's Maida Vale flat.'

'In the middle of the night?'

'She couldn't face the police, I told you.'

'Who *is* Monique?' Lady Grylls asked.

There was a pause. Major Payne said, 'It's been assumed that the Merchant shot Maginot in her panic, having no idea who she was, but what if she killed her because she somehow knew that Maginot was Corinne? What if she did manage to take her revenge? Could somebody have told her? Somebody who *knew* –'

'Jonson knew,' Antonia said.

'What d'you mean, *Maginot was Corinne*? Is this some game?' Lady Grylls said, looking round. 'Or have all of you lost your marbles?'

'Jonson was well aware of the impersonation,' Antonia said. 'I personally don't think Eleanor killed anybody . . . How did Monique know that her mother had been killed?' Antonia turned to Peverel. 'You said she phoned you in the small hours of the morning . . . Was she perhaps in the greenhouse, when it happened? Or did her husband-to-be tell her about it?'

'She wasn't in the greenhouse –' Peverel broke off. There was a silence.

'Does Monique inherit her mother's fabulous fortune?' Payne asked his cousin.

'I have no idea,' Peverel said. 'What business is it of yours?'

'Corinne Coreille was an extremely rich woman . . . A fabulous fortune, yes . . . An outlandish wallop,' Payne went on in a thoughtful voice, 'to be shared by Monique and her husband-to-be. Do forgive me the old cliché, old boy, but people have killed for less.'

'You are being a bore, Hugh,' Peverel drawled. 'Are you suggesting that Monique killed her mother?'

'She might have – or he might have. I mean Jonson. They had a good motive. I mean, they both stand to gain by her death. It isn't as though either of them was particularly fond of the good Maître.'

'You are being a terrible bore, Hugh.'

'Eleanor Merchant brought a knife with her,' Antonia said slowly. 'I doubt if she ever had a gun in her bag –'

'So much like Cluedo, isn't it?' Peverel interrupted in mocking tones. 'Mrs Merchant, the mad American widow, with a knife.'

'On the other hand,' Payne said, 'Mr Jonson, the English private detective, could easily have obtained a gun and brought it with him from London. One with a silencer.'

'Andrew has nothing to do with the murder. Nothing at all. Better get that notion out of your thick head. Andrew is a good and decent man.' Peverel sounded exasperated.

'He knew about the impersonation. He was well aware of Corinne and Monique's secret, and yet he kept it carefully. He colluded with them.' Payne paused. 'Why didn't he expose them as frauds? If he is indeed, as you say, a good and decent man?'

'He is in love with my daughter, that's why he kept her secret. Why are you acting like an oaf, Hugh? Didn't you hear what I said?' Peverel raised his voice. '*They are getting married*. Andrew knew it would cause Monique great distress if their secret became known. He was afraid that it might get her into trouble.'

Payne nodded. 'I can certainly see why he should have her interests at heart . . . What about Corinne? Are you suggesting she wasn't aware that he knew their secret?'

'Corinne had no idea that he knew their secret –' As soon as the words were out of his mouth, Peverel looked as though he regretted having uttered them.

'Corinne didn't know that he knew?' Antonia said. 'So Jonson and Monique –'

Lady Grylls cut her short. 'I don't know what this is all about – it all sounds totally potty to me, but you seem to be trying to cook up some ridiculous rigmarole against Andrew! Now then, if you've got it into your heads that he is a killer – that he shot that American woman in my greenhouse, and then shot Maginot, who, you say, is Corinne – you couldn't be more wrong.' She glared at Payne and Antonia. 'For once I am on Peverel's side . . . Peverel, you can have that damned Pugin stool, if you still want it . . . You only have to look at Andrew. He is *not* a killer. I think you should go and talk to him. Put a straight question to him and I am sure you will get a straight answer. Don't give me such condescending looks, Hughie. I am *not* drunk.' Pushing her glasses up her nose, she started heaving herself out of the armchair. 'No, I don't need any help . . . Let's go and find him.'

# 32

# Love Story

They found Jonson in the drawing room, sitting in a chair beside the fireplace. He had a forlorn air about him. He rose to his feet as soon as he saw Lady Grylls who was leading the procession. He was extremely pale. On a small table beside the chair there lay a folded copy of the *International Herald Tribune*.

'Do sit down, Andrew,' she boomed. 'Sit down, everybody,' she ordered. 'What they have been trying to say –' She gestured towards Payne and Antonia. 'What they have been *suggesting* is that it was you who killed those two women in the greenhouse.' She paused. 'Did you kill them?'

'No, I did not.'

Lady Grylls cast a triumphant glance at her nephew and niece-by-marriage. 'What did I tell you?'

Antonia couldn't help smiling. If only things could be resolved as simply as that! And yet, Jonson sounded nothing but truthful and sincere. He looked exactly as his future father-in-law had described him: a good and decent man. Was he, after all, a good actor – or was he a psychopath?

Peverel turned to Jonson. 'They know practically everything. It's none of their business, but there it is. They are suspicious of Monique because she inherits Corinne's money. They are also suspicious of you because you are going to marry Monique. They say people have killed for less.'

'I see,' Jonson said.

'When did you first know that Corinne was not Corinne but her daughter?' Payne asked in conversational tones. 'Or was it la Maginot's cover that was blown first?'

'It was the kitten in the photograph, wasn't it?' Antonia said gently. 'You knew about Corinne's allergy to cats?'

Jonson had seemed lost in thought but now he looked up. 'No. I hadn't discovered the photograph then. I learnt about the allergy later. Monique told me about it. Oh God –' He broke off and passed his hand across his face. 'All right. It was the third day of my investigation of the leaked stories. I had been going to Corinne Coreille's Paris house every day. It was the afternoon of 7th December. I had left the house and was buying an English paper at a newsagent's opposite Corinne's house. I happened to look back and I saw a side door in the wall open and a girl leave. I thought I had seen everybody in the house, but this girl was completely unknown to me. I knew she was not one of the servants. She was very striking-looking. Very slim and fair, with short hair. She wore a silvery-grey belted raincoat. She started walking down the street and I found myself following her. She didn't take the Métro but walked – all the way to the XVIth Arrondissement –'

'The XVIth Arrondissement. Am I right in thinking that's where the Cinémathèque Française is?' Major Payne said. 'That's where I saw Billy Wilder's *Fedora*,' he added inconsequentially.

'She didn't hurry. I kept up with her. We passed by the Place du Trocadéro with its illuminated fountains. There were groups of people there – they were watching a juggler – there was also an acrobat doing somersaults. It was only a fortnight to Christmas. A busker somewhere was playing the accordion – a sweet melody – "Plaisir d'amour" . . .' Jonson paused. 'At one point the girl stopped and bought a small packet of chestnuts, then she walked on. I continued to follow. She hadn't noticed me.'

'Being a detective must have helped,' Antonia said.

'Perhaps.' Jonson managed a smile. 'She was like someone who was enjoying their freedom, after a long period of incarceration. It was the way she raised her chin, shut her eyes and smelled the air – like a puppy. It was also the way she looked round, with delight and wonder. She finally sat down at a café – part of the monumental Palais de Chaillot, where the Cinémathèque is. I sat down at a table not far from hers. I heard her order a cup of Earl Grey tea. Eventually she looked down at her watch, paid her bill and got up. I followed. She went back exactly the same way, only this time she didn't stop anywhere. When she reached Corinne Coreille's house, she took out a key and let herself in through the door in the wall . . . It was clear she was an insider, though I had no idea who she could be.'

'You didn't recognize her?' Antonia said. 'I mean as Corinne Coreille?'

'No. The idea never occurred to me. I had met Corinne Coreille only once – very briefly – in a darkish room. Her hair was dark and done in a fringe, and she had heavy make-up on. She was a completely different physical type . . . The next day I asked one of the gardeners if they knew whether a fair-haired girl worked at the house, or whether there was a visitor of that description, but he said no.'

'You were interested in the gel? You found her attractive?' Lady Grylls gave an approving nod.

'Yes. I was interested in her. I also wanted to find out who she was. That afternoon I stationed myself some distance from the house and again I saw her come out – at exactly the same time – half past five. The same journey as the day before. She went on to the café next to the Cinémathèque and, again, she sat at a table by herself and ordered a cup of Earl Grey tea. This time, as luck would have it, most of the tables were occupied and I found myself standing beside her table, asking her if I could sit on the chair opposite her. It was then that it happened.'

'You recognized her?'

'No.' Jonson smiled. '*She recognized me.* It was very disconcerting, the way she looked at me. She blinked and her eyes opened wide. She gasped. Her hand shook and she spilled some of her tea. I saw her hands clench into fists and she hid them under the table. As she told me later, she had been convinced that someone was paying me to expose her and her mother for the frauds they were. I sat down and ordered a cup of coffee. I couldn't bear to see the girl looking so frightened. She was trembling, like a little bird. I kept my eyes on my coffee –'

'You spoke to her?' Payne said.

'She spoke to me. She gave a little gasp and said, *Please, tell no one.* She spoke like a child. I looked up – there was an expression of absolute terror on her face. She was staring at me. Her eyes looked imploring. I opened my mouth but I couldn't say a thing. My mind had gone blank. Then, suddenly, I *knew.* The thought came into my head. It was her scent, I think. I'd smelled it when I'd met Corinne Coreille . . . *Violets* . . .'

'That was the real Corinne's scent,' murmured Antonia.

'I said nothing. I knew I was dealing with impersonation, but I was damned if I was going to do anything about it. I didn't care . . . We remained sitting. We went on staring at each other. I don't know for how long. Probably only for a minute or so, but it seemed much longer. She was trembling. It was then that I – I –'

'Reached out and held her hand?' Lady Grylls suggested. 'It's a long time since I've enjoyed a story more,' she told Antonia as an aside. 'I *am* a silly old romantic.'

'Yes. I held her hand. She let me. Neither of us spoke . . . I can't remember what exactly happened next. I think she blurted out the whole story. *I am Corinne's daughter.* She told me what had happened – about the nuns and the video. She even told me about you.' He turned to Peverel.

'She had her father's photograph on her dressing table,' Antonia said.

'Yes. We sat talking for a long time. I told her about my fiancée who had died five years ago in a car crash. She admitted that she'd never had a serious boyfriend. I can't say how long we sat like that. Then suddenly her mobile phone rang. It was her mother, asking where she was and did she know what time it was. Then she had to run.'

'You did see her again, didn't you?' Lady Grylls said.

'Yes. The next day. That was when I found the

photograph in Emilie's locker. Maître Maginot – the real Corinne Coreille – was there of course, so we couldn't talk at all. I handed over the photograph and the film. I had made a copy of the photo for myself – I wanted to have a photo of Monique. As she thanked me and shook my hand, Monique managed to slip me a piece of paper with her mobile phone number and her email address. I tried to arrange to meet her but it was impossible. We were never alone. Her mother was there all the time, hovering over her, watching . . . Her mother was extremely suspicious, Monique told me later. After she was late that night, Corinne stopped her from going out altogether.'

There was a pause. 'Did you stay on in Paris?' Antonia asked.

'I wanted to but couldn't. I had to come back to England. I had business commitments. I tried to ring Monique on her mobile on Christmas Day, but it was her mother who answered, so I rang off. Monique then sent me an email saying that we must be very careful. She told me more about her mother. Corinne's behaviour was becoming more and more erratic. She had been making grandiose plans for more concerts abroad – for appearances on French television – for singing a song about Paris on top of the Eiffel Tower, then jumping off with a parachute . . . Corinne required total submission and the most rigid discipline from Monique. She controlled what Monique ate and drank. She insisted on regular workouts in the gym. Corinne had started monitoring all Monique's movements round the clock.'

'Poor gel,' Lady Grylls wheezed.

'Corinne was volatile, manic, frequently hysterical. When she realized that Monique had been in touch with her father – she had seen the photo on the dressing table – she accused Monique of betraying her. She ranted and raved for an hour, apparently. And it was worse when Monique brought the kitten into the house – this time her mother accused her of trying to kill her!'

'I suppose visitors were discouraged?' Payne said.

'They never had any visitors. Monique had to wear the

Corinne make-up at all times even when there were only the two of them, and the make-up had to be flawless. Her mother checked it several times a day and always managed to find some fault with it. Monique was made to watch recordings of old Corinne Coreille programmes again and again in order to perfect her act . . . Corinne was becoming more and more paranoid . . . Only young people were employed for fear that anyone older might in some way recognize Corinne in Maginot or alternatively tumble to the fact that Monique was not Corinne. After the Emilie incident, Corinne started changing the maids every month. She mistrusted the maids and had rows with them, though, unaccountably, the latest maid, a Filipina called Imelda, was allowed to stay on, and Corinne had been showering her with gifts – bottles of scent, boxes of chocolate, sweet liqueurs and dresses –'

'Did you say Imelda?' Lady Grylls interrupted. 'I heard Maginot phone someone called Imelda yesterday evening, soon after they arrived here. On her mobile phone. I remember the name because it made me think about the other one – the famous one – the Marcos woman. I read somewhere that she was down to her last billion. You know – the one with the shoes . . . Don't suppose it's the same one?' Lady Grylls guffawed.

An accomplice, Antonia thought. Yes . . . Would she remember?

'Monique gave Imelda as an example of her mother's increasingly strange behaviour,' Jonson went on. 'Monique had started hating the whole thing. She felt trapped. Singing in these circumstances was no longer fun. She hated her mother – she was scared of her.'

'Why didn't you tell her to get out and go off with you?' Lady Grylls asked.

'I did. She said she'd think about it. She – she – needed time. She still felt some kind of obligation. She said she didn't want to let her mother down. She had enjoyed the singing part of the arrangement and that she owed to her mother. We – we made tentative plans. Then – then something happened. A bolt out of the blue.'

Antonia said, 'The death threats?'

'Eleanor Merchant's letters, followed by the death threats, yes.' Jonson paused. 'Monique was very upset. She contacted me at once – she threw all caution to the winds – she emailed me – phoned. But,' Jonson went on, 'something good seemed to come of it. I received a phone call from Paris, from Maître Maginot. She said she wanted to employ my services once more urgently – as Corinne's bodyguard and protector. It was going to be another commission. She sounded extremely pleasant and friendly and I did believe that she knew nothing about me and Monique. She said they'd be coming to England, to a place called Chalfont Park. She wanted me to join them. I couldn't believe my luck. I was going to see Monique! That was all I could think about, that was all that seemed to matter. I was delighted – delirious.'

'You were not worried about the death threats?'

'No. Not really. I couldn't see how Eleanor Merchant would possibly be able to find this place,' Jonson said. 'I thought it a virtual impossibility –'

'Eleanor Merchant was *meant* to come here,' Antonia interrupted. 'She was given the Chalfont address and phone number.' She looked at Jonson. 'It was all part of the plan.'

'Sorry, old thing, but I've got to ask my aunt a very important question.' Major Payne leant towards Lady Grylls. 'Aunt Nellie, did you hear exactly what Maître Maginot – I mean Corinne – said to her maid when she phoned her?'

Lady Grylls blinked behind her glasses. 'What Maginot said to her maid? I have absolutely no idea.'

'I am sure you have. Your French is perfect.'

'You aren't suggesting I eavesdropped?'

'You know you always do, darling, especially if you are curious about the person.'

'It's important,' Antonia said. 'Extremely important.'

'Oh nonsense. It wasn't in the least important.' Lady Grylls stared. 'Goodness, Antonia, you can't possibly know what Hugh means, can you?'

'I can – I was about to ask you the very same question.'

'You were? Goodness. One of those telepathic thingies, eh? All right. Let me see . . . Maginot spoke in French. I had shown her to her room and I was back in the corridor. The door was ajar. I didn't mean to listen, you understand, but I couldn't help overhearing. It was something exceedingly trivial. Maginot said, *Imelda, c'est toi?* Then she asked whether there had been any phone calls for them. Then she said, *When was that? And you gave her both? Good girl.* Words to that effect. She said it all in French of course. She seemed jolly pleased with Imelda's answers . . . Oh yes, she also said she would cover Imelda in gold, or words to that effect, which I took to be a jocular exaggeration. Well, that was it.'

'Thank you, darling,' Payne said. 'You've just solved the conundrum for us.'

'What conundrum?'

Antonia said, 'Thanks to you we now know the identity not only of the killer but of the intended victim as well.'

'What are you talking about?' Lady Grylls frowned. 'There's no mystery over the victims' identities. We know it was Maginot and the Merchant who got shot in my greenhouse. Or are you saying Maginot and the Merchant weren't Maginot and the Merchant?'

Antonia turned slowly towards Jonson. 'It was you, wasn't it?'

He bowed his head. 'Yes, it was me.'

'What do you mean, it was you, Andrew?' Lady Grylls boomed, her voice like the thunder of waters from a subterranean cave. 'You aren't confessing to being a double murderer after all, are you?'

Jonson said, 'No. I am not the murderer. I was . . . the intended victim. It was I who was meant to die in the greenhouse last night.'

213

33

# Appointment with Death

There was a silence. All eyes were on him.

'You'd better explain,' Lady Grylls said.

'The phone call, which came last night, while we were having coffee –' Jonson's voice sounded very hoarse. 'Maître Maginot – Corinne Coreille – went to speak to the woman who had introduced herself as Tricia Swindon. Corinne suspected at once that it was Eleanor Merchant, so after the woman rang off, she dialled 1471 and obtained the number from which the call had been made. It was a mobile phone number. She wrote it down and later, after you'd all gone to bed, she asked me to ring it.'

'She asked you to phone the Merchant?' Payne said.

'Yes. Corinne Coreille had a brainwave. She thought she could trick Eleanor into revealing her whereabouts. She knew I was a good mimic, so she asked me to put on an American accent, muffle my voice and pretend to be Eleanor's dead son. Griff . . . She got the idea from one of Eleanor's letters. Eleanor had written that she expected her dead son to appear to her.'

'Of all the diabolical wheezes!'

Jonson passed his hand over his face. 'I am not proud of what I did, but the trick worked. Eleanor did fall for it and revealed her whereabouts. She seemed to have no doubt I was Griff. She asked me where I was – *was I in the greenhouse?* Corinne Coreille was standing beside me, listening.'

'That was how she knew where to find Eleanor,' Antonia said.

'Yes . . . I said I would go but she said no, she wanted to apprehend Eleanor herself. She asked me to make sure all of you were in your rooms. She didn't want people milling around the house. She told me to keep my mobile switched on – she'd give me a ring on her mobile when it was all over, or if she needed help. She was going to the greenhouse by herself. I thought that unwise – dangerous – utter lunacy in fact. I decided she'd had too much wine. Her eyes were extremely bright and she kept referring to the "capture". She gave the impression she regarded it as some kind of adventure. The only weapon she seemed to have was the niblick –'

'You didn't know she had a gun?' Antonia interrupted. 'She didn't show it to you?'

'No. I had no idea.' Jonson swallowed. 'I went on arguing with her for some time. I insisted that it was my job – my duty – wasn't that why she'd hired my services? She gave me a look of such malevolence, it froze me. She spoke to me very slowly – like to an idiot child. *You needn't be concerned on my account. I shall be fine. I can cope.* After that I – I did as asked. I had a word with Provost – told him not to leave the house. I checked on each one of you. Then I went to my room. I sat and waited . . . I didn't wait long. Her call came about midnight.'

There was a pause. Payne said, 'She didn't tell you she'd shot Eleanor, did she?'

'No. She said Eleanor was there all right – she'd got her trapped in the greenhouse. She did need my help – she said she didn't think Eleanor Merchant was armed, but she couldn't tell for certain – would I go to the greenhouse, at once?' Jonson looked round at their eager faces. 'I immediately suggested I call the police but she said, *On no account.* Again, she sounded angry. She told me not to breathe a word to anyone. She didn't want any fuss. She wished this done as quietly and efficiently as possible. We'd call the police *after* we'd done the job. She asked me to get some rope – to tie Eleanor up. She seemed to be –

215

she seemed to be enjoying herself.' He paused. 'I found some rope in one of the kitchen drawers, then I slipped out of the house. I had my torch with me, but turned it off. I started walking across the lawn. It was a very clear night. I saw the greenhouse door was open . . . It was very quiet . . . There wasn't a sound . . .'

'There was a full moon,' Lady Grylls said.

'Yes. It was so bright, it felt like day. I then stopped. My eyes were fixed on the greenhouse. I tried to make out what was inside. At first I couldn't see a thing. Suddenly I caught sight of a tiny flash, bobbing up and down – like a firefly.'

'The silver brooch on her beret . . . It must have caught the moonlight,' Antonia said.

'It was a Cartier,' Lady Grylls said.

'Yes. The brooch gave her away. I suddenly saw her, standing very still, her shoulders hunched forward – extremely tense-looking – furtive. She didn't move – she was waiting – that's what it looked like. Nothing else stirred inside the greenhouse . . . I too stood very still. I didn't dare breathe. I had no idea whether she had seen me or not. A minute passed, then another. The more I waited the less I liked it . . . I had come to Chalfont unarmed. Stupid of me, but I never thought of bringing a gun. It just goes to show you how seriously I was taking the Eleanor Merchant menace.' Jonson shook his head. 'I went on looking at Corinne Coreille. I was afraid to blink. Then I realized she was holding something in her hand.'

'The gun?'

'Yes. It gave me quite a shock when I saw that she had a gun. She was holding it aloft. For a moment I imagined that she was stalking Eleanor Merchant, but the thought then came to me that Eleanor Merchant either wasn't there or else she was already dead . . . She hadn't said a word about having a gun . . . I then remembered the look she had given me earlier on. The sheer malevolence of it – the scorn – the hatred! I started remembering other things . . . What Monique had told me about her mother's egomania and ruthlessness – about her obsession with her career – her determination to live her life through her daughter – her extreme disapproval of anything that distracted Monique from following the path she had mapped out for her – her suspiciousness and paranoia. I also remembered the two nuns.' Jonson swallowed. 'About the way they'd died. Monique had told me about it.'

'What two nuns?' Lady Grylls said. 'Goodness. Do *nuns* too come into the story?'

'Sister Felicia and Sister Fortunata. They brought Monique up,' Peverel explained. 'They died in a car crash. They died together. There was something wrong with the brakes of their Citroën, apparently.' He looked at Jonson. 'You don't think . . .?'

Jonson shrugged. 'I don't know . . . I really don't, but I wouldn't put anything past her. Corinne might have paid someone to do it, or she might have done it herself. I may be wrong – still, it's rather curious that the only two people who could have recognized Monique in the guise of Corinne died a month before her comeback concert.'

'They weren't the only two. What about the doctors and nurses who operated on her face and made a hash of it?' Antonia pointed out. 'They too would have known that the woman making her comeback as Corinne Coreille must be an impostor.'

'No, they wouldn't. Corinne Coreille had registered under a different name at the clinic. You'd be amazed at the number of crazy people who have plastic surgery to make themselves look like somebody famous. There are agencies specializing in celebrity impersonators all over the world. There is even a clinic in Thailand, apparently, that promises to give you the face of your favourite celebrity. Well, the deception wouldn't have lasted for very long,' Jonson went on with a tight little smile. 'Sooner or later Corinne Coreille's whole carefully constructed edifice would have collapsed like the proverbial house of cards. Someone would have realized that either Maginot was Corinne – or that Corinne was not Corinne. Something *would* have gone wrong. It wasn't a question of if but of

217

when. Monique would have slipped up. In fact she did slip up last night, didn't she? She told me about it. She got confused and talked about her mother singing "Love Story" . . .'

'She did,' Lady Grylls said with a sigh. 'She did. Poor gel.'

'A rumour would have got around. People would have become curious. They'd have started asking questions.' Jonson paused. 'Corinne Coreille, however, seemed to believe the scheme she'd devised was entirely foolproof. She told Monique she saw no reason why the impersonation shouldn't continue indefinitely – for another thirty years at least. Monique was terrified when she heard that.'

'As misshapen inside as she was on the outside,' Payne murmured. 'Monstrously delusional.'

'Do get on with the story, Andrew,' Lady Grylls prompted. 'You were standing outside the greenhouse and . . .?'

Jonson frowned. 'I went on wondering . . . What if Corinne Coreille had managed to read the emails Monique and I had been exchanging? She could have got hold of Monique's password. What if she knew that I was aware of the double impersonation? What if she knew that Monique and I were in love – that Monique was terribly unhappy – that I had been urging her to run away and come to me? *What if she knew everything?'* Jonson looked round the table. 'What would she do?'

'Goodness me, this is all terribly exciting.' Lady Grylls lit a cigarette. 'I can't bear the suspense!'

'I knew then with absolute certainty that it was for me Corinne Coreille was waiting inside the greenhouse. *She wanted me dead.* She intended to shoot me. She had called me to Chalfont in order to kill me. She had several extremely good reasons for desiring my urgent removal. I knew too much! Why, I was putting her whole enterprise in danger! I wanted to kick myself for not thinking about it earlier.'

There was a pause. 'You were to die in the execution of

your duties,' Antonia said slowly. 'Corinne intended to make it look like an open-and-shut case. She had thought the whole thing through down to the smallest detail. I do believe it was she who sent the death threats in the first place – and she put *Herald Tribune* cuttings inside Eleanor Merchant's bag after she killed her . . . She meant it to look as though you'd been shot by the demented avenging mother – who then committed suicide.'

'Corinne wouldn't have shot him on the lawn, would she?' Payne frowned.

'No. It *had* to be done inside the greenhouse to suggest that Eleanor did it in her panic and confusion, after he had discovered her hiding place . . . Corinne chose Chalfont Park because she believed it would be easier to put her plan into operation in England. The house is isolated. Her godmother had always complained there weren't enough servants. Besides, her godmother had bad eyesight, so she wouldn't have recognized her in Maginot in the first place.'

'Her godmother wouldn't have recognized her even if there'd been nothing wrong with her bloody eyes!' Lady Grylls cried and she shook her head. 'She'd become a monster! I can't believe it – I really can't! It's just hit me – I mean, little Corinne! The beauty turning into a beast –' Lady Grylls broke off. 'She instructed her maid – Imelda – to give my address to Eleanor Merchant, didn't she? She must have bribed her . . . You said she kept giving her presents?'

'She did . . . What if things hadn't gone according to plan?' Jonson turned to Antonia. 'What if Eleanor Merchant had failed to take the bait?'

'Well, that was a chance Corinne was prepared to take.' Antonia smiled. 'It seems she had inherited her parents' gambling streak.'

'Would she still have tried to kill me?'

'I believe she would. *You were too dangerous.* It wasn't only that you knew too much – you'd been giving Monique ideas – you were about to take Monique away from her!' Antonia paused. 'Well, I think she'd have laid a false trail suggesting that Eleanor was behind your murder. She'd have made it look as though Eleanor had been here, killed you and fled. But she knew from Imelda that Eleanor had swallowed the bait, so everything was going to plan.'

Payne put up his forefinger. '*The Corinne doll*. It was found on the stairs inside the house. Maître Maginot – Corinne – must have accidentally dropped it there last night. It must have slipped out of her pocket. She knew all about it from Eleanor's first letter. She must have intended to plant the doll somewhere near your body – in the event that, say, Eleanor had managed to skedaddle.'

'Tell us what happened next, Andrew,' Lady Grylls said.

'What happened next was that I too had a brainwave. I took my mobile out of my pocket. I'd decided to call the police, but then I thought of Monique – of the complications . . . So,' Jonson went on, 'I rang Corinne's number instead. I heard her phone ring inside the greenhouse. I was watching her. I saw her start up. She clearly didn't want to answer the phone, but she was afraid the ringing might be heard by someone in the house. I saw her lower the gun as she tried to get her mobile out of her pocket. That was the moment I had been waiting for. I ran – I sprinted into the greenhouse and turned my torch on. I flashed it into her face. It blinded her. She cried out, raised her hand. She pointed the gun at me as best as she could, but I managed to get hold of her hand and twisted it upwards – away from me.'

'Bravo!' Lady Grylls applauded, her hand going up to her bosom. 'What a relief!'

'I heard the gun go pop, like the sound a toy gun makes, and I felt Corinne's body go limp. I heard a gurgling noise . . . She slumped down to the ground. I knelt beside her – lit her face with the torch.' Jonson swallowed. 'There was a bullet hole in her throat – black blood bubbling out of it.'

His eyes strayed down to his hands. 'I never wanted to kill her,' he said. 'All I meant was to disarm her – to talk to her – to try to – I don't know . . . I was angry with her

– because of the way she'd been treating Monique – because of what she'd been subjecting her to . . . Perhaps – perhaps I *did* intend to kill her?'

'Nonsense!' Lady Grylls boomed.

'I could have run back to the house – she wouldn't have shot through the glass . . . I could have roused everybody – I could have exposed her – told you what had happened, but I didn't – I didn't want to run away. It was between me and her – I wanted to have it out with her – bring things to a head.' Jonson ran his hand over his face. 'I am not sure what exactly went through my head. I honestly can't say. It all feels like a dream now. I twisted her hand, but it was she who pulled the trigger . . . I then discovered Eleanor's body behind the palms . . . I had an idea . . . I removed the gun from Corinne's hand, wiped it clean of her fingerprints and placed it in Eleanor's hand. I made it look as though Eleanor had killed Maginot and then herself. It was much – neater that way.'

'You did absolutely right. And damned clever too! You did it for that gel's sake, didn't you?' Lady Grylls said quietly.

'Yes. I did do it for Monique's sake. If it hadn't been for Monique, I'd gladly have told the whole story to the police. If I had left the gun in her mother's hand, a different line of inquiry would have followed – the suicide theory wouldn't have worked with Corinne – people don't usually shoot themselves in the throat. The impersonation and the deception would have come out. Questions would have been asked about Monique's involvement. They might even have suspected her of her mother's murder – because of all that money . . . Or they'd have suspected me . . . Our romance would have been put under a magnifying glass. My motives would have been questioned. Then the newspapers would have got hold of the story. Monique wouldn't have been able to cope. It would have been too much for her –'

He broke off and shook his head. 'No. *No.* I couldn't allow it . . . You were right about the *Herald Tribune* cuttings.' Jonson addressed Antonia once more. He picked up the newspaper that had lain on the table beside him. As he unfolded it, they saw that parts of it had been cut out. 'I found it in Corinne's room this morning, on her bedside table. You were right – it was she who planted the cuttings in Eleanor Merchant's bag.'

'What about the gun?' Antonia asked. 'Do you know how she got hold of it?'

'When they arrived at Heathrow, Corinne met someone . . . Monique saw her talking to a man. It was only a brief exchange. Monique didn't actually see any package changing hands, but Corinne dropped her bag and her things spilled out – the man helped her pick them up. Monique didn't see anything, but the man must have put the gun inside Corinne's bag then. That was the only time it could have happened. Corinne must have arranged for the man to bring her a gun before she left Paris. When you are that rich, that is nothing – a mere bagatelle. Later she told Monique that the man had mistaken her for someone he knew.'

'You told Monique what happened in the greenhouse, didn't you?' Payne asked.

'Yes . . . I went up to her room. I was badly shaken. I had blood on my hand. Corinne Coreille's blood. Monique got extremely upset. She started crying. She said she couldn't face the police. She didn't want to stay in the house. It had all been too much. She had taken off the Corinne make-up . . . I gave her my car keys.' Jonson paused. 'She is in London – in my flat. She is all right . . . We are planning to get married next month . . . Well, Corinne Coreille will never be found now. Corinne Coreille no longer exists. She's gone, like a puff of smoke.' Jonson brought together three fingers of his right hand and blew at them, then spread out his hand. '*Disparue.*'

'Well, I hope you ask me to the wedding,' Lady Grylls said.

Provost appeared at the doorway. 'Lunch is ready, m'lady. Do you wish us to serve?'

# Coda

It was very warm now, real spring weather. The sun was shining and the nightingales sang. The magnolia tree outside the open study window looked like a giant wedding cake, covered with solid pink and white sugar icing. A spruce-looking elderly gentleman in heather tweeds, a green pork-pie hat and driving gloves could be seen talking animatedly to Major Payne in the drive, beside an ancient Bentley.

'Is that *all* you want? Are you sure, my dear?' Lady Grylls said in some surprise.

'I am. I've got quite a yen for it,' Antonia said.

'What an extraordinary thing to have a yen for! Of course you shall have Rory's desk. Goodness. Glad to be rid of the ghastly old object . . . I'll have this room turned into a boudoir or something equally jolly. You know – one of those muslin and primrose affairs with lots of silk cushions? I need to get something off my chest.' Lady Grylls pushed her glasses up her nose. 'It was I who killed Corinne.'

Antonia stared. 'What – what do you mean?'

There was a pause. 'If I hadn't given Ruse that brooch all those years ago, Corinne wouldn't have worn it on her beret,' Lady Grylls said slowly. 'Corinne then wouldn't have been noticed in the greenhouse and then – then she would have remained alive – poor dear Andrew would have died instead! It's a dreadful thought, I know.'

Antonia breathed an internal sigh of relief. 'Oh, it never works like that,' she managed to say lightly. 'Something else would have happened – she'd have given herself away in some other way – the gun would have glimmered in the moonlight – he'd have noticed it.'

'You think so? He would have, wouldn't he?' Lady Grylls brightened up. 'He is such a clever young man . . . And now,' she went on, 'we must go and look at Bobo Markham's new pigs. He's come all this way to collect us. Such an old bore!'

But she was wearing lipstick, her hair was freshly coiffed and earlier on she had asked Antonia to help her choose what dress to wear.